THE SIGNATURE LINE

NICOLE ANNBURY

As is true with many books of fiction, events that appeared in the news inspired parts of this book. However, all the actions in this book, as well as the characters and dialogue, are products solely of the author's imagination.

Edited by Meg McIntyre (Phantom Pen Editorial)

Cover Design by Hollowe Studios

First Print and Electronic Edition: 2026

www.nicoleannbury.com

To my husband. Your support means the world to me.

CONTENT WARNING

The Signature Line contains some themes and depictions that might be sensitive to certain readers. Please go to my website for a full list of content warnings.

www.nicoleannbury.com/books

THE SIGNATURE LINE

BY

NICOLE ANNBURY

Prologue

Dear Dr. Carey,

You are a vulgar bitch. I keep hearing your voice and seeing your face on my TV, and that needs to end. You think you ooze sex appeal when all I think of you is how disgusting you make me feel. You're what's wrong with this world, and mark my words—you will pay for what you've created. The only positive thing you've done is to awaken the beast within me and the army of men behind me. Now that I've accepted my mission to annihilate you, there's no stopping my force. I've already thought of the ways to go after you and your radical hags. A gun would be too quick and easy. You're not worth the pressure or energy of my hands squeezing the life from you. But I think I'll take after a hero of mine, Jack the Ripper; his knife was so nice and sharp. It did the trick, and that's the tool you'll get.

I hope my knife and I haunt you until the day we show up at your door. You had a chance to end this, but now it's my turn to show the world what I'm made of.

Can't wait to meet in person.

A really nice guy.

Chapter 1

Carmella

The percussive drumbeat sounded throughout the open-air field, willing women to open their hearts and wallets to a new way of living. Dr. Carmella Carey had five minutes to convince a crowd of women to join her revolution. A last-minute fill-in, she had plotted for a moment like this—manifested it, you might say. The call had come late yesterday evening. Mother Luna, the slotted speaker, had fallen ill with strep throat and wouldn't be able to attend, as her herbal tea wasn't healing her in time. Dr. Carey was on a short list because of her book, *Year of Self*, which helped her gain followers nationally. Her growing popularity in the wellness community had landed her on TV to discuss women's empowerment. That her former sorority sister was an organizer also helped make her a shoo-in for a spot.

Dr. Carey stuck out like a sore thumb. Her black pantsuit and bone off-white camisole were the polar opposite of the floral-patterned hippie garb the other speakers wore. She was a buttoned-up doll amid a sea of muted, pale-faced women. Carmella's blonde hair was styled in a chic blowout, accentuating its highlighted layers. She'd achieved flawless skin with recent fillers and had refined her makeup routine. Her body fat was at a perfect ten percent thanks to her weekly Pilates. The only sugar intake in her diet was her morning coffee order, an addiction she felt she deserved. The other thought leaders attending the mountain retreat had likely traveled from communes in the desert, while Carmella drove in from Beverly Grove.

Carmella paced backstage holding her prepared notecards, although she knew the speech by heart. A trained psychologist with only a couple of years of experience, she yearned for a different future—one that meshed psychology with the world of self-help, and this summit would be the perfect launching pad. She could hear a roaring crowd of women as the speaker before her wrapped up. *My soul is in alignment with this very moment and opportunity,* Carmella thought as she rested her right palm on her belly, performing a bellows breath ritual to energize her.

"Namaste, my love." A woman walked by, closing her eyes and bowing to Carmella, who smiled back.

Carmella breathed in the patchouli-filled air and raised her arms in a salutation pose to welcome fresh energy.

"Dr. Carey? You're on in one minute," a young woman with a headset informed her.

"Thanks." *You've got this.* She grabbed her cards from the ground and walked toward the stage.

"Unfortunately, Mother Luna has fallen sick, so please let's all send up healing offerings to her." The speaker folded her hands and gave them a kiss before releasing them to the sky. "Now. We're in for a treat. We have a bit of a different speaker for you. Dr. Carmella Carey is a women's psychologist specializing in cognitive-behavioral therapy. However, she's got an innovative program that she promises will forever make its mark on women's history. Please welcome Dr. Carmella Carey."

She stepped on stage to a smattering of applause. *I'll win them over.*

"Thank you. Let's start by saying I know I don't appear like the others. I'm definitely no Mother Luna or anyone else you'll see on this stage today." Dr. Carey looked around at the hushed crowd full of women from all walks of life: soccer moms in sweatshirts, muumuu-wearing astrology nuts, and granola ladies in yoga pants.

"That's the way I prefer it. I'll never be like anyone else. I'll never sell you the same garbage I know you've heard. If what you're doing is working, great. If you're still struggling, then follow me." She paused. "Are you still stressed about your relationships? Are you dissatisfied with where you're at in life? If so, follow me. You don't have to give up your dreams, hopes, or anything you've manifested. I believe in that. I believe in you." She placed her hand on her heart.

"I'm one of you. I may dress differently, but trust me—I suffer. I've had guy trouble, work problems, and guess what? Life is really, really hard for women." She took a deep breath before speaking more quietly into the microphone. "Being a woman in this world is so hard. The world is against us. But I am with you, and if you need someone to fight and be in your corner, follow me." Dr. Carey glanced at the stagehand, who flashed two fingers to show how much time she had left.

"My bold plan will give you a new life. A rebirth of yourself. We will say goodbye to the person you are today, and you will become a new woman. Gone is the old baggage you've been carrying from one relationship to the next. Through me, you'll finally be free!" Dr. Carey jumped around on stage as the audience erupted with applause, rising from their seats.

"You may question, 'Why my plan?' As a licensed therapist, I've heard so many women tell me they want radical change. I teach you the skills to be a strong, independent woman who will know her worth. You get one-on-one sessions with me as well as a community of women who are on the same enlightened path." Carmella stared out at the pensive crowd.

"Who wants to be free with me?" Some audience members jumped with excitement. Carmella didn't hear or see the stagehand waving that time was up.

Finally, Dr. Carey announced, "My time here is up, but please follow me. I'm set up at the vendor booths behind the stage. Thank you, ladies." As she turned to hand her microphone to the stagehand, several women got up from the audience to follow her.

Along the route to her booth, Dr. Carey noticed the smiles she initially encountered on her way in had turned to frowns. The hippie-clad organizers didn't feel as welcoming after her speech—less namaste, more "on your way."

Carmella smirked to herself. *It's working.* She looked behind and saw some women craning their necks to see where the woman wearing black was headed. As she arrived at her booth, her former sorority sister, Gracie, met her. "Carmella, I see you're up to your old tricks. I thought maybe you would have aged out of that tribalism now that you're a doctor, but I guess old habits die hard?"

"What are you talking about? Aren't we here to help women better themselves?" Carmella shielded her eyes from the sun.

"Of course! But you didn't need to shit on the other presenters," Gracie said under her breath.

"I simply told them that if they wanted something more or if it wasn't working for them, then follow me. What's wrong with that?" Carmella shrugged and waved her hands as the first group of women arrived. "Ladies, welcome!" Carmella greeted them with a wide smile. "You've come to the right booth to begin the journey to a new life."

The line continued to grow throughout the day, and Dr. Carey eventually received interest from over fifty women who wanted to sign up for whatever she was selling.

On the drive home, Dr. Carey couldn't stop grinning. The wind rushed into her car's open windows as she left the San Gabriel Mountains, blowing away any remnants of the day's natural body scents and the occasional puff of marijuana that wafted toward her. She wasn't sure if a contact high was a real thing, but she floated home toward the sparkle of Los Angeles. Following her bliss had finally paid off. After turning onto Wilshire, she chuckled to herself. *I guess I should send Mother Luna flowers tomorrow.*

The launch of the *Year of Self* had revealed itself to be much easier than she could have ever manifested or believed, given the gullibility of the desperate women who sought something greater than themselves.

It's time to shake shit up.

Chapter 2

Dylan

The air bubble stuck beneath his rib cage expanded as he gulped down the warming beer. The bottle fizzed as he pounded the glass too hard on his desk, rubbing his sternum, which burned under his skin. A gnawing grew, bitterness churning above and below the pit of despair wedged firmly in his breastbone cavity. Dylan's internal clock was buzzing out of control, the countdown alerting him of Renee Baldwin's live show that he'd planned to call in to.

Dylan stood from his swivel office chair, his head dizzy from too much alcohol and poor air circulation to his brain. He grabbed the edge of his desk, bent over, and let out a soothing belch, releasing the caught air pocket. His chest swelled with a comforting full-bodied breath as he paced his poorly lit room. He mouthed the words he'd prepared all week—all his life.

Men are victims of the feminization of our culture. Public institutions discriminate against men. Men are a disadvantaged group. Men are degraded and villainized.

A knock on his door and a jostle of its handle interrupted Dylan's thoughts. "Fucking 'rents," he mumbled under his breath.

He got up to open the door to his dad, who held a basket of clothes to carry down to the basement, where the laundry room was located. Edgar scowled at his son as he quickly brushed by him.

"Can this wait? I have an important meeting coming up," Dylan said.

Edgar furrowed his brow. "Isn't it time you found a job?" He eyed Dylan as he loaded the washer with dirty clothes.

Dylan glared as his dad sorted the clothes and finally ascended the stairs. He locked the door and stomped back to his desk. He checked the time—he had five minutes until the live show began. While the lump in his chest had disintegrated, the sound of water spraying into the washing machine ignited his urge to pee. With only four minutes left, he ran to the toilet to relieve himself. With three minutes left, he paced, mumbling the points he wanted to make, forgetting key arguments he didn't think he'd needed to write down. *I've been preaching this shit for years.* When he concocted his plan, he'd arrogantly believed he'd remember all that he wanted to say. Now with only a minute to go, the air bubble was back, this time in his throat.

He logged in to watch the live feed, safe in his Indiana basement apartment. Renee Baldwin felt closer than ever, yet she was hundreds of miles away in a sunny California studio. Dylan chose her show because she often had controversial guests, including Dr. Carmella Carey, who was Dylan's number one nemesis.

"Hello, my lovers. I am so glad you're joining me today. Do I have a show for you! I'm letting you in on a little secret." Renee raised her eyebrows. "Come closer." She teased the camera and wriggled her pointer finger. "Menopause is a woman's superpower!" The audience erupted in applause.

Dylan attempted to choke back disgust but ended up spitting warm beer down the front of his shirt. "Fucking gross," he slurred at the laptop screen. If he didn't already have his sights set on Dr. Carey, Renee would make a perfect backup.

"Also, today is Fabulous Friday, where I take your calls and celebrate my amazing viewers. Be right back with one of our first." Renee winked at the camera.

Dylan had already filled out the pre-call form online to be approved for the queue. He dialed the number they gave him and an '80s song began to play—"Right Here Waiting for You." Dylan leaned forward and turned the speaker volume down. He couldn't hear sappy love songs without it taking him back, his heart panging with tenderness for Barbara. Even though he still wanted her dead.

"Hello, caller. Um, Fletcher?"

Dylan cleared his throat. "Yes, hi. I'm here." He attempted to deepen his voice, but it came out as a squeak, with the constricting air bubble still perfectly lodged. Dylan cleared his throat again and tried to wash it down with the remaining warm beer. He was suddenly stone-cold sober.

He chuckled to himself. *Fletcher. Who the fuck has that name?* He laughed at the made-up name he had given them. A fun pseudonym to hide behind.

"Great. You're up first to discuss the effects of global warming on your perennials. Renee has a soft spot for gardeners, so you picked a good topic for Fabulous Friday," the production assistant said.

Yep, I do my research. "Great. It's near and dear to my heart." Dylan continued to toy with his voice, which sounded a bit like the end stages of a cold clearing up, but his throat was still raw from excessive coughing.

"The next voice you'll hear is Renee's."

Dust particles floated around him as someone walked around upstairs. This unfinished basement wasn't intended for a resident, but it suited someone like Dylan. The spin cycle announced itself with a fury as the drum slammed next to the dryer. There were no walls or doors to contain the noise that banged throughout his space. With each moment that passed, his blood pressure rose as he waited to hear Renee greet Fletcher with her syrupy voice, ready to discuss the poor daylilies and bee balm and what the changing ecosystem would mean for their existence. Bam. Thwack. *My fucking parents. They never listen and always want to ruin my life!*

Dylan stood and paced in front of his office chair. The spin cycle spun in his head, cooling his confidence, twisting his nerves into a dangerous game of Operation. The hardened lump grew enormous in his throat. If he didn't know any better, he'd have thought he had a sudden tumor, a rapid onset case caused by a woman, no less.

"Fletcher, welcome to Fabulous Friday. You have one of my favorite topics: Gardening. How has Mother Earth been treating your lawn this season? I mean, we have fires, excessive heat, droughts, just to name a few of our man-made problems." Renee sighed.

Silence.

Dylan, as Fletcher, eked out a few words. "Men are returning to take back control." The words were much louder in his head than anywhere else.

On screen, Renee's brows furrowed, and she frowned. "I'm sorry, but I'm having great difficulty hearing you. I couldn't make out what you said."

Dylan mustered a gulp that landed in the pharynx, not deep enough to give him a satisfying breath. "Men's rights are our birthright, and we're not going to back down." While this came out a bit louder, his voice was so gravelly that it sounded like Dylan was speaking through a megaphone underwater with a washing machine with an unbalanced drum in the background.

"I heard something about men's rights. I think you're on the wrong show, sweetie." Renee chuckled to her audience. "Let's talk when men go through childbirth and menopause, and then we can discuss your rights." The audience exploded with cheers and laughter, and the line went dead.

Dylan stared at the screen as the faint voice of an operator announced that his call had been disconnected. His face flushed. The rush of water filling the washing machine gushed loudly throughout the room as the lump in Dylan's throat dissolved into a raw ache.

His face burned with the heat of humiliation. This was the

moment Dylan created his mission to eradicate Dr. Carey and the women who followed her. Today was a mistake that he wouldn't make a second time. He vowed to never again let a woman ridicule him like this. And he would make a name for himself on Renee's show next time.

Dylan walked the six feet to his bed and plopped down, replaying how everything went wrong. What women had done to him—women like Dr. Carey, his mom, and the love of his life, Barbara—had shattered his confidence, manhood, and bravado. Dylan vowed to turn up the heat on those women. He just had to find them all first.

Chapter 3

Carmella

Carmella's body instinctively rocked to the pulsating beat as soon as she stepped foot onto the celebrity-clad sidewalk. Street lights bounced off the razor-straight pink wig that hung past her shoulder blades as she walked directly to the front of the line, past Livvy Kyle-level starlets. The bouncer winked and waved her inside. Her black bustier pushed up her breasts higher than natural to give her a Jessica Rabbit silhouette. Carmella believed every man and woman turned to stare at her; she was a goddess in this club. The music hit her soul just right, vibrating the parts of her that craved sex and control. She sniffed back the special of the night, allowing her fingernail to fill with the soft powder of mercy. She loved how it took her away from all the cares of the world, leaving her in a euphoric bliss.

A few vodka shots limbered her up, not that she needed much. Carmella always came ready for action, whether the pleasure came from drugs, sex, or the erotic thump of the techno music. It didn't take long for the special to hit, and when it did, she melted into a beautiful paradise of warmth. She felt herself floating past other clubbers on her trip, all of them drop-dead gorgeous beings full of dreams and awareness. Los Angeles had a way of making the average into the glamorous in bars like this, if you had the money. And six months after creating the *Year of Self*, Carmella had lots of money. It paid for every cosmetic enhancement—her new boobs, her fillers and Botox treatments. Her glassy skin was the envy of women who longed for a fresh face free of wrinkles and the stresses of daily life. As they sat in the waiting room for their names to be called, Carmella just knew each of them would tell their esthetician, "Give me the Dr. Carey special."

The fervent mass of partygoers swarmed the dance floor as the club lights flashed neon rainbow colors. The yellow felt hot like a sun-kissed beach, drenching her with its rays of joy. White lights made her heart swell with love, and she wanted to hug everyone who came near her. The red lights intoxicated her with lust as she thrust her body into the nearest person. A muscular, mustached man danced close to her and was equally engaged as their bodies grinded to the pounding bass.

Carmella tore away from him after getting to know his anatomy better by touch. Her favorite club beat entered her ears, and she came alive as she moved her hips to the slower rhythm. As it raced faster, she threw her arms over her head and rested them behind her neck. She gyrated her body, bouncing up and down as the music flooded every inch of her with exhilaration.

She stayed out on the dance floor until the end of the song, when the next jam moved her toward the elite back room. The spot where those who entered had to know the private words. Carmella walked straight through, plopping down on the purple velvet sofa next to another regular. They knew each other well; their first encounter was when she'd worn her blue wig. A new line of powder called to her, and she sat up to take a satisfying bump. By the time her head reached the back of the couch, she felt an overwhelming sense of calm. Her body was a heavy rock, yet her mind drifted in elation.

After several minutes, she watched as others took their hits off the same table, some lying down on the floor, others being held up. They were all on the same journey toward a path of enlightenment, brilliance, and destruction. Her body slowly sank from the soft couch onto the hardened floor as she lost control of her muscles. She was emotional slush, descending farther onto the ground, landing on her cheek with a smack. The cold surface momentarily sparked her eyes wide open, then she shut them again, slipping back into her blissful journey into the deep drug-induced unknown.

Hours later, Carmella slowly came to and found herself back home. She had no knowledge of how she'd gotten there, although this wasn't unique. Her head throbbed as she squinted in the sunshine filtering into her LA condo. When she saw her reflection still wearing last night's outfit and wig, she shied away from it. The downside of partying was the next day. While she had felt only love for herself the night before, in the morning, she hated everything and everyone.

The fluorescent lighting over her desk and a glass ceiling she had only just started chipping away at replaced the sparkle of lights, the sounds of the bass, and the effects of the psychedelic Special K.

Chapter 4

Dylan

The town of Lazette, Indiana, was like most college towns—full of bars with short leases and yards littered with garbage under houses with fraternity signs. Dylan Foster was never part of that scene, although he tried. He harbored a great resentment toward sorority girls who wouldn't give him a first look, believing them too stupid to see what a catch he really was. He especially hated girls who weren't in sororities because they also wouldn't accept him as a match. The last time he'd attempted to date after Barbara, the girl immediately dismissed him, and he saw the instant smirk on her face—like she was pleased with letting him down. He should have known the type. Not good enough for a clique, but still thought she was better than him. His feelings about women didn't begin in college; they just got a lot worse once Barbara ghosted him.

After high school, Dylan had dreams of making a name for himself on the college campus, but he couldn't get past the liberal views that reverberated through the halls. He quickly found that his views and voice were not welcome there. That sent his educational and career goals careening into unknown territory, where he floundered with no solid leads. As he applied for jobs, he narrowed his eyes at some of the questions: *How has belonging to civic organiza-tions made you a well-rounded individual? How would you uphold our values in meeting the standards of diversity?* Dylan stood in the middle of an interview after being asked similar questions, flinging his chair backward until it hit the floor. He chucked the interview paperwork and took off through the front door without so much as a word. With each interview, his fury rose to new heights.

After his maternal grandparents died, he inherited a decent nest egg once he turned eighteen. Now thirty-four, he'd spent some funds on a new car and laptop, but he had no ambition beyond that. His life goals weren't of the picket fence and dad variety. He'd once dared to believe he was ready for that responsibility, but as a single, unattached man, he floundered without direction.

"Men have feelings, and they deserve to be cared for and acknowledged," Dylan said to anyone who'd listen, which consisted of a few online friends. Dylan's angst grew with particular ire toward authoritative women. The type that thought they were too good to breathe the same air, never considering him to be at their level, always rebuking any advances he dared to make. Women like this usually had an appearance that repulsed him in ways that bore into the darkest part of him, while their words incited a rage that bubbled up to the surface.

Dylan started a vlog of his rantings that he called *Guy Pact,* which he added to anytime he needed to get some frustration off his chest. "Rantings from an angry man, here," Dylan said, standing outside on the grounds of the university that he still owed a sizable amount to. The video feed showed students walking to classes as Dylan stood on a bench, yelling, "This university only teaches about women's rights and doesn't care about men. Where are the safe zones for men, and what about the false accusations that occur here on campus?" No one stopped to listen. Students just walked by. Some had EarPods stuck in their ears, oblivious to his words.

Dylan always left the university campus frustrated by the lack of attention he'd received. *Even the dudes are too stupid to see through this bullshit.* "I fear for society with people like these morons in charge," Dylan would often remark in his recordings. Driving away from campus, Dylan went on his near daily check to see if Barbara had returned home. Oak-lined side streets leading from the campus to downtown held converted apartment houses. Barbara's was one that he knew well since it was his Uncle Greg's old place that he'd renovated into rental units. The once single family-owned craftsman now housed students who didn't appreciate its historical value.

That's how he first met her. He was mowing his uncle's properties for side cash when he ran into the brunette who caught his eye. Her hair was pulled back, revealing the most delicate ears he'd ever seen. Barbara, the "love of his life," as he'd later refer to her, had left him several months ago. As a self-described "perfect boyfriend," he couldn't understand how she'd just vanished. No letter or text, and her roommate had given no indication she knew where Barbara had gone.

Losing her was a turning point for him. It had shifted his thought process from verbal activism to direct action. No woman was safe with a forsaken Dylan on the loose.

Chapter 5

Livvy

The sleek ten-story building on Fairfax housed some of the best talent management a commission could buy. It was full of starlets hidden behind sunglasses as coffee orders and movie scripts bogged their assistants down. The waiting room was full of actors, both headliners and those hoping to take their careers to the next level. Frank Shephard Artists was the hottest talent agency to land this side of the valley, and Livvy Kyle hoped to keep her spot there while the dust settled on her recent tabloid drama.

Livvy had to settle for one of the lower-tier agents, Emilio Morales, whom she was meeting with today. Frank only represented the actors who won an Emmy or Oscar.

"Livvy, your career is really shit right now. I don't know who would be willing to touch you." Emilio paced his small office.

"Tell me about it. Although getting touched is what put me in this situation." Livvy rolled her eyes.

"Look, I understand Alton is about to go on trial for sexual harassment, but until he's convicted, Hollywood isn't ready to let go of his shine. He still has the Midas touch around here. He had an uncanny knack for making careers, even with talentless actors. His genius was the prototype for producers." Emilio sat on the edge of his desk.

"Yeah, on the backs of women like me!" Livvy raised her voice, letting out a deep sigh.

Emilio crossed his arms over his chest as Livvy stared back.

"I know your hands are tied, but I can't just sit and wait for a trial that keeps getting delayed. I'm in my prime, and I have to do something!"

Emilio stood to stretch. "I hear you, but trust me, the trial will be here and over before you know it. Use this time to pick up a hobby, learn a language, join a club." He leaned toward Livvy with steepled hands. "Just sit tight, wait for your time to shine on the witness stand, and then wait for the offers to roll in."

Livvy grabbed her bag and slid her shades on. She wanted to cry, but she was fresh out of any fucks to give. The man she'd thought was her soulmate turned out to be a womanizer, complete with casting calls designed to keep his concubines content. She had always heard the stories, but never thought she'd fall prey to the infamous couch.

She liked to say she stumbled into acting since she started out as a dancer. A knee sprain turned her dance chorus role into a small speaking part, which opened up more opportunities, and she loved the attention it got her. Livvy was a natural brunette, but had been blonde since freshman year. She'd been all shades, finally landing on a butter blonde, a perfect cool tone mixed with smooth beige under-tones. Her fair skin and hazel eyes went well with the shade. While her long, curled hair was one of the first things people noticed about her, she had the most perfect cheekbones. They sat high, with exquisite shadowing underneath, giving her an impeccable pout.

Thanks to Alton, she hadn't won any major awards after her big break last year. Since that movie had earned some viral fame mostly for its poor editing, nobody was calling for a sequel. Her notoriety faded in a town always looking for the next big thing, which allowed her to stroll down any street without being noticed. Her biggest achievement was a recurring guest role as a doctor's secret girlfriend in a medical drama. That required mostly sexy scenes where there wasn't much talking involved. Plus, the scenes used minimal lighting, which meant she wasn't often noticed in public.

The first couple blocks of the walk to her apartment were a blur as she contemplated how she'd cover her rent, groceries, and cosmetic bills. While she understood where Emilio was coming from, she couldn't understand sitting around and wasting her beauty while she was still young. Although she knew that at thirty, other actors were being cast as the divorced older wife, which incensed her. Her fury toward Alton often bubbled up—anger at the grooming, the lies, the manipulation, and finally the shame she couldn't shake.

The sound of wind chimes broke her from her thoughts, and she turned to see Spiritual Gardens, a corner store inviting customers to come inside for soul healing. The wrought-iron exterior displayed a rainbow flag, a red neon sign proclaiming TAROT READINGS, and a dreamcatcher hanging near the entrance. Crystals, gemstones, incense, and sound baths now replaced the small mom and pop diner that had been there. A woman wearing a long olive dress greeted Livvy as she walked inside, saying, "Welcome in love." While Livvy had no faith prior to Alton and the scandal, she was now desperate to grab hold of something to ground her.

"You've come to the right place for healing. My name is Eden. Is there anything I can assist you with?" The natural-faced brunette behind the counter beamed.

"Oh, I'm not sure. I've never been to a place like this." Livvy glanced around at the shelves, lightly running her hands up her arms as warm tingles overwhelmed her body.

"All the positive energy flowing at once can feel intrusive. Don't resist it. Let it consume you and take you where it wants to lead you." Eden shut her eyes.

Okay, lady. Livvy smirked.

Livvy walked around the narrow, elongated shop, which was flooded with the fruity and floral scents of Indian rose and lotus flower incense. The rows of crystals shone to perfection, with everything from amethyst and tourmaline to olivenite displayed beautifully on the shelves.

"Aren't they beautiful?" Eden appeared next to Livvy. "I honestly had no idea we lived amongst such magnificence before I took this position. Since I met the owner, she's helped awaken me so much."

"Yeah, they really are beautiful. Can I hold them?" Livvy asked, looking at the onyx.

"Absolutely. They give us their power when we carry them."

Goosebumps moved up and down Livvy's arms. The palm-sized onyx felt both heavy and light in her manicured hand. "I need something to protect me from predators. From men who manipulate and ruin lives. But also, to give me confidence to stand up to men like that. Is there a crystal for that?" Livvy contorted her face.

Eden shut her eyes and lifted her head to the ceiling. "Tiger's eye!"

Livvy followed as her heart raced with excitement. Once she saw it, she was instantly mesmerized by its rich coppery tone, and she loved its leaf shape that fit perfectly in her hand or pocket. "It's stunning. I'll take it."

"It comes in a stone. But you can also get it in a necklace, bracelet, or ring," Eden said.

"For now, I want this gorgeous stone." Livvy kept admiring the shiny exterior.

"You mentioned wanting protection from a man?" Eden asked as she went to the register. "I carry crystals for the same reason. I left my own toxic relationship and created a new life, and I couldn't be happier." Eden smiled. "However, I couldn't have done it by myself. I found support through Dr. Carmella Carey. She runs an online therapy group, and it's changed my life."

"I think I've heard about her on the news." Livvy furrowed her brows.

"I'm so glad I found her when I did. I was in a really dark place, and I honestly don't know where I'd be without her." Eden looked down at her hands.

"Wow, that's amazing. Honestly, right before I stopped in here, I got some really shitty news about my career, so this was exactly what I needed. Maybe I'll check out Dr. Carey." Livvy smiled, raising her eyebrows.

"That's just how the universe works. Please tell Dr. Carey I sent you! I want her to know you're one of us and just how much I believe you belong." Eden winked, smiling with her eyes.

With her new armor in hand, Livvy's steps were airy, as though she were levitating on her walk home. She had a shield she didn't know she was looking for to help her regain the confidence she'd lost this year. She squeezed the tiger's eye in her pocket, hoping it would give her the fortitude never to let a man rob her of her true self again.

Livvy threw down her mail, which was filled with bills, made some coffee, and logged in to watch some videos of Dr. Carey. "Do you need a life refresh because a man pushed pause on the path you already started? Have you had your career completely railroaded because a man couldn't control his sexual urges, yet you're the one out of a job?" Dr. Carey said on the screen.

Livvy nodded along with each question. *Finally, someone understands!* But when Livvy saw the cost of membership, she hesitated. Her earnings from her acting stint as an ER doctor's secret girlfriend were likely to dwindle once the episodes stopped airing. But she knew this was important and banked on Emilio getting her those big gigs after the trial. For now, she'd go back to her natural brunette if it meant becoming a member.

Livvy debated the pros and cons as her cursor hovered over the application submission button. She gripped her tiger's eye in her left palm and took a deep breath. The floating stars on the webpage drew her further into the screen. *What do I have to lose?*

Chapter 6

Carmella

The ding of a fresh email cut through the morning's silence, followed by the sound of Carmella's shiny red nails clicking on the keyboard. She rubbed her cheek; a mild grimace stretched over her face as her overly white teeth glinted at her from the mirror on her desk. Emails flowed, further confirmation that her plan continued to work and her message was resonating with women across the world. As she prepared for her upcoming online interview, she straightened her puffy pink sweater, smoothed her bleached blonde hair, and adjusted the angles of her multiple lights to give her the perfect, aesthetically pleasing glow. Even though she could go in-person for her interviews, she much preferred the ease and control of being at home.

Once she logged in, the show coordinator gave her the rundown she had heard many times before. The same old song and dance she'd grown accustomed to. She was the hottest interview these days, at least in her mind. Everyone wanted a piece of her, and she was ready to give them a slice.

"Hello and welcome to *Wake Up LA*. We have Dr. Carmella Carey with us today. She's become well-known for what some are calling a controversial treatment she created, encouraging women to leave their partners. I can't wait to hear more about the reasoning behind this. Please explain, Doctor," Renee Baldwin, the talk show host, probed.

"Thank you for having me. It's more than just leaving their partners. I encourage women to experience freedom like they've never had before. Many women have never lived on their own. They've gone straight from their parents' home to living with their boyfriend or husband. Granted, some women have gone off to college and lived in a dorm or with a roommate, but I believe women should experience life as a professional making it on their own—paying their own bills. Women no longer need men like we did decades ago. If we want a baby, a house, or to live off a single income, we can have it all. We don't need to live like our grand-mothers did, accepting a marriage for convenience because of financial security."

"Okay, but can't a woman have some of those things *with* a man? She can still have everything *and* love, right?" Renee asked, tapping a pen against her pursed lips.

Dr. Carey blinked rapidly. "It's rare. There are some men who can handle strong and vivacious women. My experience is that men rarely like these kinds of women and, once in a relationship, they try to change them. But if a woman is on her own and knows who she is without him first, then she's much less likely to allow a man to change her." Dr. Carey straightened. "Besides, if they're good-quality men, then they will have done their own work toward being their best selves." Dr. Carey stared back at her image on the screen.

"One rule I've read is that you tell women in happy relationships to leave. Why would that benefit them?" Renee's brows furrowed.

"That's how my therapy works. If you want me as a therapist, that's part of my program. You must be single for one year and show that you can make it financially and emotionally on your own before getting back into a relationship. If you were in a happy relationship before, then they'll still be there if they're the right one."

Renee frowned. "Wow. I really think that sounds harsh. What if there are children involved? This could really break up families."

"That is for the woman to decide. I am not actively seeking clients, but my calendar is booked. So, women are definitely interested in this program. All women would benefit from a *Year of Self!*"

Carmella signed off from the interview. It wasn't the first time she had encountered some resistance. She understood others found it difficult to understand the power of a woman who had awakened to her possibilities. Society had brainwashed women to be more comfortable with a man in charge. She professed that the brainwashing started at an early age, going full throttle throughout a woman's lifetime. However, Carmella wanted to turn the world upside down and help women completely forget about the patriarchy's dominance. She knew it was so ingrained in all our minds that it would take at least a year for women to break the myth that they weren't powerful enough to rule the world.

Carmella stretched out on her couch and stared through her condo's floor-to-ceiling windows, which overlooked the smoggy LA skyline. She chose this unit for the impeccable views at sunset, which made for flawless evening selfies. The click of the door interrupted her musings as her assistant arrived with her coffee order.

"We need to go over the new girls and discuss the next event," Dr. Carey said.

Julissa had been with Dr. Carey from the beginning of the *Year of Self.* Dr. Carey liked the young woman's compassionate nature and had brought her on as a full-time assistant.

Julissa removed her crossbody bag and reached for the laptop on her desk, which was tucked away in the corner of the living room.

"Jacqueline Manning signed up today. I'm still processing her paperwork." Julissa reached for the last of her drink. "She wrote that she's a divorced third-grade teacher and considers herself to be an enabler."

Dr. Carey grunted. "Aren't they all! If we didn't allow them to walk all over us, then we wouldn't be in this predicament. Send her the link advancing her to the next phase."

When someone entered the program, they had to go through various processes in order to get accepted. Dr. Carey jokingly referred to it as hazing. Although no one was injured, some women were known to cry. Still, no one had publicly criticized the program to date, likely because everyone had to sign a non-disclosure agreement before being accepted.

Dr. Carey came up with the idea of the *Year of Self* because she saw how dissatisfied women were with their partners. Many of these women worked from home and concluded that they weren't in the type of relationship they had hoped for, and they resented the men next to them. She knew women needed a radical shift, and she pounced on the opportunity to offer one.

However, the rules she created for her participants weren't the same ones she followed herself. She just hoped her own secrets would stay hidden.

Chapter 7

Dylan

Dylan knew a bitch when he saw one, and Dr. Carey turned out to be the biggest. He watched her latest interview, raging when he heard her voice, surveying her movements, and listening to her words. Everything she stood for went against his stance as a men's rights advocate. As he watched each interview, every vein in his neck stood out, his jaw throbbing in pain from clenching his teeth, and he'd aggressively bounce his leg and slap his knee before pacing around his basement bedroom. Dr. Carey had become his prime target and obsession, some days even more so than Barbara. Fueled by his hatred, he devoured every frame of the recordings, replaying them over and over again to catch her mannerisms. He wanted to know everything about her, to understand every aspect of the woman he wanted to silence. His hatred aroused him so much, he had the biggest hard-on for her.

Dylan glanced around his bachelor pad, which provided little privacy. He wasn't employed and grew tired of the watchful eye of his father asking when he would find a job. He was still working things out for his future and with no real pull toward a career, he put all of his energy into becoming a leader in the men's rights movement.

But with his dad breathing down his neck to "get a real job" and "be a man" and "find a good woman and start a family of your own," he knew it was a matter of time before they'd kick him out. Anytime his dad mentioned finding a woman, Dylan's nostrils flared with renewed anger at Barbara. *My bitch ex fucked that up for me, Dad.*

As he often did with his online group, Dylan complained about his parents. "My dad has no fucking clue what it's like for men of our generation. Fossils like my parents had it so much easier. My generation has to deal with the fucking social justice warriors taking away our jobs. The government has made the economy more difficult for men and given women equality under the roof, which has forced good men like us out of their seats at the head of the table." Per usual, the other men in his online group nodded their heads in agreement.

It was fairly easy to start an online support group, as like-minded people found each other like roaches gravitating to the dark corners of a lit room. The desire to have the venom they spewed validated was as addictive as the submissive porn they watched.

Life in the basement had its perks. Not that Dylan took advantage of his man cave. There were no women willing to enter his lair. Although Dylan was unconventionally attractive in some ways, his thin frame, piercing blue eyes, and brown hair kept hidden under a baseball cap were no match for his attitude, which made it nearly impossible for women to see him as anything other than...odd. Dylan's personality had no charm to it. He was apathetic and came off as arrogant. But Dylan considered himself a catch that women were too dumb to recognize.

When he first created his online men's rights group, it gained little traction, mostly adding a few bots or scammers. Once he started posting regularly, though, he gained some attention, and he created a live online event where they could share their stories. The Mandate spawned from Dylan's growing anger over the women's movement and how it was encroaching on his rights as a man.

As he entered the Mandate chat room, Dylan imagined the smell of stale cigarettes and expired beer flowing from the taps, someplace where they could sit together and discuss their issues. He drank from his own can of beer, which tasted faintly of soured pickle juice, but he needed the liquid courage to discuss his passion in front of strangers. He got out his notepad, ready to brainstorm with his colleagues. As the time ticked down, he stared at the screen, willing men to enter and join his crusade against the feminine stranglehold overtaking their lives.

James logged in, jutting his eyes left and then right, finally aiming his gaze straight ahead. Dylan raised his hand to signal he was the man who had brought him here. James was a middle-aged man with an unkempt beard and a too-tight plaid shirt that he left tucked into his sagging jeans. He kept adjusting in his seat, attempting to hike up his pants, but they slid back down to rest on his wide hip bones.

"How's it going?" Dylan asked.

"It ain't too bad, I guess. Are you the guy who advertised this men's rights group?"

"That's me. What's your story?"

"Just lost custody of my kids to my bitch ex-wife and now I can only see them at the children's services office." James scowled.

"Fuck. Dude, that's why I created this. She probably told them some bullshit lies to keep the kids."

"Exactly. I love my kids, and she's manipulating them, making me out to be a bad guy. I'm sick of her shit." James clenched his teeth.

A new guy, Alex, interrupted them. He had arm tattoos, one side depicting a naked woman on a motorcycle. He was balding but kept his hair slicked back, which accentuated the thinness on the top of his head.

"This the men's group?" Alex asked.

Dylan nodded. "Yes, it is. I'm the organizer."

"Cool. I came to get some things off my chest."

"Great. Let's hear it." Dylan rocked back in the office chair his parents bought him for his first year of college.

"I'm suffocating at home, and I'm stuck unless I want to give up my house and cars. Why does a man have to lose so much when he wants out of his marriage?" Alex shook his head, holding up both arms and asking why.

"Exactly. Men are supposed to be the stronger sex, but now women think they deserve everything. Yet they don't appreciate a damn thing we bring home to them. They rarely thank us or see how much they need us." Dylan pounded his fist on his desk as he made his points.

The other two men nodded in agreement as Dylan pontificated about his hatred of the "feminist agenda."

"Women now believe they don't need men. It's disgusting. They have the court system wrapped in that ideology too. Men are the first to lose their rights anytime a woman makes a cry for help. What a woman reports causes men to lose their homes and their hard-earned money, even lands them in jail sometimes. It's ludicrous, and that's why I formed this group. We need a place to vent and fight for *our* rights." Dylan pointed to his chest.

James and Alex raised their drinks in unison, virtually clinking them.

"So, what's your story? You got a kid or a wife?" Alex asked Dylan as he sipped on his drink.

"No wife, no kids. I can't get a woman to go out with me! They all turned me down and think they're better than me, or they want a richer guy than me. They don't see what they're missing." Dylan flared his nostrils.

The other two men nodded. "Women think they hold all the cards, and they might be right. Back in the day, men were the dominant sex. Now women want to castrate us and spend all our money!" Alex glowered.

"You're right. It's such a sad world now that men have lost their spot at the head of the household. Feminists have destroyed our birthright, and I think it's time we men band together and take it back!" Dylan fumed.

"Since this was my idea, I'll be the president, and since James logged in first, he's the vice president. Alex, you'll be my sergeant of arms. We'll each have a role to play to make sure this succeeds. We need bylaws for this to go smoothly and to stay on track with our message. Maybe we need to come up with the rules first before we go any further." Dylan twisted his mouth, staring at his notepad.

As they discussed how they wanted this club to go, they decided their mission statement was for every man to take back the voice that the feminist regime had stolen.

The rules were simple: They did not allow women because they couldn't trust them not to be a plant for some nefarious gain. The members were brothers, and each would get his time to discuss his grievances. They would form a coalition to attract TV and radio airtime and get their message out into the world.

Dylan logged out of the Mandate event on the highest high. He floated back to his bed just feet away, knowing that he was finally working toward something he loved. He believed that this was where his skills lay, and he finally had a vision for his future.

However, there was one fact he didn't disclose to the group.

I intend to make women pay for what they've done to me, including Barbara. But I have to find her first.

Chapter 8

Julissa

Six months ago, on the morning of Julissa's first day working for Dr. Carey, the jitters hit her hard. She had to admit that Dr. Carey intimidated her; she was one of the rock stars of the wellness community. When Julissa first heard her speak at the women's retreat surrounded by the healing San Gabriel Mountains, she felt called to approach her and ask for a job. The only real calling she'd felt since college graduation was to follow her heart, which led her to cleanse her aura and seek real meaning from life. While the other speakers made her snap her fingers in agreement, Dr. Carey ignited something that slept deep inside of her. She felt pulled to the therapist, eager to be a part of the genius program.

A month before the retreat, she'd gone on her own healing journey to "find herself." She learned so much about herself, including that she was an Enneagram 1. With a strong sense of right from wrong, she armed herself to make real change in the world. She saw herself as an activist for good and fully believed in what Dr. Carey was promoting.

Chills still ran up her arms when she replayed Dr. Carey's voicemail welcoming her onto the ground floor of a revolution. "You will be an integral part of the program. In some cases, you'll be the first person the women speak with before they meet me." Julissa couldn't explain it other than to believe it was all some form of divine intervention.

My growth mindset has led me on this path of awareness.

After she parked in the visitor spot in the condo's underground garage, Julissa felt the heat rising off the concrete, moistening her skin as her sunglasses slid down her nose. She made her way to the front of the building and checked in with the doorman, who stepped aside, letting her pass. As she entered the condo's atrium, the overly cool air immediately fogged up her sunglasses. She passed the resident mailboxes along the far wall as she prepared for the climb to the fourth floor. She had always hated elevators ever since being dared to ride the Drop of Doom at Magic Mountain. Although walking up a common stairwell also gave her chills from all the true crime she watched.

She took a deep breath. "Welcome to your future," she whispered, knocking on Dr. Carey's door. She heard light steps approaching as her own heartbeat knocked loudly against her chest.

The aroma of a popular body mist—water lily and musk—hit her as soon as the door opened.

"Julissa? Welcome. Come in," a striking blonde figure said, waving her arm to come inside.

Her appearance took Julissa's breath away, as the last time she'd seen her was at the retreat.

"Hi, yes—Dr. Carey?" Julissa cleared her throat.

"Yes. That's me." She smiled, showing off perfectly straight teeth.

I can't believe I'm here with her!

"Would you like a drink?"

"No, I'm good." Julissa looked around the small condo. She calculated it couldn't be more than six hundred square feet.

"I'm so glad you're joining my revolution. Not everyone understands the power of a woman." Dr. Carey's eyes twinkled.

"I'm so down with that. Honestly, that's why I wanted to work for you. I really love the message you're delivering."

Dr. Carey went over the layout of the "office" and the workspace rules, including making sure that Julissa knew to bring her morning coffee order.

"I'll let you get set up and then I'll be back to check on you. Welcome to the team." Dr. Carey turned and shut her bedroom door.

Julissa sat in silence for a few seconds until the sound of honking horns drew her gaze to the window. One thing she hadn't noticed before was the way Dr. Carey liked to pucker her lips after certain words. Her face appeared almost like she was mid-kiss, her lips crinkled, revealing an overly plump pout. Julissa shrugged it off, assuming it was a complication from some cosmetic procedure.

I have a gorgeous view, an easy workload, and good hours. This is my dream job.

She connected to the email system and immediately found a new email marked urgent. Her mouth was agape as she read the words on her screen. A cold flush ran through her body, raising the hairs on the back of her neck as the room spun wildly. She braced herself, grabbing hold of the desk to steady the motion, but the words continued to whirl in her brain.

The few minutes of calm after meeting Dr. Carey were brief, and now Julissa knew this job had big consequences.

I hope my knife and I haunt you until the day we show up at your door.

Chapter 9

Eden

As the overhead angel bell announced a new arrival, Eden greeted the latest customer to Spiritual Gardens. She squeezed the vibrant red jasper stone tucked inside her loose off-white linen jumper, a smooth oval shape that begged to be caressed. She grounded herself, preparing to give the customers the same rehearsed message she gave Livvy. As she chewed her lip, she wondered if the starlet had joined Dr. Carey's program. It was the first time she'd recommended the program to any customer, and she hadn't been able to shake the knot in her stomach since the angel bell had announced Livvy's departure.

Later that evening, Eden had her scheduled one-on-one time with Dr. Carey, which had become a dreaded part of her routine. When she'd first started, she was excited, elated even. Now it was a burden, an expensive regret she was trying to escape. She finished her dinner of hummus and pita chips and set up her laptop to watch the required daily video, as Dr. Carey would often quiz her on its contents.

"The spirit of a man is corrupt," Dr. Carey said in the recorded video. "In part, they are not always to blame for how they've turned out. They're conditioned to be the leader and earn more than their female counterparts. This aura of chauvinism that oozes out every so often is part of their DNA." Eden took notes. She fully agreed with this part of Dr. Carey's program. It was the reason she'd fallen in love with the *Year of Self*, and how she'd made so much progress toward becoming a better person in her own life.

"We are finally at a crossroads. Our sisters in the '60s and '70s started the revolution, and we will make sure it becomes the new normal."

Eden leaned back on her couch, crossed her arms, and stared up at the ceiling, waiting for the chime warning that Dr. Carey had logged in. She always felt more hopeful and jubilant after watching one of her discussions. Dr. Carey was a master orator, and her message mesmerized Eden. What Eden could no longer tolerate were the strict rules, and leaving wasn't easy. When she joined, she'd inked the signature line on the contract without a second glance at the fine print, eager to join a movement. But within it, there were strict requirements that made it clear the program wasn't what Eden had hoped for. Every member had to sign an NDA, so they couldn't disclose any of the program rules or insider knowledge. Only Dr. Carey could determine when they could graduate and leave the program, and if she thought they needed longer than the year they'd signed up for, she could decide to add on more time. The biggest rule was that they had to leave their partners during the program, regardless of their status—married or not. According to Dr. Carey, "There's no way to know if the relationship is good or not if you aren't a single person when you join. The only way to really know if this relationship can work is to separate."

Eden admitted she had been naïve when she first moved to Los Angeles to begin her new life. She'd started her self-help journey before leaving her old life. When she first saw her on a talk show, Dr. Carey had captivated her. The words, the soft way her hair framed her heart-shaped face, and the charisma that seeped through the screen overwhelmed her. When Dr. Carey announced she was going to be at the Women's Mountain Retreat in San Gabriel, Eden believed it to be a sign.

After Dr. Carey's speech, Eden was willing to sign or join anything if it meant being part of the space she had longed for. Unfortunately, Dr. Carey's outward message didn't always match her inward behavior. It never dawned on Eden that behind the screen sat a vindictive false prophet. Prior to that, Eden had never signed a contract for anything, and now she found herself indebted to the therapist, full of guilt and anger.

Eden sat up straight and fidgeted with her hands as she waited for Dr. Carey. She always seemed to make her wait well past their meeting time. The time on her laptop showed it was ten minutes past the hour. The muscles in her neck tightened. After standing on her feet at work for ten hours, all she wanted was to soak in a bath of Epsom salts. Eden pulled her brown hair into a ponytail, revealing freckles that she never thought were as cute as magazines made out. Once she surrounded herself with other women in self-help, she stopped wearing makeup and began recycling, even eating plant-based foods on Mondays. She wanted nothing to do with her prior self and did everything she could to shed that old image.

When she moved out of her small town, she had a friend drop her off at the bus station and took the next bus west, not stopping until it did. She had been working and saving up, but only enough for six months in Los Angeles, whereas in Kansas City she could live off of her savings for closer to a year. Once she reached Kansas City, she took one step off the bus and immediately knew it wasn't where she wanted to be, and not just because Dr. Carey wasn't anywhere near there. The bus stopped outside of the city in Independence, where people were sleeping on their luggage, with others begging for change. The vibes were off. She immediately booked a ticket as far west as the bus could take her. Serendipity landed her among other kindred spirits. She met Willow, who taught yoga and took her under her wing, welcoming her into her home. But Eden's conviction to follow Dr. Carey tore her away from Willow, as she did not like Dr. Carey and tried to warn Eden.

"There's just something that doesn't feel right about her," Willow said.

"She's just misunderstood. I have so much faith in her." Eden now shuddered at her own words.

Eden's final straw with her ex was the possessiveness. It was always there, but his last threat felt different, more ominous when he told her if she didn't obey his demands, she'd pay. He'd wanted her to drop out of college and for them to move in together so he could keep tabs on her whereabouts. He grew jealous and didn't trust her when she was in class. At first, she tried to convince herself that he'd outgrow his jealousy, but he was relentless, and she knew she had to do something.

After several nights of tossing and turning, she knew it was time to break free and never look back. She immersed herself in the self-help aisle at the library, checking out books on empowerment and self-worth. She devoured every article or show that Dr. Carey appeared in, believing she needed to experience that level of genius up close. Before Dr. Carey, it took a lot of time for Eden to stop blaming herself for her ex's behavior and to realize that it had nothing to do with her. Through Dr. Carey and the library books that kept her company, she broke free from him and took her cross-country trip to personally thank the woman who'd opened her eyes.

The rent on Eden's small studio apartment kept going up, yet the crystal shop's wages weren't. When she joined Dr. Carey's group, she was at a place of reformation, so she was willing to do whatever she could to afford a pricier lifestyle than her budget would allow. She was open to all possibilities in the universe and willingly connected with the spiritual aspects of the program. Although after she watched Dr. Carey for several weeks, observing her curt demeanor, she worried she had signed up for something wayward. The once gregarious leader she couldn't get enough of slowly became a vile ruler who stood for everything she had run from. The longer she stayed, the more she questioned, *Is this a cult?*

The familiar online video chime sounded, turning Eden's stomach.

"Sorry I'm late. I was busy talking a client off the ledge." Dr. Carey rolled her eyes.

"Oh, do you need to get back to them? I can reschedule," Eden said.

"Nah. They'll be fine. A bit of histrionics, and I won't enable that kind of behavior." Dr. Carey batted away a rogue eyelash. "So, Eden. What's happened since the last time we spoke? Give me the rundown." Dr. Carey read something on her screen.

"I've really been doing great. I'm all caught up on the lessons, and I've achieved what I originally wanted. I have zero desire to go back to my ex, and I'm a changed woman." She smiled aggressively at the screen.

"Mm-hmm, what else?" Dr. Carey made clicking sounds with her mouse.

"I thought I could talk to you about something that's been on my mind." Eden twisted her fingers, her bravery dwindling.

Dr. Carey turned evenly to the laptop camera with a stern look. "I'm listening."

Chills went up Eden's spine as she grasped her rose quartz. "Can you confirm how much time I have left in the program? I'm getting concerned about finances since my rent has gone up, and I think I've learned everything I can from you. It's been really helpful, but maybe we can work on a plan for leaving early?"

This comment got Dr. Carey's full attention. "There are no breaks. In fact, you pay more if you leave the program before the year is up. You've taken a spot from a woman who is fully ready to make changes, so there are consequences to that. In fact, under the rules you agreed to, this may warrant a penalty, because only I can decide when you're ready to branch out on your own." Dr. Carey stared straight into Eden's soul.

"Okay." Eden gulped and stuttered. "Well, I hope you can see I've made a lot of progress... I actually referred someone to you, to the program. I don't know if she joined, but I thought maybe she could take my place," Eden said shakily.

"Yes, I did see her mention you, and no, that's not how the program works. Also, next time, send me someone with more clout. I'd rather have an A-list celebrity, but she could be interesting to have on my team."

"Okay. Well, I hope you can see my progress?"

"No, I absolutely don't. From what I can tell, you're a quitter. You set goals and don't complete them. I won't be a party to that behavior, Eden. I am extending you another month or two. You'll receive the invoice in your email."

Dr. Carey closed her laptop, and Eden stared at the screen as she tried to suppress her tears. *I can't let her win.*

Eden gripped her crystals until her short fingernails dug into her skin. The negative self-talk she had tried to conceal was bubbling to the surface. She didn't want to revert to old habits, to be that woman anymore. The one who always doubted her worth and place in the world. She had done so much reiki bodywork, and she was angry to find herself back in that hurtful cycle. The anger she once felt toward her ex was so quick to return. Even with the distance from him and all the emotional work she'd done, it still came boiling back. Dr. Carey knew all the buttons to push.

Eden's hands shook as she dialed a friend. When Willow answered, she could hear a man's chuckle and children playing. The familiar sound of a rush of wind from a window left ajar.

"Hello? Eden, are you there?" Willow asked when there was no response.

Eden hung up. She was interfering in a family moment, and she didn't belong there. She gulped back tears, remembering good times with her sister-friend. Willow had seen through Dr. Carey and warned Eden before joining, and she hated that she hadn't taken her guidance seriously. Eden hadn't been in a place to see Dr. Carey for who she really was: a monster behind a screen, forcing members to go into debt.

Eden missed Willow. She had been her best friend when she first moved to California. But after Eden joined the *Year of Self*, Dr. Carey told her that Willow wasn't a loyal friend and was standing in the way of her progress. Eden now regretted not following Willow's advice. Her friend had long ago left the fake spiritual world to focus on other ways to provide healing as a nurse. Eden had always wanted to be liked by others, and years of deep breathing and reiki couldn't fully cure her people-pleasing tendencies. Now she could only think of how many people she'd disappointed—her own mother for not staying in their small town, her professors for leaving mid- year when she had taken a spot from another student, and now the biggest disappointment: needing to make more money or risk losing the apartment she loved.

The scorching hate she felt for herself scalded any of the spiritual work she'd accomplished. She was patient zero and could only think of how to afford her home, which had become the safest harbor she'd ever known. The place where she cocooned herself when she needed a break from the world. The cracks in her mental health hadn't formed today. They'd been plastered over for decades. Eden had struggled to cover up her perceived inadequacies. She beat herself up with constant thoughts of "I'm not good enough" or "I don't deserve good things."

Eden turned on her favorite sound bath guide and listened as she lay on the couch clutching her Afghan blanket to her chin. Lying down prevented her from rocking, which stimulated her brain too much.

"Deep breaths," she told herself as the soothing gongs took effect.

I will get out of this cult one way or another.

Chapter 10

Dylan

The last guest spot ended and Dylan watched the morning show anchors prepare for the next segment, Renee Baldwin refreshing her nude Bare Kiss lipstick and Bob Suney adjusting his shiny red tie. *Wake Up LA* gave the audience a bird's-eye view of the behind-the-scenes process when moving from one spot to the next, complete with sponsor tags. As soon as they returned from break, they announced they had a surprise caller to speak against Dr. Carey and her program.

Dylan's breakfast of French toast and a side of home fries churned in his belly. The acidity of the orange juice burned from the back of his throat all the way down his esophagus as he stood, debating running to the restroom. He carefully locked his door, securing every latch and leaving a placard reading Do Not Disturb. All thoughts of a quick bathroom break dissolved when a voice rang out from his laptop speakers. "Sir, are you there?"

You're fucking doing this. You're a king among peasants.

Miles away in Burbank, Dylan's disguised voice rang through the *Wake Up LA* studio.

"Mark my words, if Dr. Carey doesn't make a statement

denouncing her program, I will have no choice but to unleash my plan to end it myself." His diaphragm tightened with the constricting power of his nerves. "I will no longer stand by while she denigrates men. I accept nothing less than an apology and a complete shutdown of her program." Dylan's hands shook. He had rehearsed his lines since he made the plan over a week ago, but speaking live, he knew he had one shot to sound convincing. He watched Renee and Bob's faces, their brows creasing as they looked at each other and around the room with confused expressions.

"Please, we are working to contact Dr. Carey. Do not hang up." Renee held her right hand to her ear. "Sir, we'd love for you to come on the show for a face-to-face. Please tell us, what did you mean by 'ending it yourself?'" Renee stared without blinking at the screen.

"She is a disgrace to women and a threat to mankind. She's left me with no choice." Dylan gulped back the hardened lump of bile that settled in his voice box.

Bob yanked on his tie. "I'm learning that we've contacted Dr. Carey, but she's declined to come on the show. Sir, please, can we talk about your demands further?"

There was silence on the line.

Dylan saw Renee mouthing something to someone behind the camera.

"Don't think about tracing my call. This is a burner phone, and you'll never find me." Dylan hung up.

More dead air filled the studio. Deafening silence.

"Sir, are you there?" Bob shook his head at the invisible people behind the camera. "I'm sorry, viewers. But we seem to have lost the caller. This is a developing story and we'll keep you updated." Bob stared blankly into the camera.

Dylan immediately jumped up from the desk and made a run toward the bathroom, barely making it to the toilet before his breakfast reached its rim.

Dylan grabbed his phone and hit record. His face was pale white as he inhaled through a sniffly nose. "Hi guys. Soon you'll know that was me. I love the look on Renee's face. She's such a kiss-ass to Dr. Carey. I loved how scared she looked when I threatened death. She nearly pissed her pants." Dylan audibly chuckled. "One day you'll all replay these videos and look back on them with pure pride at what I've accomplished. Remember, this is for all of you men out there. For guys like me with no direction in life, fed up and left behind by the new wave of society. I do this for you." A still frame of Dylan's half-grin stayed frozen on the video screen.

Dylan laid out his laptop on the freshly made bed in his hotel room overlooking the city skyline. He had made the red-eye out to LA the previous night for his secret mission to gather reconnaissance on Dr. Carey, and this morning's call-in to *Wake up LA* was the first item on his to-do list. When he logged in to the Mandate, the fervent chatter was gaining traction as members posted about the anonymous caller. Anytime Dylan logged on to the Mandate, he always used an outer space background so there would be no indication of where he was. No one knew he was in a basement before, and now no one knew he was in a hotel room just steps away from where Dr. Carey lived.

Men from all over the country were in awe of their new hero, who stood up to Dr. Carey and her program and threatened her and her members. They ridiculed her for not having the guts to come on and debate the caller one-on-one. "She's a fucking coward. She hides behind her fancy laptop screen and pricey treatment plan, but won't answer the tough questions!"

Dylan sat back, reading the comments, which were mostly on his side. There were only a few who questioned the violent nature of his message. "Are we really talking about murder? I mean, Dr. Carey and women like her are scum, but they don't deserve to be killed." Most members quickly turned on them. The mob mentality was strong, and the mention of death didn't deter the majority of them. Dylan had accomplished more in the last five hours of his life than he had in his first thirty-four years. His nerves from earlier faded away, and he felt a rare wave of tingly confidence.

Dylan had never intended to make this his message. He didn't have murderous inclinations before, but the more he watched and read about Dr. Carey, the more he couldn't deny those feelings. At the very least, he'd hoped that today's message would scare her straight. Although the thought of ridding the world of women like her was enticing.

Over the last few weeks, the Mandate's membership had grown as word got out. With nearly a thousand men following the group both in the United States and around the world, Dylan believed he had a true mandate.

He logged on for a video chat. "Hey my dudes. Today is a great day. Whoever that guy is, I wish we could all buy him a round of beer." They all cheered in unison as Dylan's head swelled.

"The other day, some bitch asked me why I was angry. Can you believe that?" Several men shook their heads in disbelief. "I told her, 'Fuck yeah, I'm angry.' Look at what society has done to men. We have no rights. They take our rights as soon as we're born by removing our foreskin, teaching us about women's liberation in school, and then giving us rules on how to woo a woman."

Dylan watched the faces on the screen as more cheers came from the Mandate members. Dylan shook his head. His heart expanded with pride.

"I created this group so men can get back to their rightful place in *our* society. Other countries don't tolerate the bullshit that American men have had to deal with. Look how far our country has fallen since we've installed equality in the classroom, workplace, and home. The woman's role is to support her man, not to surpass him. Many men I've spoken with cannot transform back into who they were after they've been demoralized by the institution." Dylan scowled, shaking his head. "They are shells of themselves. Gutted, lost, and laid bare for women to walk all over them." A pang of emotion swelled from Dylan's throat upwards as his eyes teared up.

Several men on the screen wiped away their tears and others pumped their fists in the air.

"If it wasn't for women like Dr. Carey and women in society who never gave me a chance, maybe I wouldn't have created this, so I am thankful for that and to all of you," Dylan said.

Again, a few members thumped their fists on their chests and wiped away their tears.

"This group is here because my mom wasn't there for me. Because society allows women to trample all over men. So, I have them to thank for us finding our brotherhood. Without those failures, we wouldn't have found each other and created the pact we have today."

They all cheered, cried, and raised their drinks together. Dylan checked the clock. His schedule was running right on time. He said his goodbyes and shut his laptop, gathered it and his hotel card, and headed to the Buzzed Bee, a local coffee shop that Dr. Carey's latest assistant visited daily.

Time to launch the next phase of my plan.

Chapter 11

Bailey

Bailey walked into her second-floor office, which she shared with Matt from the tax evasion unit. When she left the public defender's office, she'd thought it was a vertical move. She grew tired of the lengthy cases where she sometimes met the defendant mere minutes before their trial. She could represent a murder case, a robbery, and an assault all within the same week. At Wright & Morgan, her goal was to make it to the top-floor office and be brought on as a partner in the firm. The top-floor lawyers were elite, including her boss, Richard Wright. He was an old colleague of her dad's, and this time nepotism had gone her way. She'd secured the job through that relationship, but now that she was there, she had regrets—lots of them.

After graduating from law school at the top of her class, Bailey had dreams of winning exonerations for the most innocent in society. But within hours of being shown to her desk, she was already jaded. The stacks of case files and the never-ending ring of the telephone made her hopeless. She sipped more wine each evening and woke to find herself in yesterday's clothes. She let her personal grooming habits slide as she bit her fingernails down to the nubs. Each morning she had knots in her stomach over returning to the stuffy, dusty office. Her depression ramped up, a ride-along passenger like the ugly friend who dutifully followed the cool girls around. The villain who always ruined a good time.

Bailey downloaded some dating apps, but she was far too busy for a relationship. She barely recognized her profile: a 28-year-old woman with a silky black bob haircut, often reaching for the phantom locks she'd cut right before starting her new position. She had the same style pantsuit with shirts in various colors; thanks to her former position, she hadn't been able to purchase newer clothes just yet. Her first nepo paycheck paid off her credit card debt. Most lawyers she knew were broke or faking their wealth anyway. Unless they reached the upper echelons of their firm, they were barely making ends meet.

When she received the call that Richard wanted to chat, it completely surprised her.

"Bailey, come in. I have a case that I need you to represent," he said, opening the file.

"Great. I'm looking forward to it." Bailey tugged on her sweater as she sat down.

"Well, not so fast. I have reservations about this one, so this is a trial run." Richard threw down the pen in his hand.

Bailey took a quiet, deep breath.

"Dr. Carmella Carey is looking for representation to oversee her *Year of Self* program." Richard used air quotes around the title. "She's already started the business, but it appears she's recently come under attack." He arched an eyebrow.

"Dr. Carmella Carey? I actually just heard about her. She was doing a TV interview, but I wasn't paying close attention." She fidgeted with the rings on her fingers.

"Yeah, apparently she's anti-men and makes lonely women pay a lot of money to cover her rent." Richard rolled his eyes.

Bailey glared, biting her tongue. "Oh, yeah, that's an interesting concept," she said, shifting in her chair.

"Something about her feels off to me. But she specifically asked for a female lawyer, and I thought it might be an excellent case for you to sink your teeth into."

"Thank you, I'd be honored." Bailey reached for Dr. Carey's contact number that Richard had written down.

"Just so you're aware, she's had some threats, but I'm really not concerned for your safety; it's just something to consider." Richard leaned back with his hands behind his head. "Honestly, it's a bunch of women's lib drama, and we're not about that here at the firm."

"I've heard about the threats. Honestly, I thought little of it. But I think I'm up for it." Bailey twisted her mouth.

Richard leaned forward, narrowing his eyes. "Well, it's not up for discussion. We believe you're the one to represent her. I went to great lengths to honor your father's request, seeing as DEI is all the rage." He slumped back into his oversized leather chair. "I need to take a call, though. Keep me posted, hon." Richard picked up the phone and asked his assistant to contact a client.

Bailey left the office wringing her hands. She had always heard of bosses treating women like pawns, but now that she was the one being used, it wasn't a great feeling. *He's from a different century*, she kept telling herself, but the more she replayed it, the angrier she became. As an Asian woman in a law firm full of white men, she stuck out. Now she knew they didn't care about her skills; they were just happy to check a box for HR.

Before leaving work, she stood outside her office door. She ran her hand over the gold nameplate that read Bailey Lake: Hard evidence of her parents' own ambition. Her successful parents had encouraged her to strive for perfection. The first sign of stress came when she didn't get a perfect mark in kindergarten. Bailey sat in the corner shaking her head, crying, "I don't want to fail." As an only child, she decided she would have to forge this life all by herself—until her dad got her this position, that is. Part of her took the job because he'd got it for her. Solving white-lady problems wasn't as rewarding as helping to exonerate the innocent, but it paid better.

Back home, Bailey poured her nightly glass of wine, which sometimes became two or three. She powered up her laptop and searched for Dr. Carey. A radiant blonde with long wavy locks stared back at her amid flashing buttons encouraging her to enter the website. Bailey pushed play on a video that was prominently displayed on the screen.

"Ladies, welcome. Today is your day to take back your life. Are you in a relationship that has become toxic? Do your male bosses and colleagues always seem to get farther ahead? Are you tired of being in last place? If so, you are home. Join me and a fantastic group of women as we kick life's ass and clear a path to regain control."

Bailey didn't think there was anything wrong with what Dr. Carey said. In fact, she nodded along during some parts. She typed in a new search for Dr. Carey and added the word "controversy" to the bar, which pulled up a thread from anonymous former members.

She kicked me out because my ex came over. I didn't even invite him.

She's just in it for the money. I am in such debt now.

My family disowned me once I joined, and they still haven't welcomed me back.

Bailey considered that more people go online to complain than leave a positive review, but there were a few perfectly curated ones.

Dr. Carey gave me my voice back. I will never stifle it for a man again.

I got rid of my deadweight husband and now I'm lighter than ever.

Dr. Carey is my light, and I'll follow her anywhere.

Bailey kept doing a deep dive to see what she said about men that might prompt death threats. She found that the main tenet of her program was that women needed to leave their relationships.

"You might think you're happy, but you wouldn't be here if you were. It's time to cut him loose and stand on your own two feet. You don't need him."

Bailey also found a list of rules that participants had to agree to. After browsing through them, she thought a couple seemed far-fetched, but nothing terrible except the financial aspect. Besides, it was all voluntary. Bailey jotted down the rules in her paisley notebook.

The more she researched, the better she felt about her assignment. Women's empowerment was her jam, and so far she had uncovered nothing she didn't already agree with.

The more Bailey learned about Dr. Carey, the more she thought about her lessons. From then on, she viewed the men in her office in a different light. Her research on Dr. Carey became an obsession. Her soothing voice mesmerized her, instantly making her forget all of her work stress. Each night, she went back to her condo, a drink in hand, and watched more of Dr. Carey's videos, only a few of which were uploaded for free.

Dr. Carey's face came into focus. With her eyes shut, she repeated, "You are worth more than they tell you. You are the driver of your life. No one can steal your light. Only amazing things will guide you."

Bailey hated to admit it, but she felt better listening to Dr. Carey. Her shoulders relaxed and warm fuzzies melted across her skin. After a second glass of wine, Bailey punched in her credit card information to join Dr. Carey, her cursor hovering over the "submit" button. She reasoned with herself that if she had to represent her, then maybe it would be a benefit if she were also a client. Curiosity overtook her. As she drifted off to sleep, she thought of the rules that she would have to sign. She wasn't a fan of signing any contract, but she accepted losing the rest of her dues if caught breaking any of the rules.

Just before succumbing to sleep, she panicked, sitting straight up. *Fuck. What the fuck am I doing?* She gnawed on her already too-short nails as she considered what a violation of attorney-client privilege it would be to join. But no one knew the real her, not even Dr. Carey. Their relationship up to this point had been via telephone and email, but thankfully, modern technology could change her image and voice. Under the name Val Frost, she joined the group and began working on herself.

Chapter 12

Julissa

A wave of nausea swelled as Julissa dumped discarded coffee into the sink. The bitter drink splashed toward her and she turned her head, grimacing. The scent of coffee repulsed her, but this job required getting used to it. After reading the death threat on her first day, she pushed through, assuming it was a disgruntled man who was making baseless threats. She already knew the media criticized Dr. Carey, and didn't all strong women face scrutiny?

Julissa hated mornings, but she wanted a job that made a difference. She loved everything about Dr. Carey's message, at least what she knew of it so far, and she still pinched herself at being in such close proximity to her.

Prior to working for Dr. Carey, Julissa had floated through temp jobs, never finding the perfect fit until now. The 25-year-old was fresh out of college with a marketing degree but was still "finding herself," as she'd recently told her mom. She was striking, with brown skin, short wavy hair that she shaved on the sides and left longer on the top, and brown eyes with a fleck of amber around the pupil. She wore a diamond nose ring and was almost always wearing her Chuck tennis shoes. Working for Dr. Carey felt natural for her since, as a queer person, she considered herself part of the women's liberation movement.

Julissa watched all the online videos and interviews with Dr. Carey. "Women of all shapes, sizes, races, ethnicities, and backgrounds have come together to unite against the patriarchy. We resist the norms society has placed on us from birth to death. We stand united as women who are tired of the bullshit!"

Julissa's cheeks hurt from smiling after she watched the latest video. Her eyes glowed, mesmerized by the thought leader who voiced all the things she felt and believed. *I can't believe I get to work for this rock star!*

But concerns about the program began to creep in, and Dr. Carey's façade quickly crumbled. When her humanness showed, her true self was pure ugliness. Julissa soon realized that Dr. Carey was a narcissist who spent hours perfecting her image while destroying the egos of her clients. She spoke down to most everyone in the program and seemed to only care about how much money it made her. While Julissa initially loved the program, once inside Dr. Carey's lair, she could see the program was a cult.

The hardest part of Julissa's job as an assistant was reading through the daily emails, with requests mounting from members who wanted to leave the program. The requests were heartbreaking, many of the messages begging to leave, from "I miss my husband and family" to "I hate everything this program stands for." Initially, Julissa brought these requests to Dr. Carey. Once Dr. Carey learned who the clients were, though, she would penalize them by adding more time to their program. When Julissa realized she was responsible for further punishment, the guilt haunted her day and night. She'd wake up thinking about these women, racking her brain for ways to help them escape. As an empath, Dr. Carey's behavior poked every sensitive nerve in her.

Julissa's other duties as an assistant were ordering Dr. Carey's morning coffee at the Buzzed Bee and then returning for the daily meeting, which was a rundown of the day's events. If it was a live interview day, she'd block out Dr. Carey's schedule for hair and makeup, as this was "the most important aspect to nail," according to Dr. Carey. Julissa also scheduled and arranged online therapy sessions, both one-on-one and with the group. She was also responsible for sending out contracts and onboarding new members. Most of her position could be managed anywhere with her laptop, but Dr. Carey wanted Julissa to be present at her condo most of the time, available for any errands she might need. In the small one-bedroom condo, Julissa's workspace was a corner of the living room. Her compact desk wasn't much bigger than a fold-out tray.

Julissa answered her vibrating business cell. "Dr. Carey's line, how may I assist you?"

"This is *Wake up LA*. We are trying to reach Dr. Carey on an urgent matter. We have a man who called in requesting that Dr. Carey denounce and shut down her program or, quote, 'There will be death on her hands.' Would she be willing to come on and speak with him now?"

Julissa's stomach dropped at the news. She pressed the mute button and walked to Dr. Carey's office, gasping upon entering. A stream of blood rolled down Dr. Carey's upper lip and she saw several red-soaked tissues wadded in the trash. "Are you okay?" Julissa asked.

"Just a fucking nosebleed," Dr. Carey dismissed as she held her head up, pinching the bridge of her nose.

"We have a situation." Julissa informed her about the threatening caller.

Dr. Carey laughed. "Absolutely not. Tell them I won't be giving him the dignity of my time. It's a ploy for airtime, and I won't be playing his game. Just hang up."

Julissa turned back to her desk. "I'm sorry, but she's not interested."

In the few months she'd worked for her, Julissa wasn't a stranger to receiving threats against Dr. Carey. Some of the email complaints from members had turned menacing. Many outsiders, both men and women, also wrote in saying the program was a sham, detailing what they thought should happen to Dr. Carey and any woman who followed her. Julissa felt the worst about the members, who only realized their mistake after signing the contract and had to endure their year, or longer if Dr. Carey tacked on more time. While Julissa had considered quitting nearly every day, another side of her wanted to stay and help. *Maybe I can figure out a way to set them free.*

Julissa's own mental health was affected. She'd wake up with the words from the emails in her head. In the shower, she couldn't escape the pain of replaying the voicemails. She'd be driving on the freeway and hear their pleas during one-on-one therapy sessions as they begged to be freed from the contract.

"I don't think I can afford rent this month. I don't know what I'm going to do. If I can't afford my apartment, I'm going to have to go back to my ex, and he's the reason I came to you. He's not good for me, and I'm afraid of what will happen if I go back and I don't have any savings."

"You've ruined me. I was so much better before I joined this cult. Now all of my friends have disowned me, and the man you forced me to give up for this *Year of Self* is now with someone else. I just saw their picture online, and I'm gutted. I am absolutely miserable. How can you do this to people?"

"You should have your license taken away! You've brainwashed my daughter into thinking that this is the only way to be healed. Meanwhile, her children and husband are living away from her and only have the memories of their mommy. Her children deserve to have her back. I'm going to contact the state board and tell them to revoke your license."

As a Gen Z kid, Julissa was accustomed to disgruntled people airing their grievances online. The latest threatening email was like the others, but now she suspected that whoever wrote it wasn't joking and was likely the caller on *Wake Up LA*.

Death on your hands. Julissa couldn't get the words out of her head. The ominous email had said the same thing as today's anonymous caller.

"You may have convinced the weaker sex to believe your bullshit, but a man can see right through you. Believe me when I say that I will never stop until you and your program are silenced. You have caused enough harm, and I have the support of my army of men, so we will no longer put up with your shit. Consider this a final warning to shut down your program."

Julissa reread the email and went back to Dr. Carey's office, where she was reapplying her lip gloss. Julissa lightly knocked on her doorframe. "Dr. Carey, I need a quick minute."

"That's all I have," Dr. Carey retorted.

"I wanted to make you aware of an email we got last month. I didn't think much of it because it seemed like a typical complaint, but maybe it's connected to the caller from today? The email was a threat against you and the members of the program."

Dr. Carey let out an enormous sigh. "I'm completely uninterested in both the phone call and this email. It's a nonissue for me, and I'm not concerned. Thank you, Julissa." She dismissed her and signaled for her to close the door.

Julissa closed the door and twisted her lips. She walked back to her makeshift desk and shrugged. *If she's not worried about it, I'm not going to.*

But Julissa knew better. The email and the phone call looped in her mind throughout the day. She dialed the lawyer Dr. Carey had hired, Bailey Lake, and left a voicemail. "Hi, Bailey, it's Julissa Sanchez. I just want to reach out to you about some complaints that Dr. Carey and her clients are receiving. She's not concerned, but I guess I just want to know if anything can be done?" Julissa furrowed her brow. "I guess I'm just getting worried because of the anonymous caller...." A beep alerted Julissa that her message had gone over the allotted time.

Julissa felt more like a manager than an assistant. Dr. Carey's program had grown so much that she needed a larger team, much more support than Julissa's assistant position entailed. She couldn't have foreseen adding legal discussions to her daily job responsibilities, but here she was.

She packed up to leave for the day and walked through the apartment doors, nearly barreling right into someone's chest. It was a man. "Excuse me." It spooked her to see him standing right outside the door. She barely got a good look at him as she immediately glanced down, averting her eyes from his face. She noticed a leather jacket and a strong, masculine cologne.

His arm, raised to knock, drifted to scratch his head. "Oh, my bad. I must have the wrong address." He walked off in the opposite direction toward the stairs.

Julissa clutched her phone, punched the button in the elevator, and peeked through the door to make sure she was alone. She snapped her head back inside the elevator when she saw the man staring back at her.

Chapter 13

Dylan

D ylan settled into a corner spot at the Buzzed Bee as he waited for Julissa to make her daily coffee run. The beauty of the youth of today was that social media revealed their every move, and Dr. Carey liked to post and tag a lot of selfies. The day before, Dylan scoped out a spot at the coffee shop until he felt comfortable with his mission. He also put to use a couple of his courses in IT, specifically the ones on cybersecurity. He created a fake profile of a woman who wanted to join the *Year of Self*, complete with a backstory and profile picture: Veronica Dixon, a newly married, 27-year-old brunette who'd just learned her husband was having an affair. Dylan had so many photos to choose from online. He landed on a plain brunette with glasses. She had a welcoming smile, but he didn't think she was hot enough to raise red flags.

Dylan thought her profile would draw enough pity to get him an easy acceptance should there be a waitlist. It didn't matter if she became an actual client—Dylan just needed her to appear believable. He needed her application to get through to the next stage so that he could send Julissa an email to infiltrate Dr. Carey's system when he sent more documentation for the membership questionnaires.

Dylan watched the crowd at the Buzzed Bee get their caffeine fix. He marveled at the various women who came and went. Some in tight yoga pants. *She's probably a big tease.* Another woman appeared professional. *Probably took a job away from a deserving man.* He checked his email and found a response inviting Veronica Dixon to enter the next phase of the application process. The next step would allow Dylan to send off his phishing email. Hopefully Julissa wouldn't notice. The questionnaire asked "Veronica" to explain why the program should accept her as a client. It requested details about her goals for the year and her vision for her personal transformation. Veronica could provide links to any inspirational stories that summed up what she hoped to achieve, which was how Dylan planned to launch the hacking attack. Once Julissa or Dr. Carey clicked on the compromised link, Dylan would have access to their files, which he hoped included a list of all the members, including their home addresses.

Not a typical coffee drinker, Dylan didn't realize how often he'd have to run to the bathroom. He didn't want to lose his table, so he hurriedly used the toilet. When he returned, he immediately recognized Julissa—the slender, toned Latina walking toward the counter. He had scanned her personal social media pages, where she had random sunset pictures and old posts with friends at a Pride event. Dylan had hoped to find newer posts with Dr. Carey, but Julissa had posted nothing in over six months. He watched as she picked up several cups, reading them and putting them back down before grabbing two and walking back out. Dylan quickly slammed his laptop shut and followed.

She had long strides, which meant he had to pick up his pace to keep up with her, but he went slow enough so it didn't look like he was chasing her. While he knew where the Buzzed Bee was, he didn't know where Dr. Carey's residence was. Luckily, the area was fairly busy with morning strollers, so he didn't seem too out of place. Plus, he'd bought dark khakis and a navy polo to fit in with the working crowd. Julissa walked up to a condo building and gave a nod to the doorman, who nodded back, holding the door open. When Dylan got to the door, the guy began to close it. "Can I assist you, sir?" the bald doorman, who was Black and muscular, asked.

"Oh, sorry. I'm here on a work order. I'm with tech support and came to fix a laptop." Dylan raised his own laptop in hopes it seemed convincing.

The doorman eyed him up and down.

Dylan's left eye twitched, a nervous tic he'd dealt with since childhood. He'd rehearsed this scenario so many times on the plane ride to California. *Come on, man.*

"What's the name?"

"Damn. I knew you'd ask me, and I left the ticket in the car. I'll have to run and get it because I parked all the way around the corner."

"Nah. It's okay. You look alright. Just don't cause any trouble." He opened the door.

"Thanks, man." Dylan slipped inside, looking around to find Julissa, but she was long gone. Along the wall were the building's mailboxes. He went straight to them, glancing back at the doorman, who was chatting with someone else. He peeked at the names until he found Dr. Carmella Carey. Condo 413. He took the stairs up to her floor; grateful the stairwell was empty. He strolled by her door, but it was quiet. A large palm plant stood outside her secluded entryway, which was fairly dark, lit only by a flickering hallway light.

He stood only inches away from the woman he hated more than anyone in the world, maybe slightly more than Barbara, even. As he stood outside the door, the sound of the elevator notified him of someone's presence.

Chapter 14

Livvy

Livvy stared at her laptop, questioning how she'd reached the point in her life to be paying for an online therapy program. She had no hangups about counseling; she just wasn't the type to discuss her issues. Since Alton broke her heart, though, she had warmed to the idea. Besides, Dr. Carey's program felt different. She knew from friends and from just being a woman that finding genuine love was hard, and maybe Dr. Carey had the answer.

When Livvy first watched Dr. Carey, she debated whether the program was just another gimmick. The psychology community was over-saturated, and many professionals had pounced on their opportunity to claim a slice of the crowded space. Even in her field, there were famous actors on TV capitalizing on their fame, touting the latest guru that "changed their life."

The deeper she dove into learning about Dr. Carey, the more engrossed she became. The more she listened, the more she craved. An overwhelming urge deep in her gut told her she had to become a member, so she hit the submit button on her application.

"Welcome! I adore you for signing up to be a better woman. I promise I am on your side and will guide you through your journey.

Consider me like a surrogate friend, always supporting you and questioning your motivations along the way, like the fairy godmother on your shoulder." Dr. Carey's smiling face was paused on the screen. Several tabs appeared for Livvy to book her first one-on-one session, as well as to attend the monthly all-member team meeting, which was mandatory. Livvy clicked through to view all the prior videos in the content library.

A psychic told her once that the person who held her destiny would have the greenest eyes she'd ever seen. It was ridiculous how much that statement stuck with her. She ignored brown and blue-eyed guys because she wanted to believe that fate would bring her a soulmate. For the entire next year, she judged guys based on eye color alone, and it seemed that none she met carried the magical hue. Until there was one—her Alton. He sold her on making it big just like she'd dreamed, finally landing the big break every young actor hoped for, complete with the house and car, and love to boot. It didn't matter that he was married because in her mind, it wasn't an affair. Livvy believed every word he told her, especially the ones about his marriage being a legal technicality that he was doing everything he could to dissolve.

"Baby, I promise you I am only married on paper and it only matters to the state of California."

Alton's ex was the reason it took so long for them to move forward, Livvy assumed. All of Livvy's ire was directed at her, which was why she didn't feel bad when she and Alton ran into her at his kids' dance rehearsal one day and Livvy whispered in her ear, "Your kids will call me mommy one day."

Livvy thought back on her behavior and cringed. *I was a fucking asshole.*

She now knew that Alton was a predator and had abused women for decades. At least, that's what the reports kept saying. But losing him and her career still hadn't sunk in, nor had the depression subsided. For the first few weeks, she slept on and off, unable to will herself out of bed. While the world went crazy with the news of

Alton's arrest on charges of sexual assault against various actors, Livvy sat at home waiting for her agent to call, vowing never to date a green-eyed man again. Her heart ached the most in the hours before she fell asleep. She missed the nightly texts, the calls, and knowing someone was hers. Each morning, she'd pick herself up again and do busy work, but by nightfall, she'd rip the band-aid off her heart and let the pain pour out once again.

Livvy's online footprint branded her as Alton's girlfriend, implicating her in his crimes. Anyone who searched his name found their pictures together, the interviews where she proudly proclaimed him the "best lay she'd ever had," and other interviews where she defended the early sexual abuse rumors. Eventually, Livvy found herself on the other side, with calls for her to be canceled for shielding and supporting an abuser. *I didn't know. I'm a victim, too!* She'd plead with anyone who'd listen, but the pool of people who would grew smaller each day.

All the people who once wanted to be close to her distanced themselves. The once clingy new money friends who wanted to attend concerts and be seen together at the hottest restaurants were nowhere to be found. Everyone removed her from their group texts, making it the loneliest time of her life in one of the world's busiest cities. The last message she wrote to her so-called friends was, "I am living in a pit of darkness." And even that didn't get a response. Her lonely existence bred lonely comforts—the bed to herself, watching what she wanted in a pit of despair knowing she was isolated with no one to love her.

Two months after Alton's arrest, Livvy was still recovering from the shock. Her once perfectly groomed eyebrows and fresh eyelashes were now mushed to her face from weeks of tears and lack of love from her favorite aesthetician. Her face grew puffier each day from crying and constant panic about her future. Stuck in a doom cycle, she made a last-ditch effort to salvage her career when she went to see Emilio.

Her meeting with him was the first time she had ventured out of her apartment in over two months. She hadn't had fresh air or sunlight or the comfort of human interaction, minus brief exchanges with a delivery person. Personal banter had grown foreign, but she slowly picked it up again after forcing herself out of her apartment. And learning about Dr. Carey seemed to be divine intervention.

Livvy clicked play on the welcome video for all new members.

"Welcome to your new life. I will be your guide to becoming free from the shackles society has placed on you. Won't you join me?"

Livvy sat mesmerized as a close-up image of Dr. Carey appeared on the screen. The hairs on her arms raised, and a sensation of warmth flowed through her body. She hadn't seen this close an image of Dr. Carey, but staring back at her were the most captivating, piercing green eyes that she had ever seen.

She was hooked.

Chapter 15

Carmella

The sound of pills clattering around in amber-colored bottles cut through the quiet room. A knock at Carmella's front door interrupted the gulp of water she was about to swallow. She sighed in annoyance as she turned to rush out of the kitchen toward the noise, her silk robe and belt flowing behind her.

"You didn't tell me you'd hired a new assistant."

"Oh fuck. I forgot. Hurry, come in," Carmella said, looking down both sides of her hallway before closing the door.

"Did you say anything to her? If so, I'll have to let her go."

"Nah. I just said I got the wrong address."

Spencer picked Carmella up, set her down on the island, and gave her a deep kiss. "How's my sexy doctor today?"

"Pissed! Did you hear some fucker called the TV station threatening me? They fucking wanted me to talk to him. Yeah, right." Carmella crossed her arms.

"It's okay, kitten. Calm down. Nobody is going to hurt you." Spencer kissed Carmella's forehead.

Carmella softened. "This is why I keep you around." She bit his lip. "Let's hurry. Our reservations are coming up."

Carmella went to the bedroom to get ready, and when she came back out, she had completely transformed her appearance. She was unrecognizable in a dark brunette wig and black bodysuit, the complete opposite the soft blonde of "daytime" Dr. Carey. Carmella's new look was edgy, like a panther in leather.

Relationships were tricky, even for a licensed therapist. Carmella wasn't lucky in love. In fact, she had some of the worst luck with men. When she created her program, she and Spencer had split up, for good this time—or so she'd thought. Nights were lonely, and he always had a way of worming his way back into her sphere. Since she'd become a public figure, she'd had to keep him a secret, which wasn't difficult since he had other obligations.

It's much better if the world believes I'm a single woman, too.

She and Spencer devised a plan to sneak in dates when they could, like *Bachelor* lovers before their big reveal. "Outward appearances mean so much. The world views women so harshly, especially beautiful, confident, and intelligent ones," Carmella said, convincing Spencer of the plan. Carmella needed her clients to believe she was one of them and could relate to their struggles with men. While she understood what a terrible relationship felt like, she certainly wouldn't leave a partner like she was asking her clients to do. "I'd never be dumb enough to follow these rules myself," she admitted drunkenly to Spencer one night.

In a recent interview on a video podcast, *Max Logan Investigates*, Carmella had described her program: "Women need to take control of their lives. They shouldn't allow themselves to be controlled by societal norms or the men who dictate them."

"Explain how a woman becomes a client and the steps she takes before and during this program," Max Logan asked. His pants were snug, and he kept adjusting them in his seat.

"I accept my clients based on their life profiles. They fill out an extensive questionnaire designed to help me understand their history, and they pitch to me why they would be an outstanding candidate for my service."

"Let me interject. Why would women willingly subject themselves to such a rigid program?"

"Because I'm fantastic at what I do." Carmella puckered her lips. "Once they finish the program, they can stand on their own with confidence that they will never need a man again. By stripping down and releasing all the relationship trauma that binds them, they are reborn into themselves as a fully whole woman. Most of us have never experienced what it's like to be a woman without a male influence. We have overbearing fathers, abusive boyfriends, and controlling husbands. It's time to take back our power." Carmella sank back into her office chair.

"What about women who come from loving homes with supportive fathers, or attentive partners? Not all men are so vile," Max asked, attempting to cross his legs.

"My program won't be for them, but I'd press them to really think about their relationships. Consider all of their interactions: at school, in the workplace, at church, or in public—they most likely come into contact with a negative male influence. That interaction doesn't need to be imprinted on women any longer. I provide the tools for women to fight back." Dr. Carey raised her eyebrows with smug satisfaction.

Carmella was used to the snickers and looks she received during some interviews, mostly from male hosts who didn't understand what women dealt with. She always preferred to be interviewed by a female reporter, as she wanted to project the image of powerful women. Still, sometimes a male colleague would make remarks like, "Glad my wife is at work right now and not watching this," or "Some guy has really scorned her," always followed by a chuckle and elbow jab.

Carmella knew all too well how women blindly trusted men. She'd watched her mother, Rose, believe their obvious lies all the time. Those early days in their one-bedroom apartment taught Carmella so much. One, that she didn't want a man like any of her "dads," her biological father included. She knew that her mom would have been able to make it without one of those losers.

Carmella saw through the bullshit and hated every man her mother brought home. Bob the drunk, Ralph the womanizer, and James the mooch. She was sure her own father, whoever he was, had earned his own superlative as an absentee father. She always wondered why her mother, who she viewed as intelligent and beautiful, wasted her time on those creeps, but Carmella learned as she got older that self-esteem was a powerful drug. If you had it, you were golden. If you didn't, you just might get stuck with a loser.

Unfortunately, Carmella's DNA left her predisposed to choosing terrible men, dooming her relationship with Spencer from the outset. They first met at the UCLA quad, sitting on a concrete bench. At first, she didn't notice the cute guy sitting nearby, but her sunglasses covered her eyes and she kept glancing up at the tanned model. At least, she assumed he had to be a model. After one of her glances, he seemed to notice her too. He raised his eyebrows and said, "Nice day, yeah?"

Carmella could instantly hear that he wasn't a native to her Southern California tongue. She wanted to hear more from this guy who spoke in such a different way.

"It's always nice. Where are you from?"

"Minnesota. I guess my accent gives me away as a transplant." He laughed.

"It's cute. I'm Carmella. My accent is local," she said with a wink as she removed her sunglasses, revealing her bright green eyes.

His eyes widened as he stared into hers. "I'm Spencer. I have a class over at comp sci in a half hour, but would you like to hang out sometime?"

Her heart skipped at the speed of the invitation. "I'd love to." She paused. "Psychology. That's what I'm studying. I want to get inside people's heads and shift things around." Carmella gave a wicked laugh.

"I'm afraid you'd never talk to me again if you learned what lurks inside my brain." Spencer raised his eyebrows and laughed.

"I'm intrigued. My professor is always telling us to challenge ourselves. Maybe I've met my match," Carmella said. She glanced at her phone to check the time. "I need to get going. My class starts soon, and I can't be late."

"Will you give me your number? I'd love to take you out soon. Besides, I've got a few of those demons lurking that you mentioned," Spencer said.

"Sure. That sounds good, but no promises on how you'll turn out." Carmella grabbed Spencer's phone and typed in her number. She immediately saw an incoming phone call from Lanie, with a picture of a sultry brunette fresh out of the swimming pool. "Oh, your girlfriend is calling." Carmella handed the phone back.

"She's a friend. Totally harmless." Spencer waved his hand.

Ignoring the way every atom in her DNA screamed at her, she told him, "I'm looking forward to seeing you again." As she walked away, she hoped he was checking her out.

After their first date, Carmella was instantly smitten. She could stare into his dark brown eyes forever, listening to his stories as she studied the hint of amber in his irises that sparkled when he smiled. Their dates weren't frequent, as Spencer always had "shit to take care of," but Carmella eagerly awaited the buzzing glow of a new text. Their relationship was exciting for her, although Carmella never knew where Spencer lived and never met anyone in his life. "It's complicated," he told her one day. "My living situation isn't great, and I have a very private roommate." Spencer shrugged and gave Carmella a big grin and a kiss to help distract her from his secret life.

Carmella's face flushed. *I knew it. He has a girlfriend.*

"My roommate is a slob. The dude is the worst, so I can't bring you there. You're too precious to put up with filth like that." He grabbed her face, making puckering noises. Carmella wanted to believe it, but she'd heard it all before. *Though not from a man like Spencer.*

Even after five years of waiting for Spencer to make her his top priority, Carmella's threshold for his antics was still high. Even now she'd gladly welcome him in, even as each secret he kept from her slowly ate away at her core. With each day he didn't allow her fully into his sphere, a little piece of her died inside. The only thing that eased the pain were her late-night escapades and the drugs that made her finally feel alive.

Chapter 16

Dylan

Dylan scanned the list of Dr. Carey's clients to see if he could find Barbara's name, but he had no luck. *Damn it. That would be too easy.* He believed Barbara had set off to find refuge with Dr. Carey and her ilk, and he'd hoped to find her amongst the sea of names, as he craved the day he would confront her for vanishing without a trace. He thought constantly of the day he would track her down and watch her grovel. What he knew of Barbara's transformation before she moved out of Lazette was that a feminist had brainwashed her. Dylan's manhood was no longer empowered once Barbara believed she had a greater worth.

There were hundreds of names to choose from with their addresses attached—such easy access for a man just starting his murderous rampage. Dylan plopped back onto the lush bed, grinning from ear to ear. So far, his LA trip had been such a success. Warm tingles worked their way across his skin as he lay thinking of all he'd accomplished. Now that he had found out where Dr. Carey lived, he could continue his surveillance to prepare for his greater mission.

He was satisfied with how his anonymous phone call went on *Wake Up LA*. This time his voice had vibrated calmly through the phone. Gone was the agonizing pit of anxiety from his last attempt; this one left a lasting smirk on his face. Although he could have done that last call from his Indiana basement, it was more exciting to make the call against the LA backdrop. Now, goosebumps shot up his arms, his neck hair spiked, and his heart sped up as he prepared to select his first victim. He chose a name at random between here and Indiana, settling on Nora Marcus out of Colorado.

After he booked his plane ticket, he watched some videos Dr. Carey had attached to Veronica Dixon's onboarding email. That's when Dylan learned the strict rules that went along with being a member.

"Welcome, seeker. You belong here. In order to become a member, there are rules you must follow. I've created them to help guide you to become your best selves. These aren't meant to punish you, but rather to help you navigate this new way of thinking. It will be tough at first to break free from the old habits that got you here. With my help, this program will release you from your past way of living within the next year, and you'll be a new woman." Dylan's jaw clenched as he cracked his knuckles.

"Will you join me and the hundreds of other women who want to be better?" Dr. Carey closed her eyes and raised her hands in prayer on the screen.

Dylan sneered as he leaned closer to the image.

Dr. Carey batted away a couple of tears. "Ladies, I want to share something that's still very raw for me." She dabbed her cheek with a tissue. "When I broke up with my ex, I finally understood the emotions that my clients were living through, leaving a complicated, painful relationship. It wasn't just any relationship; it was gut-wrenching and toxic. Right before it ended, we had gotten engaged, and then he just disappeared. The psychological trauma was torture, and I had no idea if he was coming back. I thought maybe something tragic had happened to him, but I heard nothing on the news. His social media was silent, although he hadn't posted anything for several months prior. He had no family or friends for me to contact, which is such a red flag."

Dylan breathed hard through his nose. *Just like Barbara did to me.*

Dr. Carey took a deep breath. "Finally, I realized that asshole had ghosted me. That's when I knew I needed to help other women going through something like this—to stop this cycle of falling for the same loser over and over again."

Dr. Carey's tone became firmer. "Some of you may shy away from the program after hearing these rules, while others may scoff and say that I'm unfair. However, I know that all of you will be successful if you try."

Dylan glared at the screen. In the distance, he heard someone mention housekeeping, so he got up and placed the Do Not Disturb sign on his door.

Wearing a different outfit, Dr. Carey appeared in a smaller box on the screen and the rules came up one by one as she recited them off.

1. You must abstain from seeing/dating your partner, or anyone else, for exactly one year.

2. You must get rid of all items that remind you of your partner.

3. If you are married, you must meet with a lawyer to discuss future options for divorce.

4. You are not allowed to mingle with other members or form subgroups outside of this program.

5. You must adhere to a strict routine. Sleep, work, exercise, and diet plans must be approved by me.

6. If you have children, they cannot live with you. You must live alone. I allow you to have minimal visitation.

7. You must meet with me on a rigid therapy schedule, both one-on-one and in monthly group meetings.

8. You cannot tell anyone about the program rules and must sign an NDA.

9. You must pay dues on time, and only I can decide if you can leave the program early.

10. If you break any of the rules, I will either banish you with a hefty fine or your year must start over.

* * *

Dylan replayed the clip several times, in disbelief that anyone would agree to these rules, much less hundreds of women. *Any bitch who follows these rules deserves to die.* Dylan slammed his fist into the bed, making the laptop jump in the air.

Dylan played several other clips but wasn't able to find the cost of the program. Dr. Carey kept that aspect well-hidden. *Typical marketing gimmick of a cult.*

As he de-boarded the plane in Colorado, the crisp air was already a welcome reprieve from the LA smog. But he was here for business. And he had a very important person to meet.

Chapter 17

Julissa

Don't do it. It may not be reversible, and you'll regret it for the rest of your life. The words floated through Julissa's head after her mom found out she wanted a tubal ligation.

"Mom, the country is different now. Abortion isn't accessible and..."

"Julissa, aren't you gay? I mean, why would you need that?"

"No, I'm not gay, I'm ace. But this isn't about that. I don't want to worry about getting pregnant if a man rapes me. I want control over my body." Julissa crossed her arms.

"J. I just don't understand the world today or this new wave of feminism. We burned bras, but we still wanted a family. Girls today are ready to give up every aspect of what makes them a woman." Gloria shook her head.

"You just don't understand, and I didn't expect you to." Julissa frowned.

"One day, you'll meet the man of your dreams and regret all of this nonsense." Gloria sighed.

Julissa grew tired of trying to convince her mom. Gloria was set in her old-fashioned ways—she wanted grandchildren, regardless of

Julissa's happiness. Julissa was glad to have her found family of friends, who she'd immediately vibed with. Their connection was instant, and Julissa couldn't believe she'd been lucky enough to find others in tune with her.

Julissa lined up a doctor who agreed to perform the tubal ligation, but she'd need to request time off work for recovery. She gulped down the lump in her throat as the thought of telling Dr. Carey about her surgery became a reality. She'd only been working there for a few months, so she knew it was a big ask. *Maybe I can work from home?*

As she walked out of the stairwell toward Dr. Carey's door, she took a deep breath and manifested a version of Dr. Carey she hadn't seen before: One with a brilliant aura of peace and light, a beacon of warmth. Julissa fumbled with the coffee orders as she unlocked the door and immediately saw a disheveled Dr. Carey waiting for her at the kitchen island.

She handed Dr. Carey her order, which she promptly snatched.

"Dr. Carey, when you have a minute, I'd like to ask you about a few days off."

"Already? I hope it's not soon? I really can't afford to have you away right now." Dr. Carey swallowed her caffeine.

"I know. I'm sorry, but it's very important that I get this done."

Dr. Carey's eyes narrowed. "Get what done?"

Julissa looked around the room before turning back to face Dr. Carey. "I plan to get permanently sterilized and need a few days to recover."

A slow smile formed on Dr. Carey's lips. "Really? I've been hearing about women taking matters into their own hands. I'm proud of that decision. It takes guts to do that. Just mark the days you need off on the shared calendar."

After Dr. Carey left and closed her door, a wave of chills rushed down Julissa's body. She hadn't known how this discussion would go and had prepared for the worst. *A Dr. Carey lecture was the last thing I needed.*

* * *

Back at her desk, Julissa shook out her hands, which were still trembling. She took a deep inhale before marking off the days she'd need for downtime. *I can't believe she took that so well.*

She typed a text to her best friend. "Hey, P, it wasn't bad at all. Kind of shocked right now. But we're good for the days we discussed. See you later."

Later in the day, Dr. Carey came out for a lunch break and asked more prying questions.

"Does your boyfriend have anything to say about this? I mean, not that his opinion should matter. It's your body," Dr. Carey said.

"I don't have a boyfriend and never plan on having kids, so it feels like the right thing for me to do." Julissa shrugged.

Dr. Carey narrowed her eyes as she stared Julissa down. Julissa let out a quick breath as the sunlight glinted off her nose ring.

"Interesting," Dr. Carey said before turning and closing the door to her room.

Julissa wasn't ashamed of her asexuality, but she definitely didn't think she needed to have this conversation with Dr. Carey or anyone else. Her online support community always preached that employers weren't entitled to private information. *But none of them know what it's like being an employee of Dr. Carey.*

Chapter 18

Carmella

As the final beats of her favorite song mixed into a new one, Carmella headed for the bar. When she saw Spencer, she sauntered toward him, her stomach sinking. Her ribcage pressed against her lungs a bit too snugly to breathe comfortably. She ran her hands through the ends of her pink wig and puckered her lips as she ascended the two steps from the dance floor. Their eyes locked, and she felt as if she were the only woman in the world, ready to take her man.

As soon as she got within an arm's length, he blew a puff of cigarette smoke in her direction and turned to nuzzle his face in the neck of the woman standing next to him. *A basic brunette who needs a gingham filter.* Dr. Carey watched as the woman threw her head back in amusement. As they both stared at Carmella, Spencer laughed in her direction.

"Can we talk?" Dr. Carey yelled over the music.

Spencer continued to stroke the woman's back and speak intimately into her ear. The woman giggled as Spencer kissed her left temple.

Dr. Carey watched. They were only inches from her face, yet she felt she was a million miles away, stuck in a sandstorm of misery with Spencer, a mirage of the man she believed she needed. The same neck nuzzles and kisses she used to receive were now reserved for someone new. He'd informed her only a week ago. *It will always be someone new.*

"Let's see other people. Be adventurous," he'd said to her. He looked so hot she hated herself for wanting one last romp with him.

The flush of embarrassment stained her cheeks. Dr. Carey was grateful for the mood lighting; she didn't want to give Spencer or his new fling the pleasure of seeing her distress. It took all of her power to break away from the scene. She never admitted defeat, but it was clear that Spencer was no longer hers. The man she had broken up with more times than she could count now had a new sidepiece. *Not as hot as me, but more approachable. The girl next door type.* The day that they met, she never would have guessed that one day he'd completely ignore her in a crowded club.

She walked to a different section of the bar, all lit up, ready to provide the right amount of intoxication to prevent giving a damn. Her body didn't feel like it was hers. It walked in slow motion. Her burning cheeks threatened to give away her shame. *Is everyone watching me? Did they see what just happened?* She craved liquid as her tongue stuck to the roof of her mouth, desperate for saturation. She downed her vodka sour, enjoying the way it burned at the back of her throat.

Carmella turned and took three steps until she was next to Spencer again. She brushed the side of his jacket, hoping he'd reach out to her, grab her, caress her lower back and drive her wild. She paused for a second, waiting for that touch, but none came. Carmella was open to allowing Filter Girl in with them, just like old times. It took all of her self-control not to say anything to him. *I won't give him that satisfaction. I've given him enough.*

Once past him, her flushed cheeks burned even hotter. Her identity as a self-made goddess was under attack. As a powerful woman, she couldn't comprehend why he didn't want her. *Why not me?* she begged the listeners in her mind.

Somehow, another drink appeared in her hand, which she downed in seconds. After the second, she turned back toward Spencer, who glanced in her direction. *It's all a game. I'm his toy.* The total opposite of everything she'd ever taught the women in her program.

Dr. Carey debated staying and waiting for Spencer to come to her, but all she could see was the back of his head and the cigarette smoke escaping in rings. His neck nuzzles continued as she watched his hand massage the woman's back. Eventually, it crept lower. After watching for a couple of minutes, Dr. Carey abruptly turned and slammed into a tall man with feathered hair that swooped down across his forehead. Her jaw hurt from the impact. He asked if she was alright, but she waved him off and scurried out to the front where she called for a ride back home.

Inside the car, Dr. Carey felt herself slip away into a peaceful darkness. The drinks were hitting, and whatever they were laced with was exactly the mood she craved.

Early in her career, Dr. Carey wasn't an addict. She was confident because of her skills as a therapist, not because of the pseudo-bravado the drugs provided. Spencer introduced her to that flavor of life, and it was an energy she adored. She would do whatever it took to hold his interest. She was obsessed with his attention and everything that came with him. The drugs, the secretive home life, and the good times when he desired her so much—she felt him drink her in with dizzying eyes.

The toxic relationship challenged her skills as a therapist daily. She became like a teenager, swiping her phone every few minutes to see if she'd missed a call or text from him. Her heart knew better than to think he was a daytime call. He messaged only late into the darkness, single digits on her clock.

"Hey, babe. You up?" It never failed. She was always up. Up for anything he was ready for. She'd push off early morning meetings to meet up with him or invite him over.

Any questions about where he'd been or why so late earned her a remark about becoming a needy girl. "Needy girls are lonely and single." She'd hear his words inside her head and stop herself from objecting. *He's right. No guy wants a needy girl.* She'd immediately shift and become the kind of girl she coached her clients to leave behind. This internal version of herself conflicted with the woman she presented on a daily basis. While she loved being close to Spencer, it went against everything she had ever stood for. What she hated the most was becoming like her mother—accepting far less than she'd deserved. But Spencer's eyes dazzled her, hypnotizing her into the type of woman she'd never in a million years believe she'd become.

And she hated to admit it, but six months into creating her program, she was desperate for her own *Year of Self.*

Chapter 19

Nora

The small pink craftsman house welcomed Nora as soon as she turned onto her street. Her house of six years was a beacon signaling to her, providing peace and security that finally made her feel at home. Nora Marcus was an average-looking woman, or at least she thought so. Her boyfriend had ingrained that belief in her brain, convincing her she would never find anyone better than him. In fact, as her longest relationship, she assumed he was the best she'd ever find. Her low self-esteem had carried over from high school; frizzy hair and braces do that to a hormonal girl. She never outgrew the taunts from classmates that sank into her psyche. She always wondered if her home life were less chaotic, if maybe she'd have been able to choose better for herself.

Nora was the new kid so many times she lost count—though not really. She remembered every grueling time she had to walk into a new classroom with at least twenty unknown faces staring back, wondering who this alien was. She knew the anxiety of wondering where she'd sit and the pure luck of an empty seat in the back, but usually the teacher put her up front. That's when the inner voice would tell her how other kids were perceiving her, ramping up her feelings of isolation. She was great at viewing the world through her peripheral vision, afraid to turn to the side and give the world too much.

Sit as still as possible and maybe they'll forget I exist. She blended into the plastic and metal of the hard chair until the bell rang, painfully counting the ticks of the round clock on the wall.

Those early awkward days had certainly contributed to her ineptness at forming relationships later in life. She wasn't astute at recognizing ulterior motives, and when she enrolled in college and moved into her first dorm room, she entertained advances from men for company she wasn't sure she wanted.

Her recent boyfriend, David, was the cutest guy she'd ever been with, according to all of her friends. When Nora told her mother, Kathleen, that she'd thought of breaking up, Kathleen told her, "Maybe you need to reconsider, dear. He's such a handsome boy. I'd hate for you to spend your days lonely, and not every aspect of a relationship needs to be happy." Kathleen sighed as she wiped down her kitchen counter. "I mean, I spent most of my time with your father in complete misery. But we learned to find hobbies apart from each other to make our marriage work. It's better to have someone, and I think he's the best you'll get."

Frustrated with her mom and her friends, Nora knew in her heart that they didn't understand her relationship and need for genuine love. A strong part of her didn't see any reason a woman should stick with a man just for his looks, regardless of whether she was attractive.

Nora had always believed that no man would ever find her beautiful. Maybe she was cute or passed for adorable, but she always envied the women who were naturally gorgeous. But she knew enough women to know even the gorgeous ones shared the same struggles—never feeling good enough in their own skin. In some ways, it could be harder for women who grew up beautiful. As they aged, they couldn't reconcile the change in their appearance, unable to accept that their youthful face had grown closer to the one they saw in their mother. Since Nora already didn't think highly of herself, it was easier to accept the defeat of being an average woman. She was used to being passed over for dates, being the third wheel, and sitting at home on couples' holidays.

When she met David, she thought it was a prank because he asked for her number on April Fool's Day. David wasn't model hot, but he was cute enough, certainly more attractive than any man she'd ever dreamed of dating before. When he called, she was stunned. But soon after they began dating, Nora knew she'd rather be single. The demands of dating David became too much. He constantly put her down and criticized her looks. He had many late-night escapades, and his lies were getting old.

"Why are you even with me?" Nora confronted him after one of his critique sessions. This time, he was lecturing her on exercises to achieve a firmer abdomen.

"Oh, come on. You're so selfish! You're always down on yourself, but when I give you pointers on how to look better, you don't like that either. I can't win with you." David rolled his eyes and manspread, leaning back against the couch.

When Nora first came across Dr. Carey's program, she fell in love with it. *Finally, someone gets me.* She would pay as much as she needed, do whatever Dr. Carey wanted, even if her mother scoffed at her choices.

That day, when the knock at the door came, she assumed it was a routine delivery. She preferred ordering online over shopping in stores just for the convenience; clothes, home décor, and sometimes food. But for some reason, an icy chill coursed through her veins just before she unlocked her door. A man in a black hoodie zipped all the way to the top stood in front of her, a few wisps of hair escaping from the baseball cap he wore low on his forehead. When he looked up, she noticed his right eyelid twitched. "Hello, I have a delivery for Nora Marcus," he said.

Yes, of course. A delivery for me. She let out a relieved sigh.

The man looked side to side and then took one gigantic step forward, wedging between her legs and pushing her backwards. He'd somehow gotten inside her apartment and shut her door behind them all in one quick motion.

With his hand held over her mouth, he whispered, "Do not scream or say anything, or I will kill you."

Nora shook her head as her eyes widened, glancing at his face for answers. Her body went ice cold as her limbs shook. He smelled of perspiration mixed with the stench of fast food on his hands.

He pushed her toward her computer, where the members' welcome screen for Dr. Carey's program appeared. The image was of Dr. Carey dressed in a flowing garment with outstretched arms. Falling sparkles glistened as chimes played in the distance. The stranger pulled a long knife from the back of his pants and gripped Nora's hair.

Nora's teeth chattered as the tension on her hair made her grimace. She was unable to scream, an invisible vacuum in her throat sucking her breath back. Her eyes widened as the sharp knife made its way past her eyes and toward her neck.

The killer made his first cut too prematurely. Nora gasped and her hands went to her neck as blood sprayed all over her laptop screen. Nora's blood splattered across the desk with each haphazard slice to her neck until she stopped making a sound and eventually sat slumped over before her computer.

On the screen, Dr. Carey's arms stayed outstretched, but they failed to catch Nora in life or in death.

Chapter 20

Dylan

Dylan saw himself as a martyr—a real-life hero who would take on the injustices of the feminist culture once and for all. Murder was both beautiful and eerie, a small sacrifice for the ultimate good. His own parents saw no redemptive qualities in him. His dad wanted a sports kid he could show off to his buddies. But Dylan was a kid who spent remedial math time in the small room next to the principal's office. The kid with little muscle tone who barely made the height threshold to ride the scary rides as a child, which always made Dylan fume. Height was another feminine construct—that short men were worthless, that shoe size was a valid measure of penis length, and that his voice's register said a lot about his own masculinity.

These thoughts fueled his outburst, his hands tightly gripping the steering wheel, the whites of his knuckles showing the outlines of his bones. His foot was heavy on the gas, flooring it down I-65, passing semis as his car shook from driving over the rumble strips. He checked out his appearance in his rearview mirror, puckered his mouth, and hung his left arm out the open window. He drove into Prophet's Rock Park, a secluded spot with a dirt trail that led to an overlook with a view of a lake. His own thoughts of annihilation filled the deserted space.

He took out his phone and hit record.

"Women are second class, and many are overrated. We're supposed to bow at their feet and never have an opinion. Guess what, men? Fuck that." Dylan pointed at the camera. "Our opinions are the only ones that count. We deserve the respect that they forgot is our birthright. In due time, you'll know that I'm the caller and the killer." He beamed, flashing a wide, toothy grin at the camera.

Dylan looked around as the background noise of birds chirping in the trees filled the video. "When you watch this, I hope you'll all raise a glass and toast me for being an innovator." He pumped his fist.

"It had to be done. We tried for decades to slow the feminine ways, but drastic measures were required." Dylan sighed, shaking his head. "I warned her, but she refused to listen."

Dylan smiled the widest grin he had in years. His hardened demeanor had begun to crack, and glee oozed from his pores. He sat on the grass, leaned back on his elbows, and soaked in the sun that filtered through the tree branches. The momentary jubilation of a man enjoying a rare success left as quickly as it came. Two women walked along the hiking trail, their hands animated as they spoke. Dylan raised up on his elbows, snarling, and glared in their direction. He watched as one of the women's ponytails swished back and forth as she walked, which instantly reminded him of the first time he saw Barbara.

Barbara kept her espresso-colored hair pulled back in a ponytail. He walked behind her, half annoyed, half mesmerized by the hypnotic rhythm of her swaying locks. When she stopped short and he nearly bumped into the back of her, he feigned ignorance. She even told him she was sorry. "Oh, I'm so clumsy. Sorry about that." But she was actually talking to him, and it was friendly. *That makes her the most alluring girl I've ever seen.*

In his head, Dylan replayed the day she agreed to go out with him. He thought that maybe this was how it worked. He was down on his luck, and he found the right girl, and life just got better. The first few times he was near her, all he wanted to do was sniff her. He wanted to bury his nose in her hair and neck and get drunk off her scent, drink up the coffee-colored hue of her hair. Eventually, her giggles turned to annoyance. He remembered all the favors he'd done for her—watching her reality shows, giving her rides when her car broke down, paying for her meals. He did all these things she never appreciated. And then she ghosted him.

On the ride over to the park, he'd envisioned this as a celebratory outing. His first kill was now in the books, and he had finally made a lasting mark on the world. However, by his own critique, the murder had earned him low marks. The slicing didn't go as well as he'd planned. Throughout the entire plane trip home, he'd replayed how the knife had missed his target, and he chastised himself for the sloppy work. Although he got the job done, he knew he had to be better going forward.

Dylan walked back to his car feeling dejected. Thoughts of Barbara always brought on gloomy musings. He plodded over the rocks along the way, sapped of the energy he'd had when he first arrived. He shut his car door and drove home in silence, his mind consumed with thoughts of revenge and finding Barbara.

Chapter 21

Carmella

Sometimes late nights involved whiskey and techno, with a little coke for added fun. Carmella donned a silver wig and removed her jacket, exposing a skin-tight dress worthy of one of the *Real Housewives*. She had to get creative in covering up her identity because if the public caught her out partying, it could damage her empire. Besides, the outfits amped up the fun and allowed her to unleash her true self behind a shield of anonymity.

After her latest argument with Spencer, Carmella was currently on her MIF diet—Male Intermittent Fasting. Anytime she allowed herself to think of him, her heart wept and she later had to admonish herself for typing a text to him, though she did sometimes delete it before sending. It was yet another thing she hated about Spencer's aloofness toward her. She was always the one to contact him first. *I'm a fucking goddess, loser!*

At the end of her night, she stumbled out of the car, running right into the doorman. Her lips were close to his cheek as she spoke into to his ear. "Wanna follow me up?" She knew his answer because it wasn't the first encounter. Her favorite part was walking past him days later like she'd never seen him before, knowing full well his gaze followed her until the elevator doors shut. *Not everyone gets my attention.*

Carmella and the doorman found themselves enmeshed in her bed, but it didn't stop her thoughts of Spencer. Her teeth gnashed together as she tossed him onto his back. She gripped his throat, choking the doorman with a fury earmarked for Spencer. At first, he smiled, but when she didn't release her hold, he pulled her off of him and grabbed his jeans. "You're a fucking nut job." Carmella watched as he walked out of her bedroom, listening for the click of the front door. The sound signaled that she was once again alone, which brought forth the vodka bottle she stored on her nightstand.

* * *

Carmella woke with a drool stain on her pillow. She rolled over to check her clock. In another hour, she had a client meeting. Fleeting thoughts of last night surfaced—the doorman's physique and bald head, which felt like bliss when he went down on her. The look on his face when he tore away from her and stormed off. A faint smile formed on her lips until her alarm yelled at her to get going.

Shower. Makeup. Hair. Coffee.

A gnawing headache wound its way through her skull as a loud knock at the front door pierced the silence. *Why wouldn't Julissa just use her fucking key?* She swung the door open to see a female cop standing at attention, her slick black hair pulled into a ponytail under her peaked cap. A shorter male cop with a red beard stood behind her.

"Carmella Carey? We're with the LAPD; we have some questions for you," the female cop said.

"It's Dr. Carey. Can this wait? I'm about to start a session in twenty."

"We won't be long. Can we come in? It's of a sensitive nature."

Carmella waved her arm for them to enter, hoping that all traces of last night were gone.

Just as she was about to shut the door, Julissa pushed on it, holding the caffeine that Carmella deeply wanted.

"We received a call from Boulder PD and learned that someone murdered one of your clients, Nora Marcus, last night. She had your website left up on her laptop and, considering recent threats made on TV, we thought we'd bring this to your attention."

Carmella stood unfazed by their words, sniffing the air for the sweet smell of her daily caffeine.

"I mean, it really sucks, but what can I do about it? You don't know if there's a connection, and I don't know anything about it." Carmella shrugged.

"Well, has there been any discord with anyone? Could someone be trying to get to you by killing one of your clients?" The male cop cocked his head to the side.

"I have no enemies. In fact, I have excellent ratings and see no reason anyone would kill a woman associated with this amazing program. But if I find a lead, I can let you know." Carmella walked to her front door.

"Please do. We take threats like this seriously. It's a good idea to warn your clients to be vigilant." The female cop handed Dr. Carey a card.

Detective Laura Madison. "You got it." Carmella closed the door hard as soon as they stepped across the threshold.

She downed her lukewarm coffee and read through a few emails before clicking through some paperwork Julissa had prepared for her. With a wide yawn, she stretched, leaning back in her office chair. *I knew better than to party so hard with a new client meeting scheduled.*

She checked her appearance in her table mirror, dabbed on another layer of face powder, and inhaled an energy shot. She wore a high-necked collar to cover up the marks left by some aggressive kissers at last night's rave. *I need to be the aggressive one at these things.*

It was already ten minutes past her meeting time, which was still within her forgiveness window. She enjoyed making her clients wait, especially the new ones. It was healthy for them—it strengthened their minds and made them learn patience.

She fumbled with a limp strand of hair as she logged into the members' screen, taking a deep breath and putting on the fakest smile she could muster.

"Welcome! I've been looking forward to meeting you, Livvy."

Chapter 22

Livvy

At the ten-minute mark, Livvy grew annoyed. She breathed deeply and crossed her arms, staring at the screen, willing Dr. Carey to finally show up. As an actor, she had waited much longer for headliners and knew the drill. She had once waited half a day for a star who strolled in and then immediately took his lunch break. Livvy was used to playing second best to lots of people: Alton's wife, more talented actors, and now other women waiting in line to empower themselves.

The butterflies that swam in her stomach slowly calmed as her thoughts zoned in on what Alton was doing. *Is he lying in his cell? Playing cards with his jailmates? Is he managing the glutenous jail food?*

Time ticked by as she waited for Dr. Carey to appear. This felt like one of the biggest interviews of her life since it had to do with her own character. Her neck muscles ached with the tension of her past, so she rubbed the back of her neck as she slowly closed her eyes.

The ding woke Livvy, jolting her to attention, and she stretched her face muscles to appear more awake. She was disoriented, wiping sleep from her eyes when she remembered she had dozed off and dreamt of better days with Alton. *I should log off. I'm not in the head-space for this.*

"Livvy. I've been so eager to meet you. You're our first celebrity client, and I'm so honored you're interested in my program." Dr. Carey beamed.

"Oh, thank you. I'm just a regular girl, really. No special treatment for me." Livvy forced a smile.

"Don't be coy. I actually want to play up your celebrity status. Especially with your current news. All the #MeToo shit going on with you and your ex—that's exactly what my program is about. The injustices that happen to women like us..."

Livvy cut Dr. Carey off. "Oh, I really want to keep that part of my life private. I mean, my agent told me to lie low until after the trial. I don't want anything to jeopardize my career any more than this already has." She frowned.

"Let me guess. Your agent is a man? They always want to tell women to shut up, sit in the corner, and be quiet while the men do their business, and you're supposed to not make a peep." Dr. Carey shook her head. "Livvy, that's bullshit. With me in your corner, that shit won't happen. We are going to yell from every fucking rooftop what your ex did to you."

Livvy sat dazed, letting the words sink in. *Is it too late to change my mind? Fuck, the contract.*

"Let's get you back in front of the camera. You can be the face of feminism, demanding to be heard and seen. We'll never let a man silence you again."

"This is a lot of information. I do want to be back in front of the camera, but if I speak out, it could cost me acting jobs." Livvy leaned back, shutting her eyes. She already knew her agent would drop her, which would further weaken her chances at future parts. "I believe in activism, and I know it could help others in my shoes." Livvy sighed. In her heart, she knew Alton was terrible for her. But her heart also wanted the version of him her mind had created.

"I want you out there discussing my program and how it's helping you reframe what's happened to you. As you know, I've been all over the media. It would be good to have testimony from others, and an actor would be a great spokesperson to accompany me on interviews." Dr. Carey widened her green eyes and stared through the screen. "Why don't you join me for my next live show?" Livvy could hear her typing. "I'll have Julissa set this up. Talk soon, Livvy."

Livvy took a deep breath as she stared at Dr. Carey's picture on the screen, complete with a backdrop of floating stars. *What the fuck just happened?* She was disappointed Dr. Carey didn't counsel her or listen to *her* story. She hoped Dr. Carey wasn't just interested in using what little star power Livvy had to pimp her program. Livvy weighed the pros and cons and decided to take the leap of faith that Dr. Carey's plan would give her what she really wanted, which was to be in front of a camera again. She was in her prime, and waiting for Alton's court date was the least desirable option on the table. She rubbed the back of her neck, which was even stiffer than before her session.

Livvy just hoped that her role as a feminist wouldn't cost her any roles on screen—or worse, make her lose her acting career for good. She leaned back into the couch pillows and bit her lip as images of Alton swam through her mind.

Chapter 23

Carmella

The afternoon nap failed to do its job and make Dr. Carey more approachable. After Livvy's session, she opted for rest in preparation for today's all-member meeting. She felt irritated at everyone: the world, men, and one client whom she planned to make pay for what they'd done. She pushed away from the laptop as bolts of irritation zapped through her veins. Dr. Carey had always suspected that the women were forming alliances behind her back. While it was human nature, she expected them to follow the rules, which included not fraternizing. On a tip from a loyal member, Dr. Carey learned that her client, Rubina, had made social media posts indicating she was in a cult. While she didn't come out and name Dr. Carey, it wouldn't be hard for reporters to put it together.

Dr. Carey finished her steaming shower with a few seconds of freezing water, hoping to invigorate her nervous system. She shivered as she stepped out of the tub and wrapped herself in an oversized towel that smelled of lavender. She briefly felt more alive in anticipation of the two-hour online retreat.

She picked out an army-green button-up silk shirt but left on sweatpants underneath. Last night's vibe was still in her system; the drugs left a halo of disorientation that clouded her thinking. After spending a good part of the night dancing, she was opting for comfort today.

"Goddamn it," she yelled when her eyeliner ran crooked. She stared back at her face and hated it. *It's one of those fucking days where nothing looks good.*

She teased her hair and combed it smooth, eventually throwing her brush across the bathroom floor, where it landed with a thud behind the toilet.

"FUCK!" she yelled, spraying her hair with a huge spritz of hairspray.

Dr. Carey wrenched open her bedside table drawer, whipping around the pill bottles inside. She grabbed two whites from her nightstand and downed them with lukewarm water left over from this morning. She pinched her fingers between her eyebrows to ward off a growing headache. A notification on her phone warned her she had ten minutes left until the start of the retreat.

She plopped down onto her leather office chair and typed the password to log into the system. As her face appeared on the screen, she noticed her left eye seemed off. It took her a few seconds to realize her bottom left fake eyelash had slid off and was now resting on the top of her boob. She quickly yanked off the right side to match and threw it so it stuck to her wall.

Dr. Carey took a deep breath and entered the chat room.

The sound of a gong jolted many women as they sat up straight. Dr. Carey flipped her hair and put on her fakest smile.

"Namaste, loves. I'm so honored that you're all here." Dr. Carey smiled and blinked, flashing her green eyes.

"We have so much to get through today. But first, I need to speak with Rubina," Dr. Carey said.

The small faces on the screen darted their eyes at the news that one of them was being singled out. Rubina clicked the hand-raising symbol, showing she was present.

"Rubina. I've been hearing rumors you believe this is a cult?" Dr. Carey's eyes widened.

Rubina's face looked frozen for a brief second until she finally began mouthing something.

"You're on mute!" Dr. Carey raised her voice.

"Oh, sorry. I, uh, well, I don't know what you're talking about. I love it here." Rubina choked out.

Dr. Carey shared her screen, and Rubina's social media post appeared. "I am in a cult that was supposed to help women, but it's only hurting us."

"Well, I didn't mean this group. I..." Rubina said.

"What were you referring to, then?" Dr. Carey leaned close to the screen.

"Look. I'm sorry. I drank a little wine and got tipsy and stupid." Rubina licked her lips. "I don't even remember posting that. Please accept my apologies."

"And yet you denied it. You're still hiding behind the scared little girl that you keep nurturing as a woman. We've been over this time and time again. Stop making stupid choices!" Dr. Carey yelled.

"You're right. I won't go on social media anymore. I was feeling weak and lashed out. It won't happen again." Rubina looked down at her hands.

Dr. Carey's nostrils flared as she clicked start on a prerecorded video, turning her camera off. Her headache was now full-blown, and she needed relief. More whites and water followed, along with some temple massages until the video on the benefits of recruiting others ended. She turned her camera back on with a smile plastered on her face.

"Today, I want to do a one-on-one session with a member who recently joined us. She's going through something most of us can relate to: The challenge of being a woman in a field full of men out for power and fame. She's been told to keep silent, to accept the status quo and wait her turn, but why should she?" Dr. Carey took a sip from her water bottle to get rid of the pill aftertaste. "She is now one of us, which means we have her back. No one will keep any of us quiet for their own gain. She's agreed to be a spokesperson for our program and join my next TV interview. Everyone, please welcome Livvy Kyle."

The women on the screen smiled and applauded, all except for Livvy. Her eyes widened in shock as her mouth formed a timid smile.

"Don't be coy, Livvy. I know we didn't discuss this prior because I wanted your answers to be raw. What we discuss here will be private. Only between me and the other members."

Livvy took a deep breath before unmuting. "OK. I am definitely not prepared, but I'll do my best to answer your questions," she said.

"Great. I know the media has reported on several women who've come forward accusing Alton of sexual assault. At what point were you aware of his extracurricular activities?" Dr. Carey raised her left eyebrow.

Livvy opened her mouth and shut it again before speaking. "I'm not sure if I can discuss his case, but I know what I've heard. Women have come forward accusing him of requesting sexual favors for good roles. A forced pleasure exchange."

"That's an interesting way to phrase it. And were you one of those women, Livvy? Did you also do things for him to get ahead in your career?"

"I, well... He and I were in love. I would have done anything for him. When I was in a desperate situation, his help freed me from financial ruin. He changed my life." Livvy spun the ring on her finger. Dr. Carey wondered idly if Alton had given her a genuine diamond or a fake one like the relationship they seemed to have.

"You know what? I have heard that so many times." Dr. Carey closed her eyes. "There's never a lack of hardship for women, especially financially." Her eyes opened wide, scanning the screen.

Dr. Carey grabbed a tissue and dabbed at her runny nose. "Let's go through what brought you here." Her fingers clacked on her keyboard.

"There's a lot of gossip posted about you and this relationship. I realize a lot of that's exaggerated, but can you tell us what the truth is? Just start from the beginning." Dr. Carey smirked.

"Okay, yeah. Those sites get about 10% of the story right and just make up the rest." Livvy twisted her lips. "I first moved here from my small hometown to get away from the people there, especially an overbearing ex. Honestly, I don't really want to talk about my experience back home because it's too painful." Livvy rubbed the sides of her arms. "I'd rather just focus on what's happened recently, if that's fine with you." Livvy paused.

"But anyway, I started out as a hostess at a really popular restaurant, and that's when I met Alton. Truthfully, I didn't immediately find him attractive, but something about him intrigued me."

"Did you know he was married then? I mean, that's one thing I heard on the gossip show, or was that made up?" Dr. Carey batted her naked eyelashes.

"Oh, no, I didn't know he was married until much later. A couple of weeks later, he informed me of his separation from his wife and their plans to divorce. He made it clear she wasn't good for him, and I fully supported what he was going through." Livvy sighed.

"It must be hard knowing you fell for someone like that. To those of us on the outside, it seems so obvious. How have you dealt with the shame and guilt of knowing what you've done to other women?"

"Guilt and shame?" Livvy's mouth dropped open. "I haven't blamed myself. This was Alton's fault. He did this to me, to them."

"Livvy. Take ownership of your role. Your hands aren't clean. Did you receive roles for favors?"

"Look, I know that rumor has been making the rounds."

"Is it true?" Dr. Carey asked more firmly. The other women on the screen widened their eyes, their mouths dropping open in shock.

Livvy spoke through gritted teeth. "Yes. He gave me a role and bought me a car after the first month we were together." She shook her head. "But it wasn't like that. We fell hard. I loved him with my entire soul."

"Ladies, soulmates are a false construct. That word is just an overused term we throw around; it means nothing," Dr. Carey said. "Alton was never your soulmate. You created that because you needed him to be that. You've alienated yourself from your family and your past and needed an older man to save you."

"How can you say that? He's in jail right now awaiting trial for what he's done to women! Women have come forward about his lies, his sexual assault, and his manipulation, and you want to blame me?!" Livvy slumped back hard in her chair and crossed her arms.

"Livvy, I am not blaming you for his behavior; I am blaming you for yours. You had a part in the failure of this relationship. Until you recognize what you've done, you won't ever fully heal. There is no denying that he's scum, and you deserve better. Men do not deserve women like us."

Livvy shook her head. "I was hoping to feel empowered. But this discussion is making me feel horrible."

"You'll feel terrible until you're better. That's how improvement works. Do the hard work, and then you'll be thanking me for eternity." Dr. Carey closed her eyes. "Everyone. Close your eyes for a moment of respite." She stretched her head from side to side to loosen the tightness that had worked its way into her neck muscles.

"Ladies, rub your palms together to create energy. Now bring them to your face and breathe in, saying this mantra: 'No one will take away my joy.'" Dr. Carey watched as each box on her screen went from a woman's face to the back of her hand.

"Thank you all. I hope you've learned from this session today. We are all capable of taking back our joy and learning the tools to prevent anyone from stealing it from us. Use what you've learned during the *Year of Self* to be the strongest version of YOU!" Dr. Carey flashed a wide smile.

Several women clapped, while others raised their hands in prayer, saluting her.

"We are much more powerful together than we ever are apart. I love you all... until next time."

Dr. Carey logged out of the session and immediately crawled into bed, where her right eyelid slowly crusted to her pillowcase.

As she drifted off to sleep, she thought, *maybe it's time I take some legal action and sue a few women.*

Chapter 24

Dylan

Dylan logged into the Mandate hoping to read about Nora's death, to luxuriate in all the praise for the unknown killer who'd taken out one of Dr. Carey's clients. He scanned through the chat logs, which had only a couple of posts. He saw only a brief mention of the murder, which immediately put him in a foul mood. He slammed his fist against his wireless mouse and flopped down onto his bed, landing with a thud. His eyes welled and his nostrils flared. He felt both gutted and pissed off. *My army of men doesn't even have my back.*

The chat room brought him down from his euphoria. He had been on a high, and only moments before, his own father had given him a rare nod of approval when he told him he had just gotten back from a job interview. For once, Dylan felt like his dad might respect him, like his life had some purpose, although he was still living in the basement. But his own group's lack of recognition for what happened with Nora had dashed that feeling. *Maybe it was all for nothing.*

After sulking, he logged back into the Mandate and asked if anyone had seen what happened with Nora Marcus. "I guess that dude really went and killed a bitch? He put Dr. Carey and her clients on notice, and now their time is up!"

He waited. A few reacted with thumbs-up signs, and there were a couple of comments, one of which turned Dylan cold.

"Yeah, but it's probably just a one-off thing. Like it didn't even faze her, cause the home-wrecker is still doing her thing. She was back on TV this morning and said nothing about it, so it didn't stop her at all."

They think I'm a joke. Dylan felt that familiar heat flushing across his face, and the gentle flaring of his gums as his teeth clenched down too hard. Dylan's worst fear was not being taken seriously. He'd planned out all the steps, and so far, it was as if nothing ever happened.

Things didn't go perfectly at Nora's. Once he had located her house nestled in a cul-de-sac off Gregory Avenue, he drove around in his rental, surveying her block before going in. A small bungalow— pink with white shutters, a flat front with no porch, a detached garage, and a large picture window that overlooked unkempt evergreen shrubs. Privacy didn't matter, because Dylan had already planned to arrive as a delivery man. He knew that being part of Dr. Carey's program required the clients to live alone, which made his job so much easier.

Once he landed at Denver International, he rented a nondescript white minivan and made the trip to Boulder. He changed into dark denim jeans, a navy T-shirt, and a baseball cap with the word POSTAL on the front. He zipped up his black hoodie and checked himself out in the rearview mirror. The hardest part of his plan was that he wouldn't be able to carry his murder weapon with him across the country. Since the women lived all over, he had to fly, which made concealing a gun impossible. A knife was the easiest weapon of choice. Plus, he rather liked the intimacy of it, the fear it provoked. His first stop was at the closest hunting store to check out its selection. So many to choose from, but any knife would be sufficient as long as it was sharp and he used enough pressure.

No one spared a second thought for a man buying a hunting knife in America. Once he pulled up to Nora's house, he took a glance at her neighbors—no one was outside except for a couple of kids playing kickball in the street a few houses over. He pulled his baseball cap lower until it was level with his eyebrows and smoothed out his thin brown hair, which was overdue for a trim. He grabbed the empty box he had prepared with a fake delivery label before leaving Indiana just in case she had a surprise visitor. As he walked to the door, he saw flickers of light from her TV. He took another quick peek around her neighborhood, which was still quiet. After two quick knocks, a woman opened the door.

"I have a delivery for Nora Marcus." Dylan's cap was so low he could only see Nora's lower lip. He quickly glanced from her slippered feet up past her T-shirt that read Not Today above a cat lounging on the couch.

"Yes, that's me."

"Great. It's from a Dr. Carmella Carey. I have orders to make sure it's delivered inside so that she knows no one else gets their hands on it."

Nora tutted. "Oh, okay. Sounds just like her. You can set it down on my dining table." She motioned for him to follow her as she turned inside.

After shutting the front door, Dylan scanned her small house. "You're going to shut up and listen to what I say."

Nora didn't make a sound and kept her hands raised without being told. The smile stayed on her face, frozen in place. He directed her toward her laptop, where she was still logged into her account with Dr. Carey. He glared at her screen, reaching for his knife with his eyes fixed on Dr. Carey's image. Dylan watched as Nora shook violently, the sound of her chattering teeth muffling his own thumping heartbeat. The knife cuts were manic and chaotic, not smooth and methodical like he had planned.

Nora's hand went to cover her wounds. Her voice caught deep

inside her diaphragm as she attempted to scoot back in her chair, which was caught on her rug.

Dylan made one final deep laceration to her neck as Nora slumped down in her chair, sliding all the way down onto the floor.

* * *

On the entire flight home to Indiana, Dylan replayed how that first cut went. While it wasn't perfect, he was successful. Nora was dead. He grimaced when he thought of his sloppy work. Cutting into a stranger wasn't easy. As the plane landed, the mix of adrenaline and disgust had churned in his stomach. His grab-and-go bagel inched its way up as he'd downed the last of his soda to satiate the bile.

Now, Dylan swallowed back the disgust of learning that the men of the Mandate weren't raving about the murder. No one shared his jubilation at the attack on Dr. Carey and her program. He wanted to cry, but he sucked up any traitorous tears that dared to shatter his stoicism. He logged out of the Mandate and plopped onto his unmade bed. Once his stomach agitation faded, he flipped on his TV to watch the recording of Dr. Carey's latest interview, in which she never mentioned her client's murder.

He grabbed his phone and hit record.

"Hey dudes. I'm really upset right now." Dylan's bottom lip quivered as he sucked back tears and a runny nose. "I can't believe there isn't more being said about what I've done. I killed that woman for you!" Dylan stared at the screen, unblinking. "Don't tell me you guys think I'm a joke, too. I'm used to that from the females in our society, but I thought you guys had my back. Where's my support? Why aren't you praising this unknown man, me? I was really hoping for more from you guys, my brothers." Dylan took a deep breath. "It's okay. Maybe you think it's just a one-off kill. I promise I'm going to make a mark on this world for all of you."

To earn respect, Dylan knew he had to keep killing, and he wouldn't stop. Next stop, Cape Ivy, Missouri.

Chapter 25

Stacy

Stacy Wilson was a force of nature—a creative who rarely took herself or life seriously. At least, that's what others saw her as: free-spirited and jovial. She was a crafty woman who could come into a home and make it her own with her outgoing personality and a warmth that fully enveloped her friends. She was child-free, but her niece, Isabelle, was her joy. Stacy could be the fun "older sister," as she preferred to be called.

Her career at the bank had its perks. The hours were good, and the pay was decent. Her line was the longest, as customers would let people move ahead of them if another attendant became available just so they could catch up with Stacy and add a bit of joy to their day. A small deposit could turn into a fifteen-minute catch-up session. All of her customers left believing they were her favorite and that she cared about them the most.

When Stacy returned home, the silence haunted her. She grew up in Cape Ivy and never lived anywhere else, a true "Heartlander." Never having another city to compare it to, she felt secure there and appreciated her life in the city of roses. She bought a townhouse, the kind where her neighbors' garage was snuggled up next to hers.

Although once inside, it shed the modernity of the exterior, as she'd given it a hippie makeover with crafty pieces collected over the years. She'd crochet or make decorative pins that she'd hand out to anyone willing to accept them. Stacy would always say, "Gift giving is my love language," although she grew tired of not receiving any in return.

As she aged, the distance from her youth brought on a dread that ached deep in her heart. The older she got, the farther away love became. Once she joined Dr. Carey's movement, she finally felt that sense of purpose, and she hoped that the community would help her get on track, guide her toward the man of her dreams. During her first session, Stacy confessed her deepest fears, which she hadn't done before.

"Why are you here, Stacy? Please help me understand you," Dr. Carey asked.

"Well, I want a better life. I mean, I suppose the one I live is okay, but I keep thinking there could be more. Honestly, I want to make an impact, even if it's here in Cape Ivy."

"Love that. I can definitely help you." Dr. Carey smiled slowly and nodded.

Stacy watched as she closed her eyes and took a deep breath.

"Stacy? Are you currently in a relationship?"

"No. I want to be, but...no." Stacy frowned.

"That's perfect. You would have had to dump him or her, you know? So, being single makes the first step a breeze for you."

"Great. I'm ahead of the curve." Stacy chuckled.

Without reading through the contract, Stacy signed it online and started watching the required daily motivational videos.

"You're free. Take your passion and make it happen, ladies!" Dr. Carey enthusiastically said on the screen. "We all asked for a sign, and you ladies were brave enough to not only read it, but apply it!" she said, hands together in prayer.

Since she'd joined, Stacy always felt the warmth of belonging, of being part of a community. She believed she would experience love and happiness upon completing the program.

Stacy was always grateful for her little slice of heaven at home, where she felt the most like herself. Her townhome was on the far north side of Cape Ivy, past the shopping centers and along Interstate 55, where she'd exit onto the growing Lasalle Boulevard, which formerly led to cow pastures and corn crops but now was overrun with new construction. She enjoyed living outside the city limits, as it gave her the opportunity to put her convertible top down and sing along to the radio. The constant pounding of jackhammers and trucks backing up was commonplace in her new community. She once drove onto the wrong driveway, as each new home looked like the others. But she didn't mind. It made her feel included, and what she wanted most in life was not to feel like an outcast.

When she heard the doorbell, she didn't hesitate. Perhaps it was a neighbor, someone selling something, or a delivery? Dr. Carey always told members to expect anything, including mail, so she hoped it could be a welcome gift, and she was eager to see what the therapist sent. Without looking through the peephole, she quickly opened the door, which bounced off the wall.

Before her stood a man with most of his face concealed beneath a baseball cap. He had a forced smile, but as she took it all in, she felt the slightest wave of panic. A magnetic sensation shot through her body.

"Delivery for Stacy," the man said.

"Yes, that's me!" Stacy's eyes darted to his hands and found the package. A sense of relief washed over her.

"It's kind of heavy, so let me help put it inside."

Stacy clasped her hands. The panic was gone, replaced with a toothy, excited grin. "I can't wait to see what you have for me!" She stepped inside, making room for him and her delivery.

The second she turned away from the man, he appeared at her side with a knife. Her breath hardened in her chest. She could take only one step backward before she slipped and fell.

The sound of Dr. Carey's recorded daily video played in the

background. "Do you feel stuck? Me too. Let's refresh and reset. Today is that day."

The delivery man leered at the talking laptop. "All of you women are the same. Poor me, boo hoo. You have no idea how hard it is for men in this world. Women took our power, and I'm here to get it back." He pointed the sharp end of the blade at her.

Stacy choked out a breath. "Why are you here? I promise I'll listen." She gulped back the fear. Her eyes searched his unrecognizable face. She stared at him as if to say, *I see you,* but he was in no mood to be seen.

All Stacy could do was hold her hands out in front of her to shield herself from the knife as it slashed down upon her. In a last-ditch effort to escape, she ran toward her front door, but the final cut landed in her back. She slid down the Shaker-style door, leaving one long bloody handprint trail. Her final thoughts were of Dr. Carey, wondering what her special delivery was.

Chapter 26

Dylan

Dylan found himself in a maze of identical townhouses, all with the same layout and shape. The speedy exit he'd planned was foiled for another five minutes as he turned down the wrong streets, his palms greasing the rented sedan. He headed east, crossing over the Mississippi River on the Bill Emerson Memorial Bridge as sun-streaked beams cast shadows across his face. Dylan drove in silence, his hands tight at ten and two, until he made his way through Illinois, stopping for gas in Anna. He stood pumping fuel in a trance, recalling his latest kill. As he placed the pump back on the machine, he noticed a thin line of blood on his knuckle. He quickly stuffed his hand in his hoodie pocket and hopped back in his rental, scrubbing the stain with the underside of his sweatshirt.

As he made his way through Illinois, the sky opened up, and big pellets of rain fell hard into his windshield, making visibility low. The windshield wipers flew back and forth across the glass as the brake lights of cars ahead blurred before him. Dylan was an hour outside of Anna when the torrential downpour stopped and he could finally loosen his grip on the steering wheel. The sweat pooled in his armpits as he shook his arms out one by one, releasing the built-up tension he'd been too nervous to let go of.

The closer he got to the Indiana state line, the more he felt the weight of his emotions flip-flop. The heaviness before the murder, the pent-up anxiety and jitters of making the exact cut, and the great significance of it all. *I need this to make an enormous impact.* After his second murder, he felt greater pressure to perfect his mission and make a mark on history.

As he entered the town of Mount Falls, Illinois, he stopped at a place on 5th Street to get a bite to eat. The unassuming brick exterior wasn't as inviting as the sounds he heard as he opened the finger-print-stained front door. The arcade games and overhead music blared over conversations, raising the hair on Dylan's neck. The cool air conditioner froze the stiff hairs, which were still drying from the misty rain on the way in. He grabbed the plastic menu, ordered a pepperoni pizza, and walked over to a vinyl chair and table in the corner. A couple of kids were playing video games, arguing over who was winning. Dylan looked down at his knuckle, remembering the bloodstain from earlier, but it was now gone. He hid the only remnant of the murder inside his hoodie. Dylan walked around in plain sight with blood evidence on his clothes. He stuck his chin out. The knowledge that he had likely dodged detection once again was such an ego boost. He tapped his toe to the '80s song that played on the speaker above his head. "Jessie's Girl."

His mind wandered. *Fuck songs like this. Why are songs always about men seeking women?* Dylan's toe stopped tapping and his knee bounced as his mind drifted to the woman he'd like to find. Barbara was out there, and knowing she was living a life without him, maybe even married with a child, just ate at his core. *How dare she fucking do that to me?* The kids playing video games whined for their mom to intervene in their fight. Dylan glared, wishing he could teach them a lesson. He needed a target to take his fury out on.

His mind often drifted back to the smug face of Barbara's roommate, Andrea. She held a self-righteousness over him. She knew something, and he desperately needed to get it out of her.

"I really wish you'd stop coming by. She doesn't want to get back with you and didn't leave a forwarding address," Andrea said the last time he stopped in.

She can't tell me what to do. That's my uncle's house. I should tell him to evict her.

Dylan's eyes searched the restaurant. A Rocky slot machine threatened to knock him out, and a buxom blonde invited him to play in her beer garden. The constant sounds of tones, beeps, and coins kept getting louder in his ears. He brought his hands to cover them just as the server brought his piping hot pizza to the table.

"Sir, are you alright?" She furrowed her brow.

Dylan shook his head and stood up, his vinyl chair falling backwards behind him. He took off without a single bite and got the hell out of Mount Falls, Illinois.

He drove northeast, trying to escape Illinois, and followed the Wabash, which was the major river that cut through his home state, until he found a bridge. The Cannonball was an old wooden bridge, like an antique roller coaster. No room for fear or mistakes, just keep the pedal to the metal and keep moving forward. The Wabash greeted him like no family member ever had. Now Entering Indiana was his favorite greeting. There was nothing like his home state, full of sycamore trees, delicious sugar cream pies, and basketball pride. He was a proud Hoosier, through and through. He glanced down at the water. Dylan hated that the Wabash didn't get the same recognition as other rivers. It was a moody one with many tributaries, but it was a powerful river known for its limestone bottom. Dylan loved the Wabash, though it was difficult in spots. Not everyone could navigate it. It had a long history that deserved respect. Just like men.

He pulled over to the side of the road. The midday Wednesday air was misty but ghostly quiet. He took his phone out of his pocket and hit record.

"Hey my dudes. I'm feeling really nostalgic right now. Part of me wishes I could figure out a way to escape from all this and come through the other side without getting caught." Dylan closed his eyes as tears pooled at the corners.

"I dream of a life where we can be the kind of men in charge. Dominating the world. I don't want to die for this cause, but I've resigned myself to the fact that it's the only way." He looked out of his rain-streaked window. "I really wish I could be here when you watch this, but damn it, man, I love you guys." Dylan stared into the phone camera, nodding his head, eventually cutting off the recording.

As he crossed over Hood Street, the pang in his chest grew to a full-blown boulder of agony. The deep-seated pride he felt for his state and his mission all culminated in one emotional outburst. He had to pull over again to sob. His body shook so deeply that he was in no shape to navigate the streets. His shoulders trembled as he sniffed and wiped away his tears with his formerly bloodstained hand. He leaned back, pinching his nose, inhaling deep breaths before making the three-hour trip home to Lazette. His head remained cocked slightly to the left, in a dead stupor the entire way home.

Dr. Carey better take this latest murder seriously, or she hasn't seen anything yet.

Chapter 27

Carmella

The faded metal door banged back against the wall when Carmella slammed the stall shut. Her suppressed sob shuddered to the forefront as she found herself cornered in the bathroom stall, surrounded by lesser-known starlets and wannabes. Her heart ached more than ever when she saw Spencer again with his latest flavor. She'd bought this dress specifically because she thought he'd love it. It lay just above mid-thigh, showing off her tattoo of a heart with a knife stabbed through it. A fun date night gift he'd given her during a happier time.

Her sheer stockings had runs in them, so she tore them off and flushed them down the toilet, dabbing under her eyes and nose to erase the weakness she felt. She thought she was looking the hottest she'd ever been until she saw Spencer dancing with his latest arm candy. *He didn't look at me once.* She suddenly felt thankful that her mouth felt so dry as she heaved into the toilet.

Carmella punched the back of the stall door, crying out in pain. She massaged her hand before walking out to an audience of five women who pretended to be busy as she headed to the mirror. Her face showed how she felt inside. Smudged mascara ran down her neck, her bronzer was smeared across her face, and frosted pink lip gloss stained the outer edges of her lips. A woman standing next to her handed over a tissue and lip gloss, which Carmella grabbed. She did her best job at repairing her own makeup.

"I'm a big fan," the woman whispered, tilting her head to the side, admiring Carmella's image in the mirror.

Carmella's face flushed ice cold when she pivoted away from the woman and shot back toward the mirror, finally noticing she was no longer wearing the wig. She ran back to the stall and threw it on her head, checking the position before heading out.

Now armed with a new hunger to get her man back, she pushed open the bathroom door and was met with a whiff of marijuana that hung thickly in the air. She took a deep breath, smelling not only the smoke, but hours of long-worn aftershave and a faint stench of sweat. One of her favorite songs began to play as her footsteps synced to the bass's beat. Her buzz resurrected, she glided to the dance floor where Spencer and *the bitch* were still making googly eyes. Carmella watched as his hand slid down her waist, cupping her ass.

She stomped toward the couple, their bodies intertwined. Her wig was askew from getting caught between chests and shoulders. Her newly placed lip gloss was now smeared from coming into contact with someone's denim jacket. The sticky residue of a beer cup slapped from someone's hand coated Carmella's bare legs. She moved with no grace—drunk, haphazard, and reckless, caring only about getting to the man of her dreams.

Carmella stood at the top of the steps before entering the dance floor. She surveyed the area but no longer saw Spencer and the woman he was with. She stumbled down the two stairs, barreling into the back of another woman, who quickly spun around. Carmella felt smelly, hot breath on the tip of her nose as the woman jabbed a finger into her chest. Carmella kept looking around, spinning in circles trying to get her eyes on her man. She spun wildly as the room filled with floating faces, drunk on alcohol, high on drugs, with a thirst for fame they could never quench.

* * *

The next morning, Carmella still carried her battle scars with her. Her face wore last night's caked-on makeup, streaked like a woman caught in the rain. The only real downpour was the sadness of losing Spencer, likely for good this time. She gulped back a dry, sticky swallow, immediately wincing as it scorched the back of her throat. She sat stone-faced, staring at the wall as her body shook with sobs punctuated by periodic hiccups.

"Dr. Carey? Just making sure everything is okay?" Julissa questioned in a voice that sounded childlike.

Dr. Carey hopped up, wiping the thick mascara streaks from under her eyes, energized by a thought. The door swung open, and Julissa hadn't had the chance to move far from it. "Hey, so, if you send a text and it shows delivered, but not read, what does that mean?"

Julissa gulped and stared at Dr. Carey, whose eyes searched her wildly. She hadn't showered or brushed her teeth since the evening before. Her hair was frizzy on top in a half ponytail that slid down her back. Her sparkly dress had a rip on the side, and she had very dark circles under her eyes. Dr. Carey's face was a disaster.

"Hello. Earth to Julissa." Dr. Carey glared.

Julissa's head snapped to attention, and she shrugged.

Dr. Carey sighed loudly. "No idea?" She raised her arms in question.

"Oh, I don't know. Maybe he hasn't read it yet or you're blocked?" Julissa shrugged. "Maybe they lost their phone?"

Dr. Carey's face registered only one word: blocked.

"That motherfucker!" She turned, slamming her bedroom door, sending a picture frame crashing to the floor.

Dr. Carey collapsed onto her bed, slamming her fists into her mattress. "How dare he treat me like that? I'll make him pay. No man will get away with this." She cried into her pillow.

She sat up, rolling over in bed. "Julissa, do you still have that card the female detective left? I might need to make a phone call." Her smile was nearly as pearly white as some of her online headshots.

Fuck with me again, Spencer.

Chapter 28

Dylan

Dylan had been staring at the same spot on his basement ceiling for the last twenty minutes. He felt his eyes cross and his vision blur. He'd thought he'd receive much more notoriety for his murders than the coverage he was getting. *I just want to tell everyone it's me.* He wanted the glory and fame that came from being a killer.

The act of stabbing was the most intimacy Dylan had experienced since Barbara left over a year ago. After getting away with his second kill, he'd become intoxicated with murder. With the first slice, he'd felt trepidation. *Can I really do this?* The knife was sharp enough to make his job so much easier, now that he knew how sharp the weapon needed to be. The longer he was around the soon-to-be dead victim, the angrier he became as he replayed recent comments left by members of the *Year of Self* on the online platform.

"My man doesn't clean up after himself." "He just uses me for sex."

By the third, fourth slice, and on and on, the sense of order that overcame him was magical. His body could release the built-up tension and anxiety, his arm going limp until he could hardly hold up the knife. He was silencing women who had always disrespected him and men like him. She had to pay for her stance and feminist ways. Dylan was determined to be the underdog who got the upper hand. The loser who would finally win the game. The protector of men's rights whose name would go down in infamy.

"Guys, I hope you're proud of what I'm doing. I want you to know I did this for all of you." He sighed and sucked in a breath. "I really wish things could have been different. I tried. I really, really tried." Dylan wept as he talked into his cell phone camera. "You guys mean so much to me. I just wish Dr. Carey hadn't made me do this, but I can't go back now. I'm a killer."

Dylan rose from his bed and donned the wig he'd purchased to become Veronica Dixon. Undercover as Veronica, he planned to attend an all-team meeting scheduled for next week. He'd leave the program afterward as she was due for a one-on-one therapy session. While Dylan fully believed he could play the part in a non-speaking team meeting, he didn't think he could disguise his voice in a conversation with Dr. Carey. This time, he'd leave a note on the outside of the basement door—Job Interview—so his parents wouldn't disturb him. Dylan smoothed out the long brunette wig with a part down the middle and tested out the blur on his laptop, softening his masculine features. He leaned back in his chair, listening to one of Dr. Carey's recordings as soft wind chimes played in the background. Once her face appeared on the screen, Dylan's heart sped up, and his hands made carving motions into his thigh.

Chapter 29

Carmella

D r. Carey looked into the faces on her virtual call as her ego swelled, cutting the tautness of her muscles. Women from all races and backgrounds looked back at her, some with a post-divorce glow and others getting their spark back as their stress fizzled, their dreams now at the forefront of all they did. These women were living, breathing proof that she was onto something. The naysayers were out there, including the killer. But she refused to believe that she was at risk. She believed the killer needed her; he needed to hate someone. Dr. Carey was willing to be the bullseye he detested.

The killer's contempt only fueled her to keep going and add more women to her already full roster. Dr. Carey breathed in the scent of her aloe hand lotion as she gazed at the faces on her screen, imagining they were a think tank unified by the same beliefs. Life would be much easier if people trusted professionals like her. She admired people who followed the rules of an organization and went along with obedience. There was zero room for dissent in the *Year of Self*, and there were plenty of other women just begging to join. Once, when she was asked how the killer was able to find her clients, she proudly boasted, "Some of my clients provide testimonials and are proud of the work we're doing. We will not hide from anyone." Although it piqued her curiosity—how did the killer get two victims' names that weren't on the testimonial?

As she waited for one of her educational videos to finish playing, she breathed low into her diaphragm, taking a deeper check of her body systems. Her brows furrowed as she recalled the many late nights she'd been spending out. She'd really tried to curb her evening fun, but the more she resisted, the more she craved it. Her nightlife persona differed completely from her therapy life, but society ignored such things, allowing her to remain hidden in plain sight.

Her last night out may have been her wildest yet. She immediately felt the bass of the techno music as the cocktail of the house started taking effect. The rhythm intoxicated her, and she found herself in the middle of a dance floor full of hot, sweaty bodies grinding on each other. She felt their wet, smoky lips, drinking them in. Someone's rock-hard cock pressed into her as the music turned to her favorite Depeche Mode song.

"Enjoy the Silence."

Jabs of elbows spun her in time with the melody. The lights and bodies that happily invaded her space entranced her. Free drinks arrived at various times, and she drank with abandon. She hoped they were spiked so she could escape the constant complaints and drama that came with being a leader. In this environment, she was one with the pulsing crowd. The touch of their hands hypnotized her, and she eagerly kissed them, her tongue exploring their heat. She never felt more wanted or attractive than she did amid the groping hands of the vibrant group, all moving in a hypnotic tempo. The order of it all was so mesmerizing until Spencer and his sidepiece ruined her buzz.

When the night turned bright, she returned to her condo, where once again she faced the challenges that came from being a strong, confident leader. While it was everything she'd ever wanted, she also had her own desires.

After the police left her condo the last time, Dr. Carey had received a call from Detective Madison. "I wanted to check on you and make sure you're feeling safe? Also, if any further information has come to light."

"Thank you so much. It's such a relief to know I have you working on this case," Dr. Carey said.

"I really want you to consider everyone as a potential suspect. There is some concern that someone could be hiding within your program, which could warrant a police inquiry."

"What? Absolutely not." Dr. Carey's heart sped up, and she wrung her hands. "Look, there's another potential suspect, and I didn't want to bring him into this, but he was here the other night and a couple of nights before that... Perhaps we can meet to discuss this?"

When Carmella thought of her recent interactions, she considered Anthony, the doorman, as someone to look at; albeit she never intended for the police to consider him an actual suspect. She never believed it was him. But she wasn't above giving out his and other names to get the cops off her back, and she assumed if they had an airtight alibi then they'd be safe. Since the two women killed lived in different states, it could have been their husbands or boyfriends who were distraught over being jilted for all she knew. Divorce could bring out the most vile reactions, and watching your significant other be happy could invoke a quiet rage within.

Death was terrible for Dr. Carey's business. Still, it didn't stop women from joining the waitlist. It just irritated Dr. Carey that she kept receiving questions about the murders. Her program was about women's empowerment. She didn't care about the incel who wanted to eradicate women like her. Dr. Carey didn't want to give him any airtime or acknowledgement. She loved that he hated her so much because he could never attain what she had.

When she thought about the kind of guy who would prey on the women of her program, she knew the type. The guy that called her "bitch" when she turned down his offer of a date. A guy who gaslighted his girlfriend when he felt like her love was slipping away. The guy who insisted the couple go Dutch until she put out. The guy who got married and shelled out an allowance that was less than most kids receive just for existing. A guy who thought a woman's place was in an apron with a duster in hand. The guy who made all the decisions, dictating where they lived and how much they could spend on updates, even when things were falling apart, without consulting or caring about his wife's wishes. The guy who pressured his wife to get pregnant and then complained that her stretch marks made her slightly less desirable as he watched porn of airbrushed women online.

He was also the guy who would blame a successful therapist for his shortcomings even though he was a beta loser with no qualities that a woman could want.

The educational video ended, and Dr. Carey rejoined the group, unmuting herself.

"Breathe in happiness, independence, and self-love. Throw away whatever doesn't respect you and your path to fulfillment."

Dr. Carey began her virtual retreat. The women on the screen breathed in and out in unison, eyes closed, lips smiling broadly.

"Repeat: I am a queen and we don't need a king to fulfill us. We are strong on our own, and our crowns fit perfectly. We rule with our own thoughts and decisions. Masculine energy will again burden women."

Dr. Carey sat in silence to let the words resonate. Some faces were crying, while others sat quietly, basking in the affirmation.

Dr. Carey had created her program to heal her own wounds. Raised by a single mother, she never knew a father figure. She watched her mother struggle to make ends meet, yet her mother's words always uplifted her. "Aim to be the boss, Carmie. Don't settle for less. You are brilliant and beautiful, two of the deadliest attributes to a man's ego."

Carmella was a powerhouse. She loved seeing intimidation in the eyes of others as she grew taller than other girls her age and some of the boys in her class. She was at least similar in height to the most popular guy in school. When he asked her out, as her good looks didn't deter boys away from her awkward teenage height, she flatly turned him down. The power she possessed to defy his advances aroused her. She grew to be called "ice queen," "bitch," and "goddess" by many girls who admired her moxie. The boys in school couldn't hate her because of her beauty. They feared her because of her presence. She learned to crave that power and that look on men's faces as she got older. They assumed she'd go along with them because women had for ages, and they always did a double take when she flatly said, "No."

She admitted she loved being the adversarial one. She always watched movies starring women who would have been called "frisky and defiant." Those were the women she admired and wanted to emulate. Gone were her dreams of being the soft-spoken sex siren. Instead, she wanted to be the sharp-tongued villainess.

Early in her therapy practice, she realized many women had the same complaint. Their men didn't listen to them, and they felt lonely in their marriages. It became such a reoccurring arc in her office that she couldn't say what she wanted. As a therapist, she was bound by ethical rules to help the client see their behaviors and guide them toward their goals, but she couldn't just tell them what to do. As an online self-help leader, she could say what she always wanted.

"Your man is probably cheating on you." "You're giving women a bad rep." "I wish you could see how pathetic that sounds."

Carmella would scream into a pillow after some of her clients left. She couldn't stand listening to these same stories repeatedly. The burnout was real. But with her new program, she could be herself. She was an unabashed defender of women's rights, unafraid to stand up to any man, and a judgmental bitch, which she savored the most.

"Far too often, women hold or bite their tongues. I'm here to say what many women fear or have been conditioned to conceal: We are at our best when a man isn't holding us back."

She crafted all her statements and rules mostly with good intentions. But Dr. Carey knew she couldn't follow them herself. Her own heart struggled to give up Spencer. He was part of her addiction and, as far as she was concerned, she was doing her best in recovery.

Dr. Carey ended the retreat, telling the members, "Women are stuck with the choice between an alpha asshole or a beta bum. We deserve so much better! If only we could see that we don't need to settle for either. We have ourselves and that's all that matters."

A week later, Dr. Carey woke early to meet Detective Madison at the Buzzed Bee to discuss a potential suspect. She placed her usual order and settled into a corner booth, taking in the early morning chaos of a coffee shop on a Monday. She softened her appearance to match the words she wanted to convey today. When she saw Detective Laura, who wore her usual drab attire in subdued colors, Dr. Carey waved her over and slid over a black coffee she'd purchased for her. "Thank you for meeting me so early." Dr. Carey motioned for the detective to sit across from her.

"Of course. I understand you have an idea about a potential suspect that you wanted to bring to my attention?" The detective sat down.

Dr. Carey took a deep breath. "After further thought, I think you should know about my ex-boyfriend, Spencer. I don't know if he's a suspect, but I wouldn't put it past him, and I really think you should look into his background," Dr. Carey told her, feigning her deepest sorrow, batting her eyelashes with her hand over her heart.

The officer took notes, nodding as Dr. Carey relayed why Spencer could be a suspect. "He's what we call in my business a narcissist. You see, people like that don't like it when they're not admired. He could clearly see I was gaining fame and adulation, and it really ate at his core. He is manipulator in chief, and I could never trust anything he said." Dr. Carey made a show of sniffling back tears that never flowed. "I just want him to get help. If he's not the killer, he still needs to be held accountable for his actions." She narrowed her eyes at the detective's notes.

"Thank you for sharing this new information. I will pay him a visit and see what I learn. Do yourself a favor and protect yourself. I know from my experience with a narcissist that when they see us getting strong, that's when they really amp up their abuse." Laura raised her eyebrows and stood to leave.

You have no idea.

"Oh, one last thing. I know this is an odd request, but as you know, I have a reputation to uphold. I don't want word to get out that Spencer was my boyfriend. You see, it's a rule in my program, and it would really complicate things if anyone knew I was with him." Dr. Carey looked down at her hands and then coyly back to the detective's face. "You understand, right? It's hard in our position to be such strong women in a male-dominated world. I just need to keep up appearances."

The officer winked. "I understand."

After watching Detective Madison leave, Dr. Carey stood and spun around with her arms outstretched. She hadn't felt this light since the first hit of the special of the night a month ago.

She floated back home to her condo, rewarding herself with a special coffee to go.

Chapter 30

Julissa

J ulissa sat in Dr. Carey's condo parking lot contemplating driving straight back home. Her stomach simmered as she inhaled another heartburn pill. Between the increased caffeine intake and the growing stress over Dr. Carey and her program, the job was weighing heavily on her health. The car warmed in the LA sun as Julissa took shallow breaths with her head pressed against her car seat. Today was her first day back at work since being off for a week after her surgery; she was already stressing about the mess she'd walk into. With all the emails from women begging to leave, this job was like watching people on the ledge of a burning house fire while holding little more than a garden hose.

I can't quit. They need me.

Julissa mustered the courage to take the steps into Dr. Carey's condo, the walk familiar since she'd made it so many times already. With the coffee she'd picked up in the drive-through, she announced herself at the front door.

"Miss me?" She hoped to catch Dr. Carey in a rare genial mood.

No response. Julissa opened the microwave and put in the coffee cup. Dr. Carey often warmed hers up, as she liked it extra hot.

She opened her laptop still sitting on the tiny corner desk, which showed she had thirty unread messages since she'd last checked from home.

I know what I'll be doing today.

Though she knew better, since she seemed to be developing some horrible stomach ulcers, she downed her own coffee. This job kept her awake all night, so by daybreak she was a tired mess.

An email from Bailey Lake:

Hello Julissa. Welcome back to the office. I hope this email finds you well as I'd like to discuss the program and some recent complaints.

Dr. Carey believes there is a secret group meeting, which goes against the contract. I'd like your assistance in sniffing out who those ladies are. Talk soon.

Julissa reached for another antacid and walked to the kitchen sink. She turned her head, drinking straight from the faucet. Gone were all manners at this point. She dumped her nearly full cup of coffee into the trash before returning to her desk.

Julissa rubbed her belly in slow circular motions to calm the rising agitation. She collapsed into her office chair and leaned back, slowly rocking with her eyes closed. After reading that email, all hope that Bailey would make some changes on the case vanished. It had been the one thread of hope she clung to when returning to work. While she hadn't met any of the women in the program, their pleas felt personal, and now she knew she was fighting for them on her own.

How can I turn my back on women who are begging for my help?

The shuffling of keys unlocking the door turned Julissa's head. Dr. Carey walked in with a coffee in hand.

"Oh, you're back. I must have mixed up my days." Dr. Carey absentmindedly waved her arm.

"Yeah. I guess you didn't get my text?" Julissa asked.

Julissa was taken aback when she saw Dr. Carey's appearance, which was much more toned down with her hair parted down the middle and no makeup. She wore a muted gray sweatshirt and jeans.

"I'm quite busy, Julissa."

There it is.

"I picked up your coffee order, but it looks like you got it already." Julissa also noticed a business card in Dr. Carey's hand.

"Oh, yeah. Will you heat this up for me? I need a quick bathroom break." She set her coffee cup on the counter.

"Yeah, sure." Julissa got up, picked up the cup Dr. Carey brought, and glanced at the card.

Detective Laura Madison. What is Dr. Carey up to now?

Julissa spent the rest of the morning reading through emails, wishing she'd listened to her gut. The one that was rotting inside telling her to run.

I acknowledge my sensitivities, and I seek strength to navigate the negativity surrounding me.

Chapter 31

Bailey

Bailey woke extra early for today's all-team meeting. She'd given up on actual sleep after tossing and turning most of the night. She played out scenarios of Dr. Carey somehow recognizing her as her lawyer and calling her out in front of everyone, although the odds of that were extremely unlikely. Dr. Carey had declined a face-to-face meeting, and they always communicated via email or through Julissa. Bailey prepped her look: a blonde wig with a deep side part showing darkened roots, a far cry from anything she'd ever consider. A mock turtleneck covered most of her exposed skin and muted lips to blend into the sea of women on the screen.

As Vivian Frost, she transformed into a woman who eagerly awaited the genius of Dr. Carey. She sat on the edge of her chair, too nervous to eat or drink; her stomach rumbled with hunger. A countdown clock appeared as the screen floated into outer space with stars and galaxies flying by. From the moment Dr. Carey appeared on screen, she held Bailey's gaze and attention, although her display name listed her by her pseudonym. Dr. Carey unlocked something deep within Bailey that had never been unlocked before. Gone were all of Bailey's mental blocks and restraints; she actually felt reborn under Dr. Carey's tutelage.

I will follow her to the end of the earth.

It wasn't just one thing Dr. Carey said, but the entirety of her program and who she was. Dr. Carey represented everything Bailey aspired to be. On the outside, others would assume she had it all and had made it, but inside, she was living a lie. She wasn't living her authentic self. Because she focused too much on others instead of her own desires, she always lived in the shadow of her parents' dreams and didn't pursue her own goals.

"You are all unique and beautiful souls. I see you. I hear you. I love you," Dr. Carey announced on the screen.

Tears flowed down Bailey's cheeks. The feeling was foreign, as she knew the art of sucking up her emotions all too well. She was always proud, never shedding a tear, being the strong one for her family and friends.

"You are whole just as you are and welcome in my world." Dr. Carey smiled into the camera.

Bailey's lips parted, her eyes searching the screen longingly. Her emotions confused her. She wanted to reach into the monitor and hold Dr. Carey and kiss her. She wanted Dr. Carey to love her and shine her radiance into her life. Bailey didn't want to be her lawyer; she wanted to be her partner, in whatever form that took.

After the meeting ended, Bailey poured a glass of wine and thought back to Dr. Carey's words, focused on how her eyes dazzled and the way the left side of her lip curled just slightly when she finished speaking. She wanted to know every aspect of Dr. Carey and to call her Carmella. She wanted to walk hand in hand with her, go grocery shopping and out to dinner, be lovers. Bailey wanted to be whatever Dr. Carey needed of her.

Chapter 32

Dylan

Women of all backgrounds laughed big, toothy guffaws on the screen. Dylan clicked his cursor on the arrow, flipping through the screens to see all the disgusting followers of Dr. Carey. His own screen was black except for a circle in the middle with a V inside it. Dylan's mouth stayed frozen in a frown as he sneered at the women logged in for Dr. Carey's retreat. Her message and the sound of her voice turned his stomach; he leaned over his chair and dry heaved, repulsed by everything to do with the program.

The women listened intently as Dr. Carey's voice rang out. It was the same bullshit message. "We are fiercely loyal to one another," Dr. Carey proclaimed. "Our bond is sealed as a women's group, where there's always space for you at the table." Dylan frantically clicked through the screens, looking for the woman he most wanted to find: Barbara. There were a few other blank screens, but none of them displayed her name. Still, he wildly scrolled back and forth, seeking the woman who had betrayed him the most. Sweat beads formed on his temples as the erratic click of the mouse sounded throughout the room.

Dylan's jaw clenched as Dr. Carey's voice pierced his ears. He felt closer to her than ever, hidden behind his dark box. *Maybe I should threaten her now?* He debated it, but today's mission was all about Barbara.

As he scrolled the pages, the sweat rolled down his neck. At one point, he thought he'd found her. His own memory was of an earlier version of her, one who listened to what he had to say. He didn't know this side of Barbara that would join a cult, stand up for herself, and become a feminist type. Although he was angry with Barbara for falling for a con artist like Dr. Carey, he pitied Barbara's weak mind as one of the sheeple in the cult.

Dylan scrutinized the women's faces. Some had soft curls framing their faces; others had pin-straight blonde hair. He waited to see Barbara's brunette mop she never did anything with, preferring to pull it back in a clip or ponytail. When he reached the last screen, his body went clammy as his heartbeat sped up, stabbing through his T-shirt. Her hair looked different—she had cut it short above her shoulders, but he recognized her face. She was laughing, her right dimple denting inward. She tucked a strand of hair behind her left ear, revealing tiny studs. But on further examination, he realized they were ear seeds, roughly six lining the entirety of her ear.

The more she laughed, the angrier Dylan became. Her laughter was at his expense. *I just know she's making fun of me.* "Men are so lame when it comes to our feminine mystique." Dr. Carey's voice broke his trance.

Barbara kept laughing and smiling. *How dare she be happy without me?* Not that Dylan believed she'd been somewhere pining away for him. She did ghost him, after all. But he'd rather she were dead than thriving on this screen, listening to someone like Dr. Carey. He'd much prefer she joined a religious commune, swearing off society and giving up all her material possessions, taking a vow of purity. That's a group he could actually get behind. Go off-grid and stock up their own bunker.

Dylan's foot shook with fury the longer he stared at Barbara's face. There was a lightness about it. She even appeared younger. Barbara glowed like he'd never seen before. She dared to be happy and she was rubbing it in his face. He wanted to reach in and pinch her mouth so it would form the unhappy lines he was used to.

"Close your eyes and feel the vibration of the music," Dr. Carey instructed the women. Weird jungle music played, and Barbara's expression melted into a sense of serenity and peace that got Dylan fired up. His hands shook. He wanted to destroy the tranquility that swept across her face. He grabbed his laptop and shook it, but that was futile.

Finally, he clicked the volume, unmuting himself, and yelled, "Barbara, you fucking bitch! Why did you leave me? I was an amazing boyfriend, and you just used me." Dylan gulped back the phlegm that rose as bile filled his stomach.

Dylan woke with sweaty armpits and the worst hand cramp of his life, his flat sheet wrapped tightly around his wrist. Betrayed by his own dreams of Barbara, who remained elusive. Dylan's dream convinced him his plan of wearing a disguise was a bad one, and he knew he didn't want to keep hiding behind a laptop. His hand throbbed the rest of the day as Barbara's smiling face occupied his mind. Dylan's resolve to find her matched his desire to eradicate Dr. Carey and her program.

Chapter 33

Carmella

The heart-stopping pounding at the front door was undoubtedly the police. Julissa answered, escorting them inside before notifying Dr. Carey of their presence.

Dr. Carey perked up, hoping to hear what they'd learned from investigating Spencer. His text to her, in which he called her every name she'd heard before, showed someone had contacted him.

I need to play dumb in front of Julissa. She can't know any of this.

"Damn it. I have press in less than an hour!" Dr. Carey yelled from her office, fanning her flushed face.

"Dr. Carey, this is an urgent matter. The Cape Ivy Police Department notified us they have found a murder victim who was also a client in your program. In fact, she was watching one of your videos at the time of her death," Detective Madison said.

Dr. Carey emerged from her room, closing the door behind her. "That's very sad to hear. Please let Julissa know all the details, and she'll update our billing information. Anything else?" Dr. Carey raised her eyebrows in question.

The officers stood glaring at her, furrowing their brows. "We do think it would be best to make a public announcement warning your clients. We don't know how much farther this person will go, but it appears he's definitely targeting the women in your program."

Julissa's hand rose to cover her mouth.

Dr. Carey sighed. "Thank you, officers. If you don't mind, I will conduct my business as I see fit." She took a deep breath. "I do appreciate your visit, and I'll act accordingly. Hopefully you'll do everything you can to catch whoever is doing this." She stared at them, crossing her arms.

The officers glanced at each other and nodded at Dr. Carey.

"But I have to get ready for a very important interview. Julissa, will you see them out?" Dr. Carey walked to her kitchen and reached for an ice cube, placing it on the back of her neck. The coolness worked its way into her muscles, soothing the tension that hadn't left in months.

* * *

Back at her desk, Dr. Carey prepped for her live interview with Livvy. This would be her first interview to include a client. While it could be risky, she hoped the controversy swirling around Livvy's ex might be to her benefit. People could see Livvy as an underdog, a true victim of a culture of wealthy and privileged men. Dr. Carey twisted her back, releasing her spine with a pleasing crack. She savored the release of tension as she grabbed the closest pill, round and white, and chased it with lukewarm water.

The show producer began their countdown as Livvy joined the call. Her face appeared in a small box on the screen. Prior to the call, Livvy and Dr. Carey had agreed to let Carmella take the lead.

Renee Baldwin appeared on the screen, her brunette shaggy haircut jostling as she spoke. She had just finished a segment on navigating life as an empty-nester. Her demeanor was lively as she announced Dr. Carey. "Up next, one of our most talked about therapists. Dr. Carey is back, this time with one of her clients. You don't want to miss this."

Dr. Carey closed her eyes and repeated her latest mantra: "I am a fierce queen, and I will let no one dilute my dreams." She gave her neck one last massage, hoping to loosen the growing tension caused by poor sleep.

Back from break, Renee stood facing the screen. "Dr. Carey. It's been a whirlwind since we last spoke; I've missed catching up with my favorite feminist doctor. Please introduce us to your client," Renee said.

"Thank you, Renee. The world has it all wrong about Livvy Kyle. She's a talented actor who fell for a predator. We all know the type— the guy who sweeps you off your feet with lies, entitlement, and manipulation. Thankfully, Livvy came to me to change all of that."

"Livvy, welcome to the show," Renee said.

Livvy cleared her throat. "Thank you so much. I am so grateful to have found Dr. Carey when I did. I lost everything because of my ex, and honestly, I'm just at the beginning of my journey."

"Well, what I know about Dr. Carey is that she's one tough cookie, and your ex has met his match." Renee laughed, winking into the camera.

"When I get through with Livvy, he will regret everything about himself. He'll be wishing he had her back." Dr. Carey narrowed her eyes.

Renee held her hand to her ear. "I'm sorry, ladies, this was unplanned. I'm getting some news that we have a caller who wants to speak with us." Renee motioned to a production assistant. "Go ahead, caller." Renee furrowed her brows.

A man's voice came over the airwaves. It was clearly male, but he'd disguised it with a voice changer that made it deeper, almost as if it were an underwater computer. "Dr. Carey, you don't listen very well. I told you to stop, and you didn't. Now two of your clients are dead. Consider this your second and final warning. I will murder someone else if you don't cancel your program completely."

Renee gave a loud gasp. "Caller, who are you? Why are you

doing this?" The studio was ominously quiet. "Audience, we don't know if this is the same caller as before or a copycat."

"He's a coward, Renee! Hang up. He doesn't deserve this airtime. We should not give any publicity to a man like this. He's a loser and a lowlife who will never get me to stop. Listen carefully: I will never stop." Dr. Carey stared into the camera.

The producers set me the fuck up.

"Caller, are you there?" Renee repeated several times. But there was no answer.

"Ladies and gentlemen, I am sorry. This is a fluid situation, and we ask for your patience as we determine who this is."

"Only a pitiful failure of a man would be threatened by us!" Dr. Carey screamed into the silence.

Renee searched the room for answers as the cameras panned back. "I'm now being told that the caller has hung up. As you could hear, it definitely sounds like he was disguising his voice. We have called the police to see if there is any way to track him."

"Can we get back to why we're here?" Dr. Carey raised her voice.

"I'm sorry, Carmella—I mean, Dr. Carey. I just think we need to address this situation. My viewers will want to know what's happened."

Dr. Carey sat back in her chair, crossing her arms with her nails digging into the sides of her palms.

"We all know what happened. Some incel called in to threaten the pretty girls." Dr. Carey rolled her eyes.

Livvy sat frozen, her occasional blinks assuring viewers she remained connected.

Renee mouthed to someone off screen, asking if she should go to break. "Viewers, we're going to go to break. We are so sorry if any footage was harmful. We'll be right back."

After the extended break, they bumped Dr. Carey's segment for healthy lunch ideas on the go. Her fury bubbled to the surface when she learned they wouldn't finish the interview. She slammed her glass on the counter, successfully fracturing it, sending shards of glass flying.

This asshole will not fucking ruin me!

She needed to get out and have fun, but Spencer was no longer an option. After today, she wasn't a kitten or a panther; tonight, she would be a praying mantis, would tear every man's head off and sew it on backwards. A little techno, coke, and whiskey would quiet the violence she felt inside. She donned a red wig and a skin-tight dress and called a car service. Dr. Carey walked past the doorman, not looking back as she reached over and slowly scratched the side of his bald head.

Chapter 34

Bailey

Bailey's favorite part of the day was now after work when she raced home to watch the latest *Year of Self* video upload. All day, she'd sit at her desk listening to Matt's stories about his family, barely absorbing the basketball stats from his kids' games.

How the fuck does he not see I don't care?

Bailey had always prided herself on her resting bitch face, yet Matt seemed to be immune to it. He plowed right through with story after story, regardless of how much work she had stacked in front of her. Ever since she'd discovered Dr. Carey, the hours ticked by slowly. Her wisdom and luminosity drew Bailey in like a moth to a flame. When five o'clock came, she'd march to her Mercedes, make the fifteen-minute commute to her high-rise condo, and get into comfortable clothes for the evening. A generous pour of wine, a healthy salad, and an entire evening with the divine Carmella was all she wanted.

Bailey was fixated on the daily videos, which were always far too short—usually between five and fifteen minutes. No matter the length, they gave her what she craved.

She wasn't sure when the obsession began, shifting from just part of her job to a full-time fascination, but once it hit her, it never faded. Dr. Carey's face, her words, her mannerisms, it all combined in one unhealthy loop inside her brain.

She cued up tonight's video. "Welcome, namaste. Tonight, let's discuss life paths. I bet most of you want a switch. You want to flip the switch on your life to begin living the one you dream about. I'm here to tell you that it's not a dream. It can be yours."

Bailey grinned and took in a deep breath, savoring the way her entire body relaxed as she exhaled.

"Ladies, I was in your position until I founded this program. Stuck in the rat race, falling for losers, and putting myself last. Now, I've learned the precious power of saying no, and yes, for that matter. I've learned who to surround myself with, and I've fallen in love with myself. Tell yourself, 'I love you.'"

I love you, Bailey thought as she sniffed back tears. She related so much to fading into the background as long as she did a good job. She'd been all too happy to be a part of the rat race; now she wanted something softer, sweeter, something more Dr. Carey-like.

Bailey ended each night much the same way, although she grew tired of not having those face-to-face meetings.

But she had a plan to get very close to the object of her desire.

Chapter 35

Dylan

Dylan loved the way his father believed he was a real businessman, always taking trips across the country. Little did his father know, Dylan was racking up massive credit card debt to afford his killing sprees since his meager inheritance was running out. Plane tickets, car rentals, and lodging weren't cheap, and some of Dr. Carey's clients lived quite far from each other. It wasn't possible to make a weekend of it.

As he sat in the waiting area at his gate, Dylan hit record.

"Hey guys. About to take a brief trip, but it's a secret for now." He chuckled into the lens. Prisms of sunlight bounced off the sunglasses he wore inside. "Someday you'll all learn how I did this and marvel at how well I kept it all a secret. For now, it's all for me and my trusty phone." He slurped the last of his drink, the straw suctioning the bottom of the cup. "I can't believe what's happening to Alton Shaw. I saw coverage of what they're doing to him, and it's barbaric. The man is a legend, and they're trying to take him down with false allegations." Dylan looked around, eyeing people over the top of his sunglasses before pushing them back up his nose. "Like, how do they get away with this shit?" He shook his head. "Like, why am I surprised? And of course, Dr. Carey got her bitch ass in this by manipulating his girlfriend, Livvy Kyle." His nostrils flared large in the fisheye lens of his cell phone camera.

An overhead announcement interrupted his musings. "That's me, guys. See you next time. Peace out."

Dylan took all of his usual steps. Rented the car, bought the knife, and dressed the part. All in a ruse to gain access to the house of one of Dr. Carey's clients. This time, he chose the East Coast and traveled to North Carolina. He considered stopping on the beach to check out the pelicans after his mission. Maybe soak up a few rays of sunshine and relax a bit. But time was precious these days, and there was no respite for Dylan or his purpose.

Chapter 36

Jacqueline

Tucked away in her bungalow on the Outer Banks, Jacqueline Manning sought the serenity of the coast. The natural terrain, the charming lighthouses, and the thrill of watching wild horses gallop along the beach sold her right away. Her home was a sanctuary given to her when her great aunt died, as a teacher's salary wouldn't have provided these kinds of views. She could never have imagined living close enough to listen to the waves lapping at the shore, to watch windsurfers floating above the sparkling water, and to hear the many sounds of tourists who packed downtown for the museums and walking tours.

While her home was the perfect oasis, her love life was another story. Jacqueline grew tired of dating apps and failed relationships and decided to give Dr. Carey a try. When she first saw her on TV, the beautiful blonde with intense green eyes intrigued her. She was instantly pulled in and wanted to be within her sphere. As a third-grade teacher, she really couldn't afford the program's hefty price tag, but when she completed her intake with Dr. Carey, she knew she had to become a member. She sold her car and opted to take public transportation in order to join.

"Jackie, I'm so impressed with your motivation. YOU are what this program is about. Women like you who find a way to make shit happen."

Jacqueline beamed, even though she hated being called Jackie. However, she felt a bit too timid to correct Dr. Carey. She accepted that Dr. Carey was the leader here, and she'd be open-minded to any suggestions, including changing her own name.

Jacqueline was a pretty woman herself, with icy blonde hair since birth and an athletic build. Her perfect hourglass shape made every dress fit like a glove. Yet Jacqueline was unlucky in love. She'd lost count of how many relationships had ended because he was already married or she caught a flirty text flash across the screen when they were watching a rom-com. The last time she saw heart emojis, she threw him out. "Good riddance," her mother told her on the phone. "You always took in the riffraff, and hopefully you learned some lessons."

Jacqueline wasn't sure what she learned except that being single wasn't terrible, at least for the first few months. She often questioned whether she had an addiction to men or, at the very worst, was codependent. When she took an online test that showed she was 80% an enabler, she knew it was time to seek professional treatment, which was how she came across Dr. Carey.

"I am weak and exhibit zero self-control" was her mantra for her first week. Unlike most therapists, Dr. Carey broke the person down. It was about "breaking away from the core," which meant being real. "Be real" was a common statement that Dr. Carey made to her clients, and as someone who preferred privacy, Jacqueline thought she heard it the most. Not used to being an open person, it took a lot of work to get to her core self.

When Dr. Carey announced there was a contest for the ultimate prize, where one lucky client would receive a lifetime of treatment, she submitted as many entries as possible. Winning the prize became her new obsession, and her free time consisted of submitting entries. Her phone's dying battery plus work slip-ups led to a new rule: one submission per hour. However, a week into the new plan, she started doing two entries to make up for her sleep time.

When a knock at the door revealed a delivery man with high cheekbones and eyes hidden behind sunglasses, she rejoiced; every fiber of her being cheered. She grinned from ear to ear, believing this was the big win she had been counting on. Then she had a fleeting thought that perhaps Dr. Carey was testing her, and Jacqueline wanted to make the absolute best impression. She opened the door with a smile and let him in, making sure to say only positive things about the program, not that she had anything negative to say anyway.

When the first cut of the knife sliced her neck, it was far too light of a stroke and it only made her bleed onto her shirt. However, the subsequent slices were much deeper and cut straight into her veins, one even reaching her neck bone. As she slumped to the ground, her thoughts wandered to who had been the winner of Dr. Carey's prize. Jacqueline hoped she'd made her proud.

Chapter 37

Eden

The secret support group of clients from Dr. Carey's program watched the Renee Baldwin interview together online. Eden stared without blinking at her computer screen, filled with fear and a sense of responsibility. Her body anxiously rocked back and forth, bracing under the weight of her regret. Each time she thought back to the day she'd recommended Dr. Carey's program to Livvy, her guilt balloon would inflate. *I was desperate.* She felt immense remorse for referring Livvy to Dr. Carey and now carried that burden around like she did her trusty rose quartz.

Eden had been dealing with an increase in headaches in the past few months from the stress of being in the *Year of Self,* and even more so since going behind Dr. Carey's back. The constant fear of getting caught woke her nightly with the sensation of a screwdriver in her skull. Sometimes she threw up so much she was afraid to eat or drink coffee. After admitting she had actually joined a cult, her only solace was connecting with a few other members who'd also come to this realization and formed the secret support group.

Eden turned down her speakers as she tried to control her meandering thoughts of what she could have done differently. After creating the group, Eden couldn't help but feel a sense of betrayal toward Dr. Carey. *We are the good parts of your program*, she often reminded herself.

The support group allowed them to be open and speak freely without being chastised, either emotionally or financially. It was what they'd hoped for when they signed up for Dr. Carey's program. Some of them were new members who caught on quickly that it was all a sham, and others had been in the program since its inception. Some members had asked to leave Dr. Carey's program and were being penalized with more fees. They each knew that if Dr. Carey found out about their private group, it would mean more financial setbacks. The *Year of Self* had strict rules not to fraternize with each other outside of the group, but they were willing to risk it and trust each other. The group didn't have a designated leader; they took turns expressing what was on their hearts. As a reformed rage-a-holic, Eden had learned to let love flow through her and welcome a clean aura, wiping away the trauma of her past. She embraced this style of community.

The women could talk about the things that really mattered to them. For Eden, it was moving past the abuses of her ex. The trauma of that relationship wasn't fully gone, his phantom control still gripping her today. His words replayed in her head. She could still hear his voice telling her she would never be good enough, saying, "You're not capable of making decisions without me," or, "You'll always need me to fix things."

Eden's arms trembled as she pictured her ex's smirk, remembered his scent, two days overdue for a shower because "girls love the pheromones," and how he never put her first.

One of the other members noticed Eden was looking off to the side and called out to her. "Hey, Eden, is everything okay?" Regina asked.

"Oh, yeah. Sorry. I got wrapped up in thinking about my ex and damn, it just gets me so angry. I'm mad I still let him get to me like this."

Regina breathed a deep sigh. "Oh man, I had one of those. I couldn't escape fast enough. The constant berating and name-calling was soul-sucking."

"Yes. These men make me want to join a convent and give up the opposite sex. Although, I question if we're following the right person." Eden put her palm to her forehead.

"I get it. Dr. Carey and her program wouldn't have attracted us if resolving trauma were so easy. Unfortunately, we just found the wrong person to help guide us toward healing." Regina shrugged. "Speaking of which, I get the glorious pleasure of meeting with her in just a few. The truth is, I actually love her program. I love her message and everything about it. I just wish she wasn't our leader." Regina frowned.

"Ugh, I totally understand. Peace be with you, friend." Eden waved her goodbyes.

Eden logged out of the chat with her chakras cleansed, but the pit in her stomach grew bigger each second.

Chapter 38

Regina

Regina Soloway had spent years working on the person she now presented to others. She appeared as a reserved and pleasant woman, but beneath the surface, desperate, painful longing pulsed through every fiber of her being. She just wanted to be loved. When she first discovered Dr. Carey, she was eager for a relationship and willing to follow any rule if it meant finding "the one." She found the rules easy to follow, but it was hard to watch Dr. Carey attack other members. However, Dr. Carey had a brilliant way of convincing them to strip down their outer shells until there was nothing left but a hollow carcass she could manipulate.

Thanks to "the rules," she led a lonely existence, where the familiar trickle of wine hitting the flute glass was the only thing that broke the silence. While she didn't understand the reasoning behind Dr. Carey's decisions, she always felt a rush of giddiness and excitement at being in her presence, even if online. Her own emotions were a constant tug of war—torn between wanting to continue with the program because of the benefits or quit because of its toxicity. Still, therapy was thrilling for Regina. "Working on myself is fun," she'd told her mom during their last lunch date. She always logged in early, hoping Dr. Carey would see her signed in as available and they'd get in extra time together, but that had never happened in the six months she'd been a member.

As she stared back at her face on the meeting link, she thought she was attractive, but her shyness held her back. Naturally, her mom tried to convince her she was a catch. Regina had voluminous brunette hair that she kept parted on the side, which had a natural bounce to it after she washed and dried it. She often hid her looks behind her glasses, and whenever she greeted someone, she averted her eyes, unwilling to hold their gaze too long so no one could get too close.

Regina grew up with health issues that only got worse with age. Being diagnosed with rheumatoid arthritis was not only physically painful, but it became a secret she tried to shield from others. She pushed herself to take the stairs, stand with others around the water-cooler to discuss the latest Bravo show, and agree to make appetizers for an upcoming work party, all to say, "Look over there" when it came to her illness. She always paid dearly. No one saw the tears that formed in the soothing hot shower or the deep sigh as she closed her apartment door, which was akin to unbuttoning her pants after a big Christmas meal.

When Regina first saw Dr. Carey, she was in awe of the beautiful blonde with the perfect button nose and exquisitely done hair and makeup. Regina's cheeks flushed pink with excitement, as the message was exactly what she wanted to hear. Dr. Carey's demeanor and words were perfection. *She's the type of woman I want—no, need —in my corner.* Like other women, Regina believed Dr. Carey was the rope that would pull her out of the rut she found herself deeply wedged in. A lifeline to free her from her stale existence.

When Regina became one of the founding members, she finally felt whole, a part of something grand. Love shone upon her in the brilliant UV rays, and she didn't care if it caused cancer. *I need this.* As she prepared for her session, she watched the rain fall, streaking her window. Seattle was normally rainy, but she didn't mind because she'd get to decompress with Dr. Carey soon. Her relationship with the program was a love-hate one. She loved the message, but she could see how Dr. Carey's treatment affected other members, which was why she joined the secret group. "Maybe my presence in both groups can build a bridge," she told Eden when she joined. She sipped her immunity tea and curled her socked feet underneath her. Her lazy long-haired cat, Albert, strolled past her, yawning, throwing a scent of fish in her direction.

The chimes of the virtual sound bath followed by stars floating around a translucent countdown always got her. The glow from the screen shone on her face. Her eyes twinkled in anticipation.

"Namaste, my love. Thank you for joining," Dr. Carey said, breathing in with closed eyes.

"I'd never miss my time with you." Regina smiled.

If someone passed by, they'd think they were lovers stuck in opposite worlds.

"Regina, have you been following the rules? Be honest, because I will find out if you haven't." Dr. Carey's tone turned.

Does she know about the secret group?

"I have absolutely been following the plan to a T, including my evening tea." She held up her mug, which was no longer steaming. "I am single and in no way ready to mingle." She chuckled at her own joke.

Not returning the smile, Dr. Carey began, "I just sanctioned two ladies for not following my rules; let's hope that's all there is." She narrowed her eyes. "As you know, I am silencing and penalizing them."

Regina gulped and thought, *I hope to be a member for life.*

"Today I want to discuss daddy issues. Specifically, what has your dad done to put you in this position? Let's talk about his failures and how we can reverse those effects in your life today." Dr. Carey relaxed her mouth and sat back in her chair.

"Daddy issues? Hmm, I don't know." Regina quickly scanned her childhood memories but couldn't place a specific incident.

"I understand. Human nature is a miraculous thing. We can forgive, forget, and create a whole new existence, regardless of whatever horrors we've experienced. If you can't come up with anything, we may need to go to the next step of hypnosis. It's a wonderful tool to draw out the demons hiding inside of you."

"Well, my dad was...fine. I mean, we get along, and he didn't do anything horrible to me. I can't really say I have daddy issues." Regina shrugged.

"Regina. Stop covering for him. I can see right through you. I know there's more than you're letting on. If you can't be honest, then maybe we need to stop today's session."

"Trust me, I'm thinking. But honestly, nothing is coming to mind. I had a good childhood, except for my health. My dad drove me to every infusion appointment, and we got ice cream afterward. He was a quiet man, but if I needed gas money or financial advice, his accountant side came through and he always helped me. He was a stable father to me and a good husband to my mother." Regina frowned.

"Dig deeper. Women don't turn out like you by chance. There's always something in a woman's childhood that led her to where she is today. What did your dad do?"

"Honestly, he was a wonderful dad..." Regina said, but Dr. Carey cut her off.

"DIG DEEPER! I don't have time for these games. Maybe you're not right for this program after all. I had you pegged differently." Dr. Carey shook her head.

"No, please, I am right for this program. I mean, it's been helping me. I feel like a new and better woman."

"Yet you refuse to open up about the pain you've been holding onto since childhood."

"I mean, my dad ran over my favorite dog when we were growing up, but he was heartbroken over it too."

"Did he do it to teach you a lesson?"

"Oh God, no. It was an accident."

"Keep digging. It's there, but you've locked it away in a vault."

Regina bit her lip. "He and my mom fought when I was younger, but they worked things out. I found out years later that he cheated, but he changed his life."

"There. Your dad was a cheater, and you learned to accept that in a man. He broke your spirit and let you live your entire life with trauma, believing that was how you were to be treated." Dr. Carey pursed her lips. "See, this is what I need. I need you to reach into your core. I understand how hard it can be, but I can't help you unless I know everything."

"But I wasn't even aware that he cheated until I was an adult. My parents got help and worked things out." Regina gaped.

"That kind of thinking is exactly why you're stuck in this mindset today. It was just simple cheating, only once, or my boss only grazed my ass, but he won't do it again. This bullshit mentality needs to stop!" Dr. Carey raised her voice.

"I honestly never thought of it that way. I still love my dad, though, and don't think he's a dishonest man." Regina shook her head.

"Mindset and reframing take time. But first, honesty. We broke through a wall today, and I'm proud of you. You don't deserve infidelity. You deserve love and respect. Repeat that."

"I deserve love and respect." Regina gulped.

The session ended, but Regina didn't feel toasty and warm like she normally did. She felt guilty for exposing her dad. He was a good man, and he didn't deserve to be labeled a cheater. But she also wondered if that's how she was forced to think. Maybe her sensitive nature really was covering for him. Maybe this was all his fault.

Chapter 39

Bailey

Bailey jerked in her office chair when her phone rang. She was on edge after another night of sleep deprivation because of watching Dr. Carey and her escapades.

"Bailey, it's Julissa with Dr. Carey's office. I wanted to talk to you about the Cutthroat Caller. Umm, Dr. Carey isn't too concerned, but honestly, I feel like I need to do something. I..."

"Julissa. Take a breath. Why do you feel the need to go over Dr. Carey's capable head?"

"Well, she's blowing it off." Julissa grew quieter, nearly whispering into the phone. "I have members calling all the time wanting out of their contracts, and I'd like to help them."

Bailey audibly sighed. "They willingly entered into those contracts. It's not Dr. Carey's fault there's a lunatic out there. If anything, they need the community more than ever now with a killer on the loose. There's power in numbers."

There was silence.

"So there's no way to help the women who want out?"

"Unless they want to pay a sizable fine, they have to wait their contracts out. It's much cheaper for them to stick with the program.

Besides cost, it's better for their mental health. Dr. Carey is a gift. She's really an amazing person, and anyone is lucky to have her in their corner."

More silence on the line.

After the call, Bailey walked up to Richard's office to fill him in on Dr. Carey's case.

"How's working with that batshit crazy broad?" Richard laughed.

Bailey glared. "Dr. Carey is doing amazing and necessary work. I'm so glad to be on this case."

Richard looked up from his file. "Uh, sure. Any word about the killer? I heard they gave him a fancy moniker."

"The Cutthroat Caller. Yeah, it's really giving him a lot of publicity. But the media should focus on Dr. Carey and the *Year of Self*." Bailey crossed her arms.

"Sounds like you drank the Kool-Aid." Richard chuckled.

Bailey stared.

"Keep me posted." Richard shooed her away with his hand.

Back at her desk, Bailey typed an email to Dr. Carey:

"I want you to know that I think you might have some people in your program that aren't very supportive, and it may be in your best interest to weed them out."

Bailey wanted to end it with more, but left it to her thoughts.

I'm here if you need me.

Before hitting send, she hit backspace and deleted the email.

Julissa is a good pawn to have in my corner. She might not be supportive of Dr. Carey, but she's the closest to the person I want.

Chapter 40

Dylan

Dylan wasn't the king of his castle; his father was. But when his dad was deployed for many years, Dylan gladly took the throne. His mother was no queen and could barely function most days, which was a source of fury for him over the years. When Dylan was five, his mother gave birth to his younger brother, and his father came home for this birth. Which was another bone of contention for Dylan, as Edgar wasn't there for his own. This time, they gave the baby his father's name: Edgar Foster Jr., with his father becoming affectionally called, "Eddie Sr."

"Meet your brother, Eddie Jr. Isn't he the sweetest?" Reece cooed.

It was the first time Dylan was keenly aware of his temper. His heart sank into the boiling bile in his stomach. His skin turned red hot, and he immediately hated everything about his brother. He glared at the suckling baby. Dylan despised his face and the way his parents fawned all over him, and he vowed he'd never want anything to do with him.

"Don't you want to hold your baby brother?" Reece coaxed.

"No. I never want to touch him or talk to him." Dylan turned away from him.

No matter how much they tried, Dylan's parents couldn't get him to show any interest in Eddie Jr. Dylan refused to sit near him and would taunt him every chance he got. Reece's own mental health actually improved after Eddie Jr. was born. She got out of bed, went for walks, and attended social events with her friends. This time, Edgar was home during the first two years, so he could be there for all those early milestones.

Dylan refused to be a part of his brother's life; his parents told others they hoped it was "just a phase." When Dylan overheard his parents saying those things, it incensed him further. His hatred took on deeper roots—he had to prove them wrong. He was tired of pretending to be a happy family and refused to love a brother who his parents clearly loved more than him.

The family secrets had begun as early as he could speak, when his dad would coach him, "Don't tell the neighbors your mother is having a nervous breakdown again." Some kids had normal mothers, but not Dylan. His mom was often in bed with what her doctor termed "female hysteria." When she wasn't resting, she was in a frenzy trying to make sure every room was presentable when Edgar came home. Dylan never knew what to expect with his mom, and he would never tell the neighbors anything, sworn to secrecy. He wouldn't dare speak to actual people on his own, anyway. What Dylan's dad didn't realize was that Dylan would much rather let everyone believe his mom was dead; he thought she disgraced their good family name. He believed his dad deserved much better than anything his mom could provide and that a man of such military honor warranted a sane woman. *If there were any.* Her first mortal sin was naming Dylan after her side of the family and not after his own father.

Dylan would never forget his mother's betrayal.

Chapter 41

Edgar

Edgar was a highly decorated man, weighed down by medals of valor and honor. And yet, he harbored a secret from the world about his ill wife.

Years earlier, when he first laid eyes on her as he walked through the doors of the college hall, Reece was the prettiest girl he had ever seen. Wild, curly hair, cat-eye glasses, dazzling blue eyes—he couldn't resist staring at her. He did a double take when he first glimpsed her smile; it made her entire face light up as she sat under a sycamore tree laughing with a friend. He stood amid a sea of rushing students as they greedily searched for openings in the crowd, trying to avoid being late for class. Edgar had his eyes on this beauty, as well as a career in business management. It was a solid field with a nice future that would land him a house on a cul-de-sac and children—and hopefully this gem in front of him.

Edgar was an understated, debonair man of his time, passing for a second cousin of James Dean. Thick blonde hair, blue eyes, a medium build, and delicately placed chiseled features gave him a softness women found approachable. He also had the confidence of a man who had a history with women; he'd had his fair share of relationships, although he was always the gentleman.

He approached the woman who had caught his eye. "Hello, I can't recall ever seeing you here before, and I'd definitely remember a beauty like you." He smiled, his face wrinkling at the corners of his eyes.

"Oh, well, hello. I'm a new student. My name's Reece." She gave him a wide smile, revealing straight teeth and eventually puckered lips.

He stared for a bit too long. "Oh, sorry. I'm Edgar. I'm a junior majoring in accounting." He hoped to impress her with his long-term career outlook.

"I haven't decided on my major yet. Probably education, but I'm taking a few elective classes right now to, you know... figure it out!" Reece fanned her hands in the air.

"Are you free? Would you allow me to take you on a date?" Edgar asked, praying she didn't have a boyfriend.

"Oh, I'd like that." Reece glanced away toward a college building, batting her eyelashes.

They settled on a date the following weekend, sealing their status as a new couple. Days after Edgar's graduation, however, the army reserve called him up to fight an unknown enemy in an unplanned-for country in the Middle East.

Reece was only two years short of graduation, but once they found out Edgar was going to war, they quickly married at the courthouse with a couple of college friends as witnesses. She had dreamt of the big day, but in wartime, reality no longer had room for her adolescent dreams. The sudden war announcement cut into their budding love affair, forcing them to grow up quickly and make adult decisions: marriage, because Reece couldn't be an unwed mother with a delinquent father. They hadn't planned on getting pregnant, but Edgar was ecstatic about it. Reece wore white lace and carried a bouquet of tulips, touching her un-showing belly as they said, "I do."

The Foster family embraced Reece, allowing her to move in with them to wait for her husband's return from war. The pair wrote to each other as much as they could, and when Dylan was born, they had hoped Edgar could finally return home in order to raise his young family. But combat and its aftermath didn't allow for that kind of compassion. Baby Dylan wouldn't meet his father until he was two years old. Dylan would later swear that caused most of his problems, as he told them he never felt the presence of a solid male influence.

Dylan didn't inherit the beauty of his mother or the determination of his father. He was a fussy baby who rarely smiled or clapped his tiny hands. He didn't like water or the sun. Dylan hated being sung to and was grouchy when his mother tried to calm him down for a nap. Reece would write to Edgar, telling him how difficult Dylan was and that she just couldn't take his fits most days. She'd write in detail about how crazed his incessant crying made her feel—that she no longer felt like a strong woman with such a weakling baby to watch over. She made pleas to send Dylan to an orphanage. "At least for the time being. Until the war is over, and then we can pick him up, and maybe he'll be better. For both of us."

The letters weighed on Edgar as he fought in battle, staring into the eyes of the enemy, yet he was the unwanted guest there. He knew he was a stranger to his son, and he was missing out on the bonding that should be happening. He had a strong bond with his own father, who he hoped was filling in as a strong male role while Dylan was under his roof. But he knew a grandfather was nothing like a dad, so he did his best to return home as soon as he could, hoping to turn Reece's pessimistic view about Dylan around. However, after the war ended, things improved little between Reece and Dylan. He was a difficult baby who became a terrible toddler, and Edgar hated to admit to himself that he disliked his own son. So when his second son was born, he hoped things would be different. He made it a point to be home for the birth and to be around for as long as possible, staying for two years until he took a position overseas. "I promise I'll be back after six months," he told Reece. But he could instantly see the familiar look of fear in her eyes.

"Don't leave me alone with him."

Edgar's return home was sudden, a tap on his shoulder from his superior, accompanied by a chaplain. His heart lurched; his lips quivered as they alerted him to an emergency at home. "Sir, we regret to inform you that you're needed back home. There's been a death in your family and you're being allowed to return home."

Halfway to the airport, he sat in the back of the cab, silent. *I forgot to ask who died.*

Back home, the scene was chaotic. He found Reece whimpering, balled up in a corner in baby Eddie's nursery as the police milled about the room. Baby Eddie's lifeless body begged to be held, loved, or resuscitated. Dylan stood just outside the nursery doorway, watching as several officers walked past him. Edgar overheard conversations confirming his son's death: "Looks like the mother suffocated the poor thing."

"Never had a fighting chance."

"Saw something like this over in Crawfordtown where the mom went berserk."

Edgar glanced between Reece and Dylan, who still stood stoic, but the words didn't seem to cause any shift in his demeanor. He slumped to the floor and cradled Reece, who collapsed into his arms. She stayed there until the police officers requested statements from the family, including Dylan. That was when he finally showed a new emotion: a flash of a grin across his face.

After Edgar's return home, life was forever altered in the Foster household. After her release from a required hospital stay, Reece mostly remained bedridden. While the police on the scene initially blamed Reece, the coroner stifled their investigation. Sudden Unexplained Death in Childhood (SUDC) was a possibility, according to the coroner, and he wasn't willing to level accusations of homicide against the grieving mother. However, the initial police statements spread quickly, and the gossip mill did its job—anyone who'd been Reece's friend immediately turned on her. Circumstances compelled

Edgar to retire, requiring him to raise a troubled son, support a grieving wife, and mend a broken family.

Dylan always walked awkwardly near his father, as they never did form a close bond. The two were nothing alike, which became painfully obvious as the years went on. Reece left her bed a little more over the years, but she was always a shell of herself, crying out for the son she wanted instead of the one still alive in front of her. "There, there, it's okay. Go rest," Edgar would often say, patting his wife tenderly on the back. The decorated man feared by so many was such a gentle soul to his dear wife and wanted little to do with his living son.

Edgar no longer answered to his short-lived name of Eddie Sr. It died along with his son.

Chapter 42

Carmella

"Are you saying Dr. Carey is a suspect?" Renee Baldwin gasped.

"Everyone's a suspect at this point. The police and the FBI will thoroughly vet anyone who has a relationship with the victims," FBI profiler Dominique Hay said.

"I fucking hate that woman!" Dr. Carey hissed over Julissa's shoulder. She stood watching the viral video clip that was calling her out as a potential killer.

"How would Dr. Carey benefit from killing the women she's trying to help?" Renee asked.

"People murder for many reasons. Again, I'm not accusing Dr. Carey, but she hasn't made things easy." Dominique pursed her lips.

"It's not my fucking job to make your life easy!" Dr. Carey grabbed the back of Julissa's chair. "This woman is so close to getting sued," she said, seething.

"Well, I certainly wouldn't defend a killer, but I just can't imagine a therapist doing this." Renee frowned.

"Thank you, Renee. Julissa, send her some flowers or something. This is beyond ridiculous. Like anyone would believe I was the killer and set up some men's rights caller? Give me a break." Dr. Carey leaned her head as far back as she could until there was an audible crack.

Julissa quickly scooted her office chair closer to the window, away from where Dr. Carey stood, and jotted some notes.

"People of all kinds of backgrounds kill every day. Killers don't follow a checklist regarding appearance or motivation," Dominique said.

Dr. Carey watched, shooting death glares at the two discussing her. "The actual killer is loving this! Two women talking about me as a potential killer? Come on!" Carmella yelled at the laptop.

"Julissa, contact Bailey and explain the situation. See what she can do about this. People can't just go around and ruin reputations because they don't like me," Dr. Carey said.

Dr. Carey lay across her couch and draped her arm over her forehead.

Julissa punched in the lawyer's number, taking quick glances back toward Dr. Carey. "Hello, Bailey. It's Julissa from Dr. Carey's office. Hey, um, give us a call back. This is regarding an unflattering interview in which a guest named Dr. Carey as a potential suspect..."

"We need to sue, Bailey!" Dr. Carey yelled in the background.

Julissa put her hand over the receiver as Dr. Carey spoke, ending the call.

Dr. Carey stood and snatched her own phone off her desk, sending off several text messages. The room remained quiet except for the clicking sounds of her fingernails on her screen and the clunk of her front door as Julissa left for the day. After a ding cut through the air, she audibly chuckled, and rose to get ready for an evening out on the town.

Purple wig. Backless dress. A new elixir of the night awaited her.

Chapter 43

Bailey

Bailey glanced at her image in the floor-to-ceiling mirror at the end of her narrow hallway. The skintight pleather catsuit accentuated aspects of her body she hadn't outwardly shown the world. Usually hidden by pantsuits or oversized shirts, she embraced this free, wild version of herself.

Thanks to Dr. Carey, I'm now unbound by societal obligations. Even the ones I've created.

Forced into a career by overly rigid goals on a path carved for her long before she had any idea who she actually was. Bailey was, for once, untethered from the corporate world she thought was her nucleus. Now she'd learned to strip away that cast-iron thinking, all thanks to her idol, Dr. Carmella Carey.

She slid into her Mercedes. The heated seats toasted her ass while her gloved hands tapped her lit cigarette, her red lips forming an oval to blow out the billowing smoke. She hadn't smoked since a dare in college, yet now it was part of her nighttime ritual. With her inhibitions so low, she was determined to set out on the prowl, hoping to run into Dr. Carey at one of her favorite clubs.

Her pleather-clad leg squeaked against her leather-bound car seat as she scooted out the car door. A quick glance in the mirror revealed a woman she had dreamt of becoming: a vixen free of burdens. A short line formed at the entrance to the club. She made sure to get there early, avoiding eye contact, concealing her gaze under the bangs of her wig, a short blonde bob. Bailey didn't think anyone would recognize her in this outfit, but she didn't want her boss or parents to get word of her new alter ego. She sized up the people in front of her in line. There were a couple of jock-type guys with pseudo-model girlfriends hanging off their arms, nibbling their ears. Another guy in front kept checking his cell phone and searching the parking lot. The bouncer stood without emotion behind all the power of his red rope of hopes and dreams.

The bouncer motioned for Bailey to come forward as the suited cell phone guy let out a sound of audible disgust.

"You," the bouncer said.

Bailey sauntered forward, the sound of her heels slicing through the wishes of the few she'd cut in line. Once past the red ropes, a gust of cool air hit her face, forming goosebumps up and down her arms, her nipples hardening at the excitement of entering the club. A spray-tanned brunette with dead eyes stood at the coat check and handed Bailey a blindfold.

"These are for the main event."

Tonight was Exploration Cove, where all who dared entered the dance floor and put on their blindfolds for some consensual fun with whoever they wanted. Bailey drank in the mesmerizing lights as the few bodies already on the dance floor ahead of the event moved in rhythm to the sounds floating from the speakers. She made her way to a back corner where she could spy both the front door and dance floor, awaiting the one woman she hoped to get close to tonight.

Bailey was straight, but infatuated. Dr. Carey was an obsession, and she wanted every part of her. After studying her program, every-thing clicked. She had never felt so free in all her life. Dr. Carey gave her permission to breathe like never before. Bailey always felt like she'd been breathing through a straw, and any mistake was a nick to its side, exacerbating her struggle to get a deep breath. Now with Dr. Carey and her program, she could enjoy a full-bodied inhale. She could soar where before she'd floundered. Outwardly, it had always appeared she had it all; inwardly, she'd lost grip of who she was so long ago that she no longer had a clue who the real Bailey was.

When Bailey first followed Dr. Carey to the club, it was just for research. She was concerned about the on-air threat. She feared for her client's safety, and she couldn't bear to lose her. Bailey was brave enough to tell her she was a big fan when she caught her coming out of a bathroom stall. It took everything in her not to grab her shoulders and tell her what she meant to her.

I'd honestly die to protect her.

It fascinated Bailey to learn about Dr. Carey's penchant for drugs, alcohol, and techno dancing. It turned Bailey on, and she'd envision what it would be like to kiss and touch her, full of vigor and zest. Dr. Carey was such a bitch, and Bailey wanted that power turned onto her. What a thrill to finally be submissive when all her life she'd been the alpha. For once, she didn't have to be perfectly in control. Dr. Carey was a masseuse for her soul, rubbing all of her erogenous zones, easing her into the role of obedience.

Bailey's breath caught in her chest, warm tingles filling her veins as she spotted Dr. Carey. There was always something about having a crush that seemed to come with built-in GPS designed to zero in on them.

She's so fucking perfect.

Bailey watched as Dr. Carey seemed to float across the room wearing a skin-tight dress and purple wig, heading straight for the bar. She had the blindfold tied around her wrist, which made Bailey smile. Bailey loved being in on the secret, knowing the true identity beneath the wig. What she wouldn't give for a real encounter—a face-to-face rendezvous. Bailey had rehearsed it so many times in her head. The last time she'd followed Dr. Carey into the grocery store, she was so close to the apples.

"I love the red ones, too."

Bailey imagined Dr. Carey's eyes would light up, mesmerized by their common bond over red apples. But Bailey knew how dumb that would be, so she never spoke and just followed her, inhaling the sweet scent of her vanilla perfume. She watched the bounce of her freshly done blowout, the perfectly plump way her lips parted, and the flawless tone of her calves as she took each step.

What I wouldn't give to reach out and turn her around and make her see me.

It was all too risky, but Exploration Cove was the perfect way to get close with no strings attached—the ideal opportunity to caress her goddess. As the minutes ticked by, she watched Dr. Carey take a few pills followed by a few drinks before making her way to the dance floor. The club was full of the most beautiful and eligible people, like the Raya app had thrown up inside. Bailey was so grateful that her look caught the bouncer's eye.

Dr. Carey laughed at a thick-necked man who held a thin-rimmed bottle. She threw her head back, exposing all her teeth, obliging a likely dumb joke from an even dumber jock. Bailey knew the type—the guy with a little girth who thought his thickness was enough to please a woman who just wanted a little more length.

Go away, loser. You'll never be enough.

From this vantage point, Bailey could see how painfully awful men struck out. Eventually, Thick Neck took off, and she watched Dr. Carey stand all alone.

A woman like Dr. Carey should never be alone.

Bailey glanced around as the crowd grew. She wanted to run to Dr. Carey and convince her to escape from this scene, but she knew her one chance to get close was coming up. She watched as Dr. Carey danced seductively in front of a man who ignored her, turning toward the woman he was with.

The problem with men is they don't know how to care for women.

It's so easy. Treat us like goddesses. Love on us, make us feel like a fucking queen, and we'll melt in your arms forever.

At least, Bailey hoped that would do the trick for Dr. Carey.

A soft voice whispered into the intercom, "Tonight is Exploration Cove, where you leave your inhibitions at the door. At the end of this next song, come to the dance floor so you can explore."

Bailey's blood pressure spiked, and she attempted to crack her knuckles through her gloved hands. While nervous, she was beyond excited for the opportunity. She had to plan carefully to get close enough to Dr. Carey to make sure they ended up together.

She's wearing a backless dress.

Bailey made her way to the dance floor, keeping tabs on the area where Dr. Carey was dancing. From only a few feet away, she could sense the connection and wished she could walk over to her now.

"It's time! Put on your masks and let's start off with our first song." Bailey donned her mask. "Spin to your left and now to your right. Walk forward and spin to the left again. Now stop and explore." The slow, sensual beat played overhead.

Bailey lost her bearings but guessed she needed to turn to her right when she ran into a barrel chest. *A man.*

He grabbed her shoulders and bent down, kissing her between her nose and lips before Bailey pushed away. She used her hands to feel through the crowd for Dr. Carey's wig and backless dress. The song sped up and hips began to gyrate into hers. Hands reached for her breasts and butt as she forced her way through the crowd. Frantic that she would miss her opportunity, she gently raised her blindfold but didn't see Dr. Carey at first. She spun to the left, then right, finally spotting her behind the tall, barrel-chested man. Dr. Carey was making out with him. Bailey charged toward them, wedging herself between them, clutching Dr. Carey's waist to pull her into her, placing a firm kiss onto her pillowy lips.

To Bailey's surprise, Dr. Carey kissed her back. Her hands reached around Bailey, grabbing and wanting more from her. Bailey felt hands searching her torso, up her ribcage, and finally resting on her breasts. She was so aroused she never wanted to leave this spot on the dance floor. As the beat melted into a faster one, a hard shove behind Bailey knocked her forward, disrupting their kiss, and Dr. Carey was gone.

Bailey left the dance floor and the club, but part of her would live there for eternity.

Chapter 44

Livvy

Livvy knew it was Emilio before she even saw the name on her lit phone screen. The TV interview was a total shit-show, and the attention was a disaster. When the caller came on, Livvy immediately knew things had taken a turn and she debated logging out, but she didn't want to turn her back on the one person who seemed to support her. Part of her questioned whether Alton had paid somebody to do this. *I wouldn't put it past him.*

"Do you know what kind of damage control I've been having to mount for you this morning? Goddamn it, Livvy. This is fucking bad." Emilio sighed into the receiver.

"Look. I know how it looks, but we had no idea it was going..."

"Dr. Carey? You know she's a fucking quack. She's in it for money and clout. I'm around fucking starlets all damn day. I know a star chaser when I see one, and let me tell you, she's a fucking fame whore."

"Look, I just want to work again. You turned your back on me. You think I can sit around and let my talent go to shit? I'm in my fucking prime; I won't be this hot forever. I need to be working now!" Livvy tossed a pillow across the room.

"Guess what? Nobody will touch you now. You might as well go to San Fernando and do porn because you aren't doing Hollywood anymore after that stunt."

Livvy hung up the phone, dejected and more alone than ever. *Maybe I've fucked up getting involved with Dr. Carey.*

She flung herself onto the couch as a headache bloomed. Nothing was going right. The car that Alton had "gifted" to her was now gone from her parking spot. She'd naively thought that maybe he really loved her enough to let her keep it. However, after discovering his numerous "affairs," or what she now termed "transactions," involving underage girls, she realized the repossessions were covering his bail and legal fees. It was expensive to fund a legal team to keep him out of prison.

None of Livvy's former friends accepted her calls or texts. Her last hope for support was to return to the crystal shop and see if Eden would go to lunch or coffee with her. Livvy hoped a new person with ties to Dr. Carey would be a positive force in her life.

She slid her tiger's eye into the front pocket of her jeans and walked the four blocks to Spiritual Gardens. When she entered, she was relieved to find no other customers. The bell on the front door sounded as she walked past a shelf of crystals, her eye catching on the brilliant amber. At first, she thought Eden wasn't working until she heard light chatter in the back room. As she approached, she heard a familiar sound: gongs cascading behind a rushing waterfall, followed by a couple of namastes. "Peace be with you," and some laughter.

"Hello?" Livvy called out. There was complete silence followed by some shuffling. Eden appeared, smoothing out her outfit.

"Oh, Livvy. I'm so surprised to see you." Eden looked her up and down as she opened her mouth to speak before closing it again a few times, finally saying, "I saw you and Dr. Carey on TV and I'm so sorry. I am absolutely shocked by what happened."

"Yeah. That still has me rattled. How do you feel about these threats? Dr. Carey doesn't mention them, but we should prepare ourselves in case the threats are real, right?"

"Oh yeah, that's a totally taboo topic. A few women have brought it up, and Dr. Carey shut them down. She swore us to secrecy about it. In fact, if she knew you and I were talking about it now, she'd sanction us."

Livvy heard muffled chatter behind the beaded entryway to the back room. Though the voices were low, she could make out parts of a conversation about the program rules and sanctions.

I didn't think that part of the contract was actually being enforced.

"Dr. Carey didn't find out about us, right?" a voice asked.

"No. Although she told us she knew about a secret group, so either she's onto us or she's fishing for info."

Livvy furrowed her eyebrows. "Wait, what secret group? There's a secret group?" Livvy pushed past Eden through the beaded curtain, walking into the back room.

"Livvy, wait. Don't go back there." Eden attempted to get in front of her.

Inside, the familiar screen of women looked back at her, searching for answers. But there was no Dr. Carey at the helm to guide this group, and it was much smaller, only a fraction of the full program with ten logged on.

"What's going on?" Livvy asked.

A few women covered their faces and immediately shut their cameras off.

"Livvy, look—we all signed a contract, and if this gets out, we'll be in financial and legal trouble, and none of us can afford that," Eden pleaded.

Livvy glanced at a few of the names: Regina, Amy, Margaret.

"So, what is this group?"

Eden opened and shut her mouth before speaking. "Well, we created this group because we feel like the *Year of Self* isn't exactly what we signed up for. We loved the message and the sisterhood; we just don't love...her." Eden shrugged.

Several of the women nodded in agreement, and the ones who had taken themselves off camera came back on.

"Oh, thanks, bitch. You got me into this. Why the hell did you recommend her to me?" Livvy stepped closer to Eden.

Eden raised her hands. "Look, I've been sick over that. I thought it was my way out, and I know that's so shitty, but I was desperate. This whole fucking cult—yes, this is a cult—has turned me into a person I hate. I am so sorry, and I don't blame you if you hate me."

Livvy stared at the wall right past Eden. "I should be angry with you, but honestly, I would have probably done the same thing. Don't worry. I won't tell Dr. Carey, but now I'm also stuck, and being associated with her is ruining my career. I came here because I'm all alone, and after that TV interview, things are worse than ever." Livvy's eyes welled up. "Before I walked over here—and yes, I walked because my fucking car got taken away a couple of weeks ago. Alton took it back, and I don't have a job, so I can't afford one." Tears streamed down her cheeks. "I actually called him. I fucking called that loser. And guess what? His wife answered. The woman he told me he hated, who I planned my future around."

Livvy sank onto the beanbag in front of the laptop, sobbing. A few of the women on the call wiped away their tears, and Eden put her hand on Livvy's shoulder.

"The absolute worst part is I still fucking love him. After all of this, I love him!"

"What did the wife say to you?"

"She hung up on me." Livvy sniffled. "Serves me right. I mean, I would have cursed myself out. She probably needs this group, too." Livvy laughed, and eventually the women joined in with their own laughter and tears. All their emotions came pouring out. It was much-needed therapy that Livvy had craved for weeks.

"Why does it hurt so much? Why does this kind of love ache to the core, ripping my heart away from its comfortable and sacred spot?" Livvy closed her eyes and shook her head. "Why am I obsessed with every inch of this man who never cared about me? I just want to move on and be the bad bitch I say I am." She sucked back tears. "Why can't he love me like I want him to?" Livvy sobbed uncontrollably again. "Why do I love him so much?"

"Oh, honey. You don't love him. You just don't love yourself," Margaret said through the laptop speaker. Some of the other women nodded in unison.

Livvy looked up. "You don't think I love myself?"

"I think most of us think we do, but if we dissect most of what we tell ourselves, it's usually shit talk all day. Language like, I'm not good enough, I'd be better if... He would love me more if I were more this or that."

"I never thought about that. I guess I'm guilty of that too. Most people would say I'm pretty tough, but deep down, I'm pretty doughy. I'm sensitive, but that makes me defensive because I don't want to let my guard down." Livvy sniffled, reaching for the box of tissues Eden passed to her.

Eden bent down to Livvy. "You trusted me, and I am so sorry. That is not how I operate, and I hope you can forgive me. I think I can speak for everyone when I say you're welcome to join our group. It's private, and we have all the positive benefits of the *Year of Self*, just minus Dr. Carey." Eden smiled.

"I get it. We're all hurting here. I'm glad I found you. Life is pretty fucked up right now, and I need all the help I can get." Livvy smiled and reached for her tiger's eye.

Livvy wasn't sure if her loneliness would be solved by fixing herself or by surrounding herself with healthy people, but either way, she was willing to do whatever it took. But letting go of her past was proving to be harder than she realized.

Part of me still loves Alton, while the other part knows he's the worst person in the world.

Eden walked through the beaded curtain and reappeared holding a lit bundle of white sage. "With the healing power within, I cleanse and purify your body, mind, and spirit. Let this smoke wash away all impurity and negativity. May this renew you as the divine woman you were born to be."

Livvy took in a deep breath, and her body warmed in a wave of love as all the women bowed and put their hands to their hearts in reverence for the ceremony.

"One question. Are you all witches or something? Kind of getting that vibe." Livvy laughed.

"I'm a witch in training." Eden winked.

"I'm just emo." Margaret shrugged.

That night, Livvy slept better than she ever had. Her body still tingled when she thought back to the group and the comforting words they'd shared. *Maybe I've found my people?*

She was flipping through her phone messages when an urgent message from Eden alarmed her.

"Did you hear? The police found Margaret's body! They think that guy who called in during your interview is now a serial killer."

Livvy's phone slid out of her hand as her eyes shot to her front door to make sure she'd locked it.

Chapter 45

Margaret

Soft clouds hung just above the tree-lined dead-end road as Margaret Palmer turned onto her almost too steep driveway. She was immediately hit with the smell of a smoky fire pit and the sound of engines revving. Her noisy neighbors had turned the once peaceful home into a nightmare. They were such a nuisance that she thought of moving every other day. However, the birds that fed in her yard, the groundhog family under her shed, and the neighborhood cat who often stopped by to visit kept her planted.

Moving wasn't foreign to Margaret. She had moved over thirty times during her life, even though her family wasn't in the military. Her two working parents struggled to make ends meet and feed the growing family. She was always the new girl in school and never the one with long-term friendships. Even today she struggled to keep friends. Being happily child-free kept her away from mommy groups, which organized get-togethers, and introverts didn't just happen upon a bunch of girlfriends. Finding similarly minded people was hard work.

Margaret was a writer in the thriller genre who loved getting lost inside her characters' minds. She hadn't made any major sales, but once she started writing, she knew she'd found her niche.

Her current project was about a killer who snuck inside women's apartments, leaving them gasping for air. While she often wrote of murderous villains, her home life was one where she cultivated coziness. She usually wore black; it was the easiest color choice since her cats were little voids. She loved to eavesdrop and spy on her neighbors, often questioning why she wasn't included in their neighborhood gossip. But anytime she involved herself, she left feeling exhausted by their interactions.

She was safe inside her cozy home decorated in shades of jade and cream, with a soft, lush couch and a hand-woven natural rug. Snuggly blankets hung over the back of the couch, with plenty of fuzzy cat beds for her cats to choose from. She'd painted her walls a creamy sparkle-flecked gray, and a large picture window provided her with the outdoor view she craved. Vanilla and cinnamon candles were often lit, gently dancing so the light reflected off the antique art prints framed on her walls. Her family lived several states away, a place she'd left behind over five years ago. However, she never felt truly at home anywhere.

As a writer, Margaret's life was sedentary, and she rarely left home. Neighbors would think she was gone if not for the occasional light turning on at dusk. She wanted to find connection, and she was intrigued when she first listened to Dr. Carey on a national news station. In real life, finding meaningful relationships had proven to be too difficult, so she thought perhaps online she'd discover others just like her.

Dr. Carey's first rule was to dump your spouse, which was easy for Margaret since she was perpetually single. She certainly craved love, it just didn't want her back. She was a member of various online groups, such as Introverted Writers and Child-free Bookworms. However, most of those groups consisted of women who also stayed at home. Margaret had almost resigned herself to staying hidden behind a laptop screen, forfeiting the vitamin D she desperately needed. Beauty came from nature, and Margaret was only enjoying it as framed by the interior wood beams of her little house.

Her first meeting with Dr. Carey wasn't great. Margaret was a stickler for timeliness, and when ten minutes passed, her frustration grew. The countdown clock kept recalibrating, and a message flashed across the screen: "Dr. Carey is eagerly awaiting the manifestation of a new journey." When Dr. Carey's face finally appeared on the screen, Margaret could clearly see she was distracted. It appeared she was reading an email, and her greeting lapsed for a minute while she finished. Margaret had a low tolerance for poor manners. She expected people to show respect, which she wasn't receiving from the therapist.

"Welcome, Margaret. I am so glad you're here. Are you ready for your new life?" The strikingly beautiful blonde stared into the camera.

"I am ready. I was ready over twenty minutes ago." Margaret sighed.

"I see. Do you understand how busy I am? I took on a few clients, including you, because it's my mission to spread this treatment plan to everyone. But if you'd like to leave, there are thousands willing to take your place. Albeit leaving would come at a cost," Dr. Carey said, still beautiful, but able to get ugly quickly.

"I'll stay. I'll just bring a book next time while I wait," Margaret huffed.

"I think our first course of action is to work on your impatience. I can sense the rage bubbling up, and I refuse to allow you to put that on me. Your fury is all your own. I am a peaceful statue." Dr. Carey breathed in with closed eyes.

"Wait. I don't have fury. I just like punctuality. But I'm here for your therapy and look forward to starting."

With a long look at the screen, Dr. Carey began. "I know you read through the rules because you signed off. I have a strict policy: if you violate any of these rules, I will decide whether you can restart or whether you pose a risk to our process."

"I won't have any issues following the rules, though I do have a question. Out of curiosity, are you also following these rules, or are you healed from your relationship traumas?"

Another long stare. "I am certainly following these rules along with my clients. I am the star pupil and intend to remain that way," Dr. Carey said. "Any more questions for me before we start?" Her eyes narrowed.

In that first session, Margaret's emotions were X-rayed and analyzed for every flaw and fracture. Dr. Carey wanted to find any breaks and heal them, although as time went on, Margaret felt like those cracks weren't set properly and would need to be broken again in order to heal.

Eventually, Margaret made plans to leave the program. She knew she'd forfeit the deposit and receive a penalty, but when she signed up, she couldn't have foreseen all that she was agreeing to. Hindsight was 20/20, and when she'd signed the contract, she would have ignored any red flags even if there were flashing strobes of light warning, "Look over here, read this fine, fine print." Her desperation to escape the daily loneliness was greater than a few tiny letters at the bottom of a page.

Margaret was definitely a skeptic about love but had hoped she'd find some benefit in this therapeutic program. However, after watching Dr. Carey conduct TV interviews, experiencing her hostile treatment, and enduring incessant emails filled with blog posts from their so-called beloved leader, Margaret soon realized that she'd been bamboozled by the brightness of hope and the never-ending quest to "be better." During her last session, the voice inside her head was very clear.

This is a cult. Time to cut my losses.

That was when Eden reached out to her about the secret group. Margaret still planned to leave Dr. Carey, but staying became an experiment. *Maybe I'll write a book about my experience.* Remaining a member granted her access to Dr. Carey and other members. It kept her connected to a community, which made her less lonely. Because of that, the program was working.

Margaret understood some of the pain that women like Livvy felt. While she didn't understand loving a man like Alton, she understood not loving herself. She'd spent most of her life hating the person she saw staring back at her in the mirror. She always wished the image were someone prettier, skinnier, or smarter. *If only I were her, I'd be better...* Margaret recognized the feeling of being unloved by others, and it devastated her. She'd put in a lot of work over the years to get to this place. A lot of self-help books, a lot of different therapists and a lot of self-discoveries to come to terms with the fact that she may be permanently flawed.

Margaret prepared one of her favorite meals and cozied up on her dark jade couch. A new lavender candle burned nearby as she sipped chamomile tea. Warmth washed over her body from the effects of a sound mind and comfy vibe; this was her peace. The knock at her door popped her eyes open. It was dark outside. Perhaps she'd fallen asleep. In her half-awake daze, she went to the door and opened it without peeking out as usual. A stranger stood before her with his index finger to his lips as he pushed his way inside. Margaret's sleepy haze lifted slightly, but it was all too surreal. She couldn't remember the last time a man had walked into her home, and now there was one making his way in.

Maybe he's just robbing me? she thought. "Please don't hurt me. Take what you need," she said as she stood with raised hands.

He never spoke. Instead, he communicated through gestures, leading Margaret down the hallway toward her writing room. Once she turned around to face him, she looked for a weak point: the neck, the knees, the eyes. A kick to the center of his legs did the trick, and he doubled over, allowing her to get away. In the struggle, her slippers came off and her recently lotioned feet slid across her hardwood floor, making traction poor. She had to make a split-second, and whether to turn to her right where he'd entered through her front door, or to keep running through her kitchen toward her garage door and escape out the back. Margaret's body ignited, an electric current that propelled her forward instead of making the turn. Her feet off the hardwood, meeting the cool tile of the kitchen floor. The streetlight cast faint shadows; the gooseneck faucet looked like an arm reaching inside from afar. She reached her garage door and unlocked the first lock, but the deadbolt got her. *Why did I need a deadbolt on an inside door?*

Her attempt to escape was futile. The first few stab wounds didn't hurt. In fact, Margaret was shocked to see so much of her own blood and questioned how she could still be alive. In her current book, the killer strangled his victims, which she'd thoroughly researched. His powerful hands would feel the pulsating vein on the side of the neck, the thumping heartbeat getting stronger right before the victim's last breaths escaped her lips.

Margaret's mind raced with thoughts of escape, attack, and survival. However, the man stabbing her was relentless. The brutality of it felt personal, yet she absolutely did not know this man. Her yells wouldn't bring any neighbors to her rescue. She'd walked through life dead some days, and now it was happening for real. She imagined the news headline: "Local thriller writer met with a gruesome fate. Stabbed over a hundred times. Now here's your weather." Yep. That's how society worked. No time to ponder things; just move on to the next. Margaret sensed a part of her soul float away, leaving her a heap of skin torn to shreds by an overly sharp knife. Her essence was now gone. Another body for the earth to bury deep underground among the bugs.

As she left this earth, she thought of all the animals left in her yard—raccoons, groundhogs, opossums, stray cats. She hoped someone kind would feed them in her absence.

Chapter 46

Dylan

Dylan didn't have far to travel for his latest kill, as his target was in the state capital, an hour south of his home. He always hated driving in Indy; he had a general distaste for its congestion and overpopulation, not to mention its liberalism. After he finished his kill, he dropped off his rental and slid into his own vehicle, muscle memory guiding him to where he wanted to go. Dylan drove along the suburban tree-lined side streets near his college town as he waited for several students to cross the street, their arms lined with books and lunch bags. He snarled at the pack of frat boys that walked in front of him, who slapped each other's backs and made grunting calls.

I should just fucking run them over. I could tell the police, "Sorry, officer, I think the brake pads went bad."

Dylan's snarl turned to a mischievous grin, but he wasn't here to exact revenge on his oppressors, at least not the non-female kind. He rounded the corner toward his uncle's house, as he'd always called Barbara's place. She was only a tenant and had no real claim to the property. Dylan parked in the gravel driveway and walked down the short sidewalk to where he'd last laid eyes on Barbara.

He knocked. Not like the delivery knock. This knock was firmer, with a lot more fury behind it. He was tired of the games he just knew these women were playing on him.

The exterior of the apartment hadn't changed. The brass number three hung in the middle of the door above a jute doormat that showed the wear and tear from several Indiana winters. Cigarette butts littered the area around the folding chair the next-door neighbor used to sit on when he came outside to smoke. Bald patches of grass where his footpath broke the growth made Dylan's jaw clench.

My fucking uncle needs to evict this creep.

Dylan knocked again, harder this time.

Andrea opened the door. If she sighed, he didn't hear it, but her body showed it as her eyes rolled back. "Dylan. Please stop. I've told you already, I don't know anything about where Barbara went." She attempted to close the door.

Dylan stuck his foot in the doorway. "Hear me out. Let's carefully go over the last week before she disappeared. What she did. Who she saw. All the little details like that so I can piece it together. She may be out there waiting for me to rescue her. Have you considered that?" Dylan's eyes bulged.

"I really think she's fine and left on her own. Look, some relationships just don't work out." Andrea shrugged.

Dylan shook his head in defiance. "Yeah, but we were special. I mean, I deserve answers." He continued to hold the door open with his foot.

"Dylan. Please. I promise if she ever contacts me, I'll beg her to send you a message."

He pulled his foot back as Andrea slammed the door. He could hear the lock catching.

Taking a seat on the smoking chair, he put his head in his hands.

When he thought back to happier times, he could clearly see Barbara wearing a dress with a large palm print that she'd been so happy to find at the thrift store. Barbara was a college student, so being economical was important, which was a turn-on for Dylan.

He'd arranged a special date, even making reservations at Anthony's Steakhouse, which was a place he'd never seen himself at previously. He found himself getting lost in her eyes as she spoke. They sparkled. Her excitement about whatever she talked about endeared her to him even more. He was a freshly made ice cream cone on scorching pavement. It didn't take much. His hardened exterior was putty with her. At first.

He didn't see what was wrong with helping her become her best self. While he thought she was the most beautiful woman in the world, he knew she could be even better if she gave up certain foods. She'd be much happier without some of her friends—they were such a bad influence and, sadly, he felt Barbara was much too naïve to see it. While he didn't believe Barbara was stupid, she certainly wasn't as astute as he was.

We were in love.

Dylan couldn't wrap his head around why Barbara had just disappeared. He never saw it coming, and he certainly never believed it would come to this. He stood to leave, taking one last look at Apartment 3. Part of him believed that maybe Barbara was hiding inside. *Maybe she's been eluding me this entire time. Laughing and sneaking around behind my back.*

Dylan's fists clenched when he realized that his own uncle had confirmed Barbara hadn't paid rent; they'd since rented out her room. He headed to his car and spun out of the gravel driveway, heading back to his own torture chamber of living with his parents.

At least he could get back to the Mandate, where they'd listen to his grievances and understand where he was coming from.

Chapter 47

Julissa

Julissa first noticed the purple wig on the living room floor when Dr. Carey came out of her bedroom wearing an oversized men's T-shirt. She rubbed her eyes, still wearing last night's makeup, her fake eyelashes clinging on for dear life. Dr. Carey immediately reached for the coffee and took a swig, with most of it not touching her tongue.

"I needed that and may need another one before the morning starts." Dr. Carey gulped.

"Rough night?" Julissa peered over the laptop.

Dr. Carey swayed behind her kitchen island with her eyes closed. "What's on today's agenda?"

"I've been wanting to talk with you about the many clients who are emailing me in a panic." Julissa twisted the silver ring on her finger. "We have a lot happening, and it's reached emergency status. I've lost count of how many women have reached out..." A ding pierced the room, alerting her to another email. "There's probably another one. They just keep coming as more news comes out." Julissa took a deep breath. "Since last night's murder, the number of members wanting out of the program has grown. The recent murder makes four, and the media is calling him the Cutthroat Caller and..."

Dr. Carey rolled her eyes and threw her empty coffee cup into the trash. "Oh, for fuck's sake, this is ludicrous. Nobody knows if they're related or if the exes are finding this a great opportunity to kill their partners for getting better without them." Dr. Carey opened her refrigerator but slammed it shut when she saw it was empty. "Let those members know no one gets out for free. They all have to adhere to the contract. So, if they want out, they have to pay." Dr. Carey rubbed her temples. "This is giving me a migraine." Dr. Carey briefly held her hand to her mouth. "Cutthroat Caller? Just great, they're giving him more power." She slammed the door to her room.

Julissa sank into her chair. She'd read so many emails that she'd hoped would sway Dr. Carey to reconsider. The pleas broke her heart, but she knew Dr. Carey wasn't built like that—her sensitivity wasn't for others. She didn't empathize with anyone else; her only care was how it would affect her and the program. However, Julissa also knew that Dr. Carey wasn't without fault and was living a secret life. She was getting sloppy. The man at the door a few weeks ago, her messy morning appearance with the wig on the floor, and the accidental email Dr. Carey meant to send to "Spencer," who sounded like someone she had a long history with.

Julissa had access to all of Dr. Carey's passwords, so if she wanted, she could do some damage. But Julissa wasn't an agent of chaos—she couldn't fathom ruining Dr. Carey. She just wished she could shake her and make her see the error of her ways. Julissa had put Dr. Carey on a pedestal when she began working for her, and she still struggled to reconcile that image with the destroyer of emotions she'd revealed herself to be. She saw the power Dr. Carey had, and it ate at her core to see how unjust she was to the members, yet somehow, she held on to the smallest thread of hope that there would be a shift.

Maybe I can make things right.

Client emails poured in all day with the same tone and message:

"I fear for my life. I need to get my name off that list. I wish I had never joined this fucking cult. I can't afford the dues or penalties. Please give me a break. I really miss my family."

* * *

At noon, there was a knock at the door with a seriousness perfected only by the police. Heart pounding, Julissa noticed it was the same two officers who'd come by before. Dr. Carey peeked her head out of her room. She'd showered and dressed in her usual attire, but her attitude was the same as this morning. "Yes. I've heard. You really don't know for certain this is the same guy, do you? Do you have DNA proof?" Dr. Carey rocked back and forth before leaning on her doorframe. "These are crimes of opportunity, and there's no way you investigated them that quickly." She crossed her arms.

"We understand we don't have all the facts. However, the man who has been calling in anonymously has admitted responsibility for these murders. While we do not know who he is, authorities have already ruled out one of the victims' former boyfriends. So your theory doesn't pan out," the male officer said.

Dr. Carey audibly sighed. "That doesn't exonerate the others. Besides, what can I do about it? Killers don't dictate my life. I don't listen to losers who want to tell me what to do because their mommies didn't love them." Dr. Carey paced around, raising her arms with each statement. "I will not stop just because they didn't get the support they wanted or because women don't want to put up with their useless asses. It's my right to do as I please." Dr. Carey placed her hands on her hips.

"Look, we're doing our best to piece this together, but it's been a challenge since the crimes cross various jurisdictions. Each department and city work differently, and I'm finding not every detective has been on the same page with our theory." Detective Madison frowned. "However, it is your right to continue your program as you see fit. We're just asking that maybe you appeal to the killer for peace and warn your clients to be more vigilant. To lock their doors, protect themselves, make sure their security is up and running," Detective Laura pleaded.

"You know I'm a therapist, right? Maybe *you* should go on TV and discuss this. I have an image to uphold, and I don't want that to be hijacked by this guy. I refuse to waste an interview talking about guns and security and murder!" Dr. Carey raised her voice.

Julissa watched from the safety of her corner desk. *Unbelievable. All she has to do is send out an email, for fuck's sake.*

Once the police left, Dr. Carey stormed back into her room, slamming the door.

Julissa stared at the red notification symbol. More unread emails were waiting. *If she won't do it, I will.*

Julissa typed as fast as she could, trying to finish the email to Dr. Carey's client list before she left for the day.

Dear beloved members,

I am heartbroken to discover that a serial killer is targeting the powerful women in my program. We are a wonderful community of women seeking empowerment, and sadly, the enemy wants to silence us. While I have been steadfast in my conviction to stand up for women's rights and to speak out against the abusive gender roles within traditional relationships, it's become clear that I need to take an alternative approach. With all of this in mind, I will tone down my message and the rules. It has come to my attention that people believe our community hates men, and that is far from the truth. In fact, we love men—the ones who've put in the work to shed their masculine trauma. Many women who complete the program go on to have healthy, productive relationships with men, and I'm thrilled for them.

For the killer. I know you're reading this. Your beef is with me. Leave the women of this community alone. If you have further grievances, you know where to find me.

Dr. Carmella Carey

Julissa read through the letter, editing it several times to make sure she got Dr. Carey's cadence right—the sweet tone dripping with the fake bullshittery that she was known for. Once satisfied, she sent it to all the members and copied Renee Baldwin. Julissa wasn't sure who else to send it to, but she thought Renee would sensationalize it the most. The rhetoric was getting to be too much, and if Dr. Carey was unwilling to stop or let any of her clients go, then Julissa had to step in.

Julissa closed the laptop. Her heartbeat was so loud she feared Dr. Carey would pounce on her, questioning what she'd done. She tiptoed the rest of the way out of the apartment as chills went through her body. She ran to the elevator, pushed the button, and kept turning back to see if Dr. Carey was coming after her. When the elevator doors opened, she jumped inside, pushing G to escape the building. Julissa moved to the back of the elevator, waiting for Dr. Carey to appear. She wanted to stick her head out to see, but knew it would only delay the doors from closing. As the doors slowly shut, Julissa's heart plummeted along with it.

"WHAT THE FUCK DID YOU DO?" Dr. Carey's text came through.

Julissa stared at the screen, unsure of how to respond. It didn't take long for the news to break. "Can you send me my last check?"

The typing bubbles appeared, but no message ever arrived.

Chapter 48

Carmella

"Against my better judgment, I'll come on live," Dr. Carey told the producer who called from *Wake Up LA* to ask about a live interview to discuss her recent statement. *I have some damage control to do.*

The producer fumbled through the on-air rules that Dr. Carey had heard many times before. She agreed to be on her best behavior and hung up to prepare for her interview.

Carmella banged on her wireless laptop keyboard. She knew Julissa was behind this because no one else had access to her email.

She punched aggressively on her phone screen, misdialing twice.

"Bailey, call me back. I'm losing it over here. My moron assistant has sent out a statement without my approval, and now I have a shitstorm to clean up." Carmella threw her phone onto her bed after hanging up.

Within a couple of hours of her interview with *Wake Up LA*, Carmella's spiral continued as she picked up her phone to call her oldest drug of choice, Spencer. But that option was off the table. *He's ruined everything. Everyone fucking sucks!* Dr. Carey screamed into her couch pillow until her throat burned. Her face turned crimson red as her breath quickened through her nostrils.

Oh baby. I know you're always the capable one. You're always taking care of shit. Spencer's last words to her during happier times rang through her mind. Her body shook and fat, ugly tears fell from her eyes as she thought of better moments with him in her life.

Carmella sniffled. "Why me? I just want to be loved, too. I want the same thing everyone else wants." She picked up and smelled Spencer's T-shirt she wore to bed. She stared at the wall, blinking back her tears as her breathing returned to normal.

The silent pause felt like a lifetime because of the years of memories that flashed through her head. The passion, both the fights and the love, all converged in an electric star of imagery. It was all she had left. She knew she'd never get Spencer back again. She'd caused too much damage for him to ever want to return. Carmella also knew she had no power over him, and that was the emptiest feeling of all.

I was never his number one. Her lips quivered.

She slid to the floor, her newly applied mascara streaking in clumps down her cheeks. Despite being surrounded by so many people, she felt lonelier than ever, though anger boiled to the surface when she remembered how he totally blew her off the last time she saw him. She gritted her teeth and seethed at the image of his smoke circles rising above him.

Fuck. The interview. Her live interview was in an hour. She couldn't cancel because at this point the fake email was everywhere. She had to face the media and make a statement.

"Please come back. I need you right now. I promise there will be changes," Dr. Carey texted Julissa.

After applying fresh makeup, she dressed in a white flowing top and added a gold beaded necklace. She applied extra concealer under her eyes to cover the puffiness of crying and poor sleep. As she put together her look, she became the familiar woman everyone knew. She felt more human, although inside she ached. Her world was being torn from her. With swollen, tear-dried eyes, she donned a fake smile to face the public.

With fifteen minutes to go before the interview, Carmella's nerves betrayed her. The pit in her throat lodged deeper as she downed a glass of water. Her knee bounced up and down, occasionally hitting the underside of her desk. An email and two men had crushed the confident woman she had been just twenty-four hours earlier. Fragile are the wounds of those whose bones never healed.

Carmella stood and paced around her tight bedroom, reciting what she'd say to Renee.

"We will continue our program and won't back down from our mission. Women have a right to stand up for themselves. I urge my clients to protect themselves at all costs. Be vigilant."

She jumped when she heard her front door lock click open. Her heart stopped for a split second as she froze, staring at the open door.

Julissa walked in with Dr. Carey's usual coffee order. "Thought you'd like a coffee before your interview." She smiled.

Dr. Carey gave a half smile as she grabbed the coffee and headed to her office, turning back at the threshold. "I don't know what you think you're doing, but you're about to watch a genius at work." Dr. Carey's eyes glared right through Julissa. "If you want to avoid being sued for this stunt, focus on writing a retraction email announcing someone hacked into our system," Dr. Carey demanded.

As Dr. Carey turned, she paused, glancing back to add, "And clean this place up before you leave. It's really been let go." She closed the door behind her.

* * *

Julissa squeezed her coffee cup as it spilled over her hand, not flinching once. *Why the fuck did I come back here?*

Back at her desk, Julissa received dozens of emails from delighted members, thankful for their pending contract releases. She also saw an email from Bailey. "Do not go on TV. Let's brainstorm this before you dig yourself in any further."

I'll keep that message to myself. Julissa laughed as she heard Dr. Carey being greeted by a producer.

Grab a shovel, bitch.

Chapter 49

Dylan

The Mandate was bustling with comments about the recent news: Dr. Carey had finally backed down from her rigid rules. Several men placed bets on what would happen to Dr. Carey once her program went out with a bang. Dylan swelled with pride at how much he'd accomplished—at his ability to take her down. He had never felt this kind of overwhelming joy that made his heart so happy. His skin tingled, and he hugged his bony frame for a job well done.

The chat flew by much too fast to keep up with, and Dylan's cheeks hurt from smiling. He'd created something successful. He wasn't his father's preferred son, but he could now look into his dad's eyes and tell him he was a man who set out on a mission and got shit done. His mission's only flaw was that he couldn't share it with anyone, but that would be okay because there were some things a man needed to keep all to himself.

The pre-interview chat had the same jovial energy as waiting for the Super Bowl or the election results. Nerves and excitement, pizza and beer. Even though the interview was at noon in Dylan's time zone, he would have celebrated at any hour. The Mandate had grown so much from the first few days and weeks. Dylan couldn't keep up with the requests to join, so he enlisted other members to help. Naturally, there were spammers that got in, mostly people looking around for curiosity's sake. The group grew by the hundreds, rivaling the pace of Dr. Carey's fame and client list. The Mandate became less its title than its subtitle: "Men against Dr. Carey and the women who follow her."

Dylan cued up the TV stream on his computer screen, grateful that it was a syndicated show he could watch. The show before Renee Baldwin's was another anchor he hated, George Coolidge, who spoke on the latest political coverage affecting SoCal. Dylan hated politics too and identified as a constitutionalist more than with any current political party, although he certainly supported conservative policies. The smug, silver-haired anchor had no clue how Midwest folks lived and didn't care. Dylan immediately hit the mute button, flipping off his screen when George appeared. In the bottom corner, he saw the banner for the exclusive interview with Dr. Carmella Carey up next, and his adrenaline flip-flopped. With five minutes left, his stomach ached and he ran to the bathroom to relieve himself.

A minute before the interview, Dylan's foot shook uncontrollably. *Why the fuck am I so nervous?* It was maybe the most excited he'd ever been, second only to the moments before he killed the women in Dr. Carey's cult. Watching Dr. Carey give up her program was like a public murder, and he hoped it would be just as satisfying.

On the screen, Renee Baldwin appeared in a royal blue top, her chin-length brunette hair parted to the left, revealing small gold earrings. "Welcome, ladies and gentlemen. Boy, do we have a doozy today. We have Dr. Carmella Carey back for an exclusive you don't want to miss."

Dylan's heart raced as Dr. Carey's face appeared on his monitor. The show patched her in via an online video. Dylan snarled at her smug pout.

"Viewers, yesterday we learned about Dr. Carey's letter allowing her members to leave the program as well as changing the rules in order to tone down some of the rhetoric. As you know, she has received backlash from men's rights groups and an anonymous caller who has claimed to be the serial killer going after women in her program." Renee turned to face the screen to her right, which displayed Dr. Carey's image. "Welcome, Dr. Carey. I can only imagine that this is one of the most difficult times for you," Renee said.

"Difficult doesn't begin to describe it. However, I need to clear some things up." Dr. Carey cleared her throat.

Dylan leaned even closer to his computer screen, studying every word and movement Dr. Carey made.

"First, that letter did not come from me or anyone I work with. Someone hacked us."

"What?" Renee gasped.

"Second, we aren't going anywhere. The women in my program are fighters. I'm a fighter, and whoever this caller or killer is will not scare us." Dr. Carey leaned toward her laptop. "We refuse to be intimidated, and we stand united."

"Let me understand. You're not dissolving the program or quitting. The *Year of Self* is going to continue just as it always has?"

"That's right. Absolutely nothing has changed. That letter was fake, and I will find out who wrote it," Dr. Carey said.

"Wow. Now this is major breaking news," Renee said, turning to the other camera. "I admit I wasn't prepared for this. Do you think it's wise to continue going about business as usual, knowing there's a serial killer on the loose?"

"Yes, I do. Let me tell you why. There's no evidence that these murders are connected to a single person." Dr. Carey's expression softened. "Look, I understand everyone wants me to issue statements and take responsibility for my tone, but let me tell you, those women who died supported me just as I am. I don't run my life or business from a place of fear, and I will never back down to a lowlife piece of shit because he's too fucking weak to get ahead in life." Dr. Carey glared at the screen.

"Oh my. I think we need a commercial break." Renee looked off-camera. "Yes, yes. Okay, audience, we'll be back."

Dylan sat staring at the screen in disbelief, yet part of him was unsurprised. Another part was giddy to continue with his original plan. Dr. Carey was exactly the woman he believed her to be, and she'd just told him "Checkmate." The Mandate chat spun by so wildly it made him ill to look at it. *Cunt, kill, hate* were just a few words he could make out on the speeding wheel of spew that flew by. Dylan received a private message from a member named Ethan.

"Can you fucking believe it? They always win!"

"I know, man. In shock." Dylan sat numb; his face slowly weighed down by an invisible tether.

"Let's find where she lives and make some noise."

Dylan thought about this. He knew exactly where she lived. Making some noise outside her condo could get attention, maybe get more airtime for men on TV. *Dr. Carey got plenty of airtime for women, but the media hasn't heard my point of view.* At least not in a sit-down style interview.

"Good idea. Maybe we should go down there with signs? Call the local news? Get some attention and make her see us?" Dylan's eyes sparked to life.

Before he knew it, he'd agreed to picket outside Dr. Carey's condo next week, but first he needed to send a message that he wasn't happy with her plan to backtrack on the program. He also decided to stop for a layover along the way, where another client would pay for today's announcement.

Chapter 50

Eliza

Eliza's lips trembled as she waited for Dr. Carey to log in for their session. She had given up so much in the past four months and gained nothing in return. The program's promises were hollow, and she was now a shell of her former self. The man she loved more than anything was still waiting for her, but self-doubt swelled—he might not wait much longer. *Why would he wait for me? Why do I fuck everything up?*

When Dr. Carey finally logged in nearly fifteen minutes later, she took her time greeting Eliza, clearly distracted by the tabs on her screen.

Eliza fumbled with her words, which came out all at once.

"I don't think I can do this anymore. I just wanted to be a more confident woman, and now I feel worse than ever." Tears ran down her face.

"We've been over this, Eliza. Do you know how many women want to be in this program? You will forever regret wasting this opportunity. It's like medicine that takes a couple of months to kick in. You'll be ashamed of your current self when you look back." Dr. Carey shook her head.

Eliza gulped back her words. "I don't know. I had some hope you were giving us a way out with the letter and..."

"That was a complete hoax. That letter didn't come from me!" Dr. Carey raised her voice.

"Oh, I know that now. I understand therapy takes time, but I'm struggling right now and I don't trust the process. I miss Walt. Can't we do couples therapy? I need him," Eliza pleaded.

"Weak and pathetic. That's not the kind of woman I want representing my program. I think you need more intensive treatment, Eliza." Dr. Carey glared.

"I want to be better, but I also want my husband back. I'm afraid he might find someone else if I wait too long."

"Precisely. Listen to your words. You should want a man who would wait years for you to return. The part of you that's lonely needs to learn to be happy with herself. You don't love yourself, and that's the problem here."

Eliza's tears flowed even harder. "I can't love myself right now. I am so sad and, yes, I'm lonely. I don't have any friends where I live and..."

"Stop. You aren't even your own friend. How can you hope for someone else to even like you?" The corner of Dr. Carey's lip twitched.

"I don't know. I feel really hopeless right now." Eliza bowed her head.

"Again, this is a flawed mind speaking. You're worse off than I thought." Dr. Carey made a tsking noise.

"But I've done everything you've asked, and I..." Eliza choked on her breath, unable to finish.

"Eliza, our time is almost up. The next time I speak with you, I need to see improvement or I'll put you on an advanced treatment plan, which is much more intensive."

Eliza attempted to respond, but the screen zapped closed as Dr. Carey ended the call. Eliza Ulrich hadn't been the same since her mental spiral last year after losing her parents in a car accident. It was difficult to get out of bed, and she let her home and marriage slide while she sank into her grief. When she saw Dr. Carey's ads and videos, she was enamored, and it gave her hope to get her life back on track. "I'm jump-starting my emotional health just like I did with my diet last year," she proudly told Walt before starting the program. He was supportive until he realized it meant he had to move out. They weren't following the plan perfectly as they'd sneak in texts here and there, but they became more like ambivalent daters who could go days without conversing. The once inseparable pair now struggled to come up with anything to talk about.

Eliza hoped the program would help her exude the same confidence that she saw in Dr. Carey. When she played the new client video questionnaire, she answered all the questions out loud with immense excitement.

"Do you want to be in a spiritually committed and mutually respectful relationship?" *Yes!*

"Do you want confidence to ooze out of every pore?" *Yes!*

"Are you a fighter and believe you have a right to be listened to and heard?" *Yes!*

"If you've answered yes to these questions, I welcome you into the sisterhood of women who have agreed to change their lives," Dr. Carey's video announced as her serene face appeared on the screen.

Although it made her unhappy, Eliza said goodbye to Walt, willfully blinded by hope for a better future. She believed in the program and was willing to do anything to feel alive again. In the back of her mind, she always believed they'd be together because she considered him her twin flame. Her destiny. However, it devastated Walt, and at first, he refused to leave their home. His efforts to denounce Dr. Carey were met with anger and frustration.

"Don't you want me to get out of bed and be more capable?" Eliza said.

Walt eventually agreed and moved to a friend's basement. Eliza became very upset when she learned the friend was Daphne and that

Walt hadn't accepted the same offer from his friend, Greg. Part of Eliza blamed Walt for sabotaging her efforts by rooming with an attractive colleague. Eliza knew how those things began. First, they were friends, then a bit of flirting turned into a tryst. Walt's address would transfer from his basement futon to the queen-sized mattress that lay above his former sleeping spot, where he barely texted his wife. Eliza's mind swirled with thoughts of what was happening in that house. *Is Walt screwing Daphne right now?* Eliza didn't know for sure that they were intimate, but she couldn't escape the images that bounced around inside her head. She defied the rules about making contact, texting and calling Walt as the negative thoughts consumed her. She sensed that she no longer knew him like she used to. Time apart had corrupted their marriage. Walt wasn't engaged during their calls, and she could only envision a naked Daphne waiting for him to hang up.

Eliza's meeting with Dr. Carey ignited the part of her she had been keeping at bay. The part that snapped. The energy came from deep within her pelvis, surging up through her stomach into her throat, where it fumed, infecting her voice. Thankfully, her home was far enough from her neighbors that no one could hear the piercing screech. Her grief was a guttural pain she had been gulping back for so long. Her pent-up tension came flooding to the surface. Every stress and torment she'd hid was on full display—her parents' death that she'd never fully mourned, burying it in depression and bedrest. The job promotion she didn't get but smiled about anyway because her work husband got it instead. Her failed pregnancy and the way she told everyone she was better off being a dog mom even though she desperately wanted her own baby. And now she'd pushed the only man who loved her right into the arms of one of the hottest women she'd ever seen. *I'll never be as beautiful as Daphne!* Eliza flung herself onto the carpeted floor, pounding her fists until they hurt. As she lay there, the image of a naked Walt with Daphne fueled her pain, and she got up and paced, searching her home for anything to destroy. She grabbed a knife and stabbed the couch over and over and over. The laughing was nearly as loud as her guttural scream, but it felt so much more therapeutic. She collapsed onto the exposed cotton; the weight of the world finally gone. She texted Walt to come home, that she was leaving the program.

"Please come back home. I'm so sorry for everything."

She waited for a response. She spiraled. *He's going to tell me he wants Daphne.* The calm she'd briefly found was gone. With fists clenched, she took her anger out on anything near her. She cleared a shelf full of knickknacks and books, which seemed to fall to the ground in slow motion as her brain sped up, fueled by a passion she hadn't felt in months. She threw dishes and laughed until she cried, eventually sinking to the kitchen floor.

When the doorbell rang five hours after Dr. Carey had hung up on her and four hours and forty-five minutes after she had texted Walt, she ran to the door, hoping it was the husband she'd sent packing just months ago.

From the moment she opened the door until she found herself seated at her laptop, everything was a blur. Her own reflection stared back at her in the black screen. No countdown this time, only a shiny sharpened knife at her throat. She logged in and the delivery man directed her to make a video. He stood behind her and with a gloved hand, he set down a notecard. "Read this."

Eliza's face soaked with tears as she spoke. "Hi everyone. I need you to know I did this to myself. As a woman, I should never push away a man, especially my own husband." Eliza cried as the knife's edge pressed into the line of her neck, stinging. "I want everyone to know that Dr. Carmella Carey has ruined my life. Her program is a cult, and she needs to be stopped. Her clients will be murdered one by one until she's silenced for good. Women of the world, don't be like me. Be grateful for the men in your life and stop striving for more." Eliza took as deep a breath as possible when the first slice went through. She watched her face on the video screen, where a man's black-gloved hand made precise work of her flesh. In a fleeting thought, she wondered if Walt and Daphne would have a beautiful life together.

A mere thirty minutes later, the silent, darkening room lit up with a text message on Eliza's cell phone.

"Honey, I'm so glad. I'm coming right home."

Chapter 51

Dylan

D ylan arrived at the meeting spot, just a block west of the Buzzed Bee. He smiled with the secret that he'd walked this path once before. The familiar route was a slight comfort to him as he located the hotel and saw the doors to the coffee shop. He glanced around to see if Julissa was there, but there was no sign of her. Several guys had prepared some signs—Support the Rights of Men and Dr. Carey is a SCAM and other provocative messages to get the attention of anyone driving by. Dylan had left an anonymous tip with the local news outlets letting them know where they'd be marching, requesting some coverage.

The Mandate had roughly a hundred men signed up for the protest, which was more than Dylan could have imagined when he first created the group. The sidewalk outside of Dr. Carey's condo was wide enough for them to walk in rows, two by two, with ease. No cars were allowed to park in front of the condo, as it was a fire lane, which made it even better for visibility. Dylan envisioned Dr. Carey stuck in her condo, begging for everyone to leave, eventually calling them off with a white flag and ending her program. Knowing they'd found her, she'd no longer feel safe. Then she'd have to retract her recent statement about the program.

On one sign, Dylan wrote in large letters, Ask Me How to Join our Men's Revolution. He hoped it would help him stand out—he'd made it clear to the others that he wanted to be the one to give the interview. He'd revised his speech multiple times on the flight in and again this morning before heading to their meeting spot. Nerves shot through him, eclipsing the thrill of his quick stop at Eliza's house, although he winced every so often as the sign's wooden post dug into the nick on his finger. He stared down at the tightly bandaged finger that had begun to bleed after the fourth slice. He'd been able to wrap it up inside his hoodie pocket. A constant reminder of his success, yet a failure in terms of what he still hadn't accomplished. Two victims' blood forever cohabiting inside his hoodie pocket, just waiting to be found.

There was no rhyme or reason to selecting his next victim, although Livvy and Dr. Carey were at the top of the list. The murders were like a game, and part of the fun was choosing a new city to stop in. When he first got the list, he'd hoped to see Barbara's name, but his heart soon sank with disappointment. He just knew she'd left him and gotten caught up in something like this.

I want her to feel pain.

When Dr. Carey wasn't Dylan's primary focus, he spent his time trying to track down Barbara. He spied on her former friends' social media pages, drove by her parents' house (which was only two miles from his own parents'), and set up online alerts for her name, but it was as if Barbara Winford had been erased from existence after she left Lazette. He wondered if someone had killed her on her journey of self-discovery. A pang of sadness ignited in Dylan's chest as he thought of Barbara meeting with that kind of demise. *If only she weren't so stupid and had listened to me, we'd be happy and together today.* Then he'd snap back into the present, rubbing the sides of his face as he clenched his jaw so tight his head hurt.

Dylan hated himself for missing Barbara, but if she was going to be out of his life, he wanted to be the one responsible.

Loud chants of "Dr. Carey is a scam. Women die for her plan" echoed across the sidewalk. Dylan fell in line, shouting and pumping his sign in the air. He glanced around at the condo he'd seen before, recognizing the doorman, who hadn't seemed to think twice about letting him walk in. He looked up at the fourth-floor windows, hoping to ruin Dr. Carey's entire day.

Several cars honked as they sped by. Mostly people stared just long enough to read the signs with confused faces. The area was upper working class, home to professionals with fancy dogs, personal Botox injectors, and novelty shops offering the various "waters of the world." Dylan hated everything about this fake plastic world. He missed the familiar roads of home. Indiana had the food, the smells, and the grit he preferred. While he wasn't successful with women back home, he absolutely hated the types of women he saw in California. In fact, Dr. Carey epitomized the stereotype of the "California girl," and any woman who joined her was his sworn enemy. His hatred for them was more powerful than anything he'd ever felt.

Dylan took charge of the men as they angrily pumped their fists, pacing back and forth in front of the condo. The doorman grabbed his cell phone, making calls as the men's voices became so loud that tenants gawked out the front door.

"What's this about?" the doorman finally asked.

One man stepped out of line. "Dr. Carey refuses to quit, so we refuse to be quiet." The words were met with roaring cheers.

Never underestimate the upheaval caused by a group of angry men who've had their rights questioned. The predominantly white group was full of men who proudly boasted that they would never be silent again. The beasts within had awakened.

"Whoever organized this, please move it to the park located just two blocks north. You can protest there without disturbing the residents of this building," the doorman said.

Dylan stepped out of line to address the doorman. "Dr. Carey is the reason we're here. If she'd like to make an announcement, we'd be glad to listen. Otherwise, it is our constitutional right to march." Several men slapped him on the back.

The doorman started typing on his phone, but a ring interrupted him; he answered, covering his free ear to listen. The chants were rowdy, and the street was full of horns blaring, with a couple of drivers shouting. A news van rounded the corner, its slogan—Action News breaks for you—emblazoned on the side. Dylan gawked to read its call sign, but he was disappointed it wasn't a bigger station. He wanted his own one-on-one interview with Renee Baldwin. If he could get on her show, perhaps he'd have a better chance of debating Dr. Carey. *I'd love to defeat her on live TV for everyone to see.*

The lesser news station brought out what appeared to be an intern, followed by her cameraman. *This isn't going to get me the publicity I want,* Dylan scoffed.

"Hi. Is anyone willing to do an interview about why you're out here today?" the overzealous reporter said in her plaid pants and chiffon shirt. Her wavy brown hair was pulled back in a decorative headband with tiny stars sprinkled across it.

"Yes, I'll speak on behalf of these men and the millions of men who can't be here but are with us in solidarity."

Another protester jammed his cell phone into Dylan's face, filming him and the reporter as the men watching from home cheered.

"I'm Megan Lyle, and your Action News team is here reporting live from Beverly Grove, where a group of men are protesting outside of one of the luxury condos here on West 3rd Street. Joining me is their spokesman, who has a message for a specific tenant in the building."

"Dr. Carey, you and your program are done. Time's up. End it now. Men will no longer stay silent about your toxic femininity. As long as I have a voice, I will fight for our rights and..." Dylan looked up toward the condo unit where Dr. Carey lived. "Mark my words, if you don't end the program, this will not be the last you've seen of us."

"What is your next step if she doesn't comply? Where do you go after protesting?" Megan asked.

Dylan grabbed the microphone and stared into the camera. "Dr. Carey doesn't want to find out. She will have an army of men coming for her, and any woman that joins her cult won't be safe. She's brainwashing women, and society hasn't done shit about it."

Megan attempted to retrieve her microphone, but Dylan spun around, holding it in the air as the men began to shout and cheer. Once Megan got her mic back, she and her cameraman took off. Dylan hoped that the coverage would garner a call from Renee and her office. He marched back into formation, but as the minutes ticked by, the protest thinned amid groans of, "My feet are tired," or "I need to get back to work." Dylan's dream of a big media production faded as time slipped away. By the end of the first hour, the remaining men were unable to shout anymore. With only a handful of men left, their hoarse voices made little impact, barely even audible to the passing cars. Their morale had faded, and the excitement of the event had worn off. No other news stations arrived, no police, and Dr. Carey never showed her face. The entire event was little more than a failed lemonade stand that garnered a couple of sales from a pair of pitying passersby.

Dylan walked back to his hotel in a sour mood. He'd envisioned at least ten reporters vying for his attention and shouting questions at him. *One question at a time, geez,* Dylan had imagined. He'd acted out the entire day in his head, but it didn't pan out that way. He didn't know whether Dr. Carey had even seen him.

Back inside his hotel room, Dylan did his usual social media checks, searching Dr. Carey and the women closest to her. He didn't find anything; however, when he checked Julissa's profile, he found a live video posted to her feed showing the tops of heads of men holding signs. She'd posted the crying laughing emoji along with the comment, "A few haters outside my job."

Dylan immediately recognized himself as he stood talking to the news reporter, although he'd never seen himself from this angle. The bald spot he hadn't realized he had was very clear from this vantage point. As the video zoomed in, he could hear laughter.

Fucking bitch. Dylan fumed at being mocked, believing Dr. Carey was likely seeing the video, too. The comments were in the hundreds, many with a skull emoji followed by a laughing one. Dylan's cell phone shook in his hands. Today's viral video would not be the one he staged but the one mocking him. Dylan punched the bed so hard he thought he might have broken his hand. He didn't dare log into the Mandate. He knew they'd see the viral video soon enough; he was just grateful it didn't show his face. And though he hadn't given Megan his name, he hoped no one would actually see her footage.

Somebody had to pay for today's colossal failure, and Dylan knew he was getting closer to the end of his mission. First, he had a few California-based *Year of Self* members to go after.

Chapter 52

Julissa

The chants grew louder as Julissa peered down from Dr. Carey's condo, counting a couple dozen men on the sidewalk. She couldn't make out the words; it sounded more like mumbled chatter as she studied their signs raised in the air. One read, Dr. Carey for Prison, which made her laugh. She knew from wrangling Dr. Carey's emails that there was plenty of hate from both members and anonymous trolls alike.

"Dr. Carey is a fraud who stole my money and offered promises she could never keep. Dr. Carey must stop, or else the serial killer will target more women. Does she really want their blood on her hands?"

Julissa knew that if Dr. Carey's clients could leave reviews, the program would go bankrupt. The ratings would kill her business because the number of dissatisfied members only grew, and some women had hired lawyers to help them terminate the contract. The constant toxic positivity angered many of the women, who felt like they didn't have a voice to bring up the issues bothering them. The sound baths and tranquil music made some women want to plug their ears. Once soothing melodies now grated on every nerve. The way

Dr. Carey lingered on certain words with a slight smack of her lips even caused some women to complain that they'd developed misophonia "because of this stupid program."

Julissa had noticed it since her first day. Dr. Carey liked to enunciate certain words with a smack at the end before licking her plump lips. Julissa just stared at her mouth, waiting to see the tongue moisten her injection-filled pout. Julissa tried to phrase questions so she wouldn't have to hear those words, but sometimes it was inevitable. Pucker words weren't always easy to avoid.

Dr. Carey was in bed during the march, so she missed the commotion, but once she woke up, Julissa informed her about the crowd of men that had protested outside. "Where's my coffee?" Dr. Carey asked, still groggy from the night before.

Julissa grabbed it from the microwave.

"I took a video of them if you'd like to see? It's actually going viral." Julissa chuckled.

After taking two large gulps of coffee, Dr. Carey motioned with her hand to be shown the video.

Julissa pushed play and handed it over, watching for any reaction. She hoped Dr. Carey would love it; maybe it would soften her mood so she'd go easy on the members. Julissa knew better, though. Dr. Carey would never thank her for making the video to shine a light on how ridiculous the men's rights movement was.

Dr. Carey just said, "Hmph," and walked back to her room, shutting the door.

Julissa left for the day, nodding at the doorman. "Hey. Did those guys say anything to you?"

"Oh, from this morning? Nah. I mean, they're mad at Carmella, but it's nothing. A bunch of disgruntled incels is what it seemed like to me." The doorman shrugged.

Julissa nodded. "Thanks. Guess I should watch out for them." She snickered.

As she walked away, she thought about the men and how they

knew where Dr. Carey lived. Of course, anonymity was an illusion in today's world. Dr. Carey was all over social media posting where she worked out, restaurants she frequented, and she took plenty of sunset selfies from her perfectly lit room.

Julissa decided it was time to shut the video down. More attention on Dr. Carey meant her clients would have to pay for it. She disabled the comments and set her account to private. *Don't want to give the killer any more fuel.*

Julissa dialed the temp agency she used to work for. "I just want to start interviewing again and see what else is out there."

"Have you told your employer yet?"

"Oh, no. I don't want to say anything until I have something else lined up. You know, I'd hate to cause any tension with her. It's already pretty hostile sometimes. Besides, she has a big TV interview next week, and I'll need to be there to help run that." Julissa let out a nervous giggle.

"I'll email you some options," the woman said. Clicking sounds came from the other end of the line. "Hostile? We really don't want you working in a hostile environment. Do you mean it's unsafe?"

Julissa thought about it as she hopped on the 10. "You know, I don't know how to answer that. There's a serial killer murdering the women associated with her program, but she doesn't seem to mind even though a group of men just marched outside her condo today. I have no idea about my own safety, but I'd have to say it's not healthy."

There was silence.

"Hello? Are you there?" Julissa looked at her phone and saw the call had dropped. *That's for the best. I don't need to talk about why I'm leaving. I just need to get the fuck out of there.*

By the time Julissa arrived home, she was already feeling guilty for considering leaving. Her lips quivered. She was hopeless, unsure what more she could do. Julissa had already escaped, but she'd returned because she felt an obligation to the women in the program. Since Dr. Carey was unwilling to do anything about the threats, her sole purpose was to figure out a way to help them get out. Julissa didn't have a clear plan, but if she had to, she would go to the media about the rules and Dr. Carey's treatment of her clients. Ultimately, she wanted to see Dr. Carey and her program destroyed.

She hoped to make a difference, even if it cost her own sanity.

Chapter 53

Ava

Ava Masterson examined her new breast implants in her Hollywood glam mirror, turning side to side to see how far they protruded from her clothing. She'd always hated her flat chest, and LA was the land of plastic surgeons, giving her the opportunity to finally get the procedure done. She always wore her cascading brunette hair parted down the middle in perfect beachy waves. Ava checked her watch, an antique Bulova from her grandmother complete with a stretch band. She remained tied to her Midwest roots, never forgetting her values even as she fully embraced the glitzy atmosphere of Los Angeles. Ava had become a fixture in the celebrity-clad nightclubs where she dabbled in extracurricular party favors and attached herself to a man she knew was all wrong for her.

When she met Spencer, she could tell he was closer to her home life than her party one since he was also from the Midwest. He was every girl's dream—the sultry model who got into every club. What young girl didn't want a guy like Spencer? To be his eye candy, dressed in a sexy gown, and attending all the latest premieres? Except as soon as the camera switched off, so did his interest.

She stared over her balcony at the couple fighting across the way. *I wonder if they watch when Spencer and I fight?* While the fights never got physical, they certainly were verbally injurious. The once suave boyfriend she'd bragged about to all her friends back home about was nothing more than a womanizing player. She reached for the latest gossip mag and flipped through it, landing on images of B-level stars leaving clubs. She scanned the pages, hope rising in her body like a fresh wish on her birthday, believing that she'd get discovered soon. However, no such luck in the latest issue.

She wouldn't be going out tonight since Spencer had distanced himself from her over the last few weeks. She didn't have the clout to get into the clubs without him. The last time they'd seen his ex there in a jealous fury, Spencer whispered, "Just follow my lead." Which included PDA and making a show of ignoring her. Ava felt sad for Carmella. How could a strong, capable woman fall for a guy like Spencer? *Then again, how could I?*

In a different lifetime, Ava likely would have become a member of the *Year of Self*, but now it would be too awkward as Spencer's girlfriend, if that's what she was. But she didn't mind admiring Dr. Carey from afar, even if she thought she was crazy. Spencer often told stories about what a bad ex she was. "She nearly ripped my head off for not texting back fast enough." "Carmella's what's wrong with chicks. She doesn't know how to play it cool." "She's got a few screws loose." He always had crazy, wide eyes when he mocked her. Ava always laughed, but there was a sense of sadness too. She knew how cruel men could be. She'd bite her cheek and hope to change the subject.

Her life was more relaxed now that she saw less of Spencer, but she also longed for the excitement he brought to her nights. She knew her role was just as a sidepiece, and now she needed to focus on her future.

The arguing across the balcony got louder. "You slept with her!" the woman yelled, followed by a slamming door. *Damn, I'm so glad to be single-ish right now.*

The distant thump of a neighbor's too-loud music vibrated in her ears as she rubbed her temples. Her tiny Glendale studio apartment didn't afford her luxuries like privacy, space, or the garden she desired. She'd grown up on a farm, more accustomed to cornfields and cow pastures versus the hustle and bustle of the city and all the crime that came with it. She didn't bother to follow the news clips on social media anymore because it only made her scared to leave her apartment, and she didn't want to live like that. Although back home had its share of problems, LA had cold cases, serial killers, and even obsessive boyfriends.

A knock at her front door woke her up from a brief nap. She must have dozed off. Not expecting anyone, she stretched, her mind buzzing with thoughts of who it might be. *Sometimes Tina stops by unannounced.* She stared through the clouded peephole she kept meaning to clean. It gave a fisheye view of whoever stood outside, but it was so distorted and grimy that the image wasn't clear. It appeared to be a man in a baseball cap holding a package. *My favorite thing!*

She opened her heavy door to the stranger outside.

"Delivery for Ava?" he said with a thick Southern drawl.

That accent sounds almost fake.

"Yes, do I need to sign for it?" *Hand it over, dude.* She reached out for the box.

"It's deceptively heavy. Let me help you get it to your table." The man feigned the box's weight, putting on a show.

"Oh, it's fine. Here," Ava said, reaching for it.

It all happened faster than she realized. The heavy door shut with him inside. He locked it quickly with ease, like he'd done this before.

Thoughts flashed through her mind like a speeding meteorite crashing to earth. *Who is this man? What does he want with me? What does he plan to do?*

Ava raised her hands in front of her as she took hurried steps backward, away from him. "Please don't hurt me," came out of her mouth in a choked breath.

The man glanced around the room, which was now dark after he switched the light off. The faint murmur of the arguing couple and the bass of the neighbor's music took turns between her own heartbeats.

"Get your laptop. I need to make a video." The man seethed.

She noticed the upward curl of his lip as he glared at her like he knew her.

Why does he look like he hates me?

She saw the veins in his forehead protrude, his temples pulsing as he spoke to her through clenched teeth.

She knitted her brows and glanced at the couch, absently giving away the spot where she'd last used her laptop. Her mind raced as to why this stranger wanted her computer. "Over there," she said, nodding toward the couch.

With an aggressive turn, he pushed her forward toward the sofa. His grip smarted as his thumb dug into the flesh of her shoulder.

"Log on to that bitch site you love so much." His cruel smirk mocked her.

She scanned the room and her brain to figure out what website he could mean. *This has to be a mistake.*

She reached for the laptop, shielding her eyes from the bright screen.

A loud door slammed across the street. She could only wish she was in that apartment right now.

"Quit playing dumb. Fucking log in!" He pulled a knife from the back of his pants. It made a switch sound as it opened.

She coughed as breath went down the wrong way. Her entire chest seized up at seeing the sharp weapon only inches from her face.

"I'm sorry, I don't know what you're talking about?" She said it like it was a question, hoping he'd give her a clue.

"That cunt, Dr. Carey. The one all you women can't get enough of. I'm the Cutthroat Caller, and today's your day." He smiled widely.

Dr. Carey? "Oh, no. I'm not in her program. I swear..."

If looks could kill, she'd be dead without him lifting a finger. "You think I'm going to believe that bullshit? I've seen your name. I know you're in the fucking program!" His voice rose at the end of the sentence.

"There's a mistake. Please, I swear. She's my boyfriend's ex. I am absolutely not in that program."

His face turned to the side. "Quit fucking around."

Ava shook her head. "I promise. I don't have an account with her. If you want, I can show you my texts with Spencer."

He gave a sinister chuckle. His once-stern mouth twisted into a clever smile, and he fell into full-blown laughter. "If what you're telling me is true, that bitch set you up."

Her mouth dropped open, and she took a big gulp. "She sent you to kill me?" Her eyes blinked rapidly.

"Basically. She added you to the list, and now you must die. She's a cold-ass bitch, and she sent me directly to you."

Ava shook her head. She'd definitely heard of the Cutthroat Caller, but she'd never feared him since she wasn't in Dr. Carey's program. She'd told Spencer, "I really hope they catch that guy. I mean, it's not women's fault for falling for a false idol. It happens all the time."

"Now that you know I'm not in the program, you can just let me go." She glanced at his hand, still holding the knife.

"No way. You've already seen me, and I'm not done with my plan yet. There's no way out for you, but she'll get what's coming to her."

She begged for her life, but once it began, it was quick. Her life-less body lay on the couch, facing the neighbors across the balcony.

* * *

Dylan slid the knife back into his pocket, straightened his hoodie, and quietly walked out of the apartment, erasing all traces he'd ever stepped foot there. He reached his rental and strapped himself into the driver's seat, with his own smug face staring back at him in the rearview.

He pulled out his phone and hit record.

"Dr. Carey is one twisted bitch, maybe worse than me." He chuckled. "She just got me to kill her ex-boyfriend's girlfriend. I guess you could say she checkmated me. Don't worry. I've got a few more plays left before this game is over, and my favorite move might be my next."

Chapter 54

Carmella

D r. Carey had heard the men protesting all morning as she peered out of her bedroom window onto the sea of rejects. The sweaty, unwashed heads walked in circles, following each other like defenseless cattle. She watched as a reporter spoke with a man, followed by cheers from the group behind him. *Pathetic losers.*

It had been a late night; they were increasing in frequency as Dr. Carey spent more nights each week out at various clubs, depending on the vibe she craved.

Dr. Carey made it a habit to scan social media each morning to see if the killer had struck again. She knew it was unethical to suggest Spencer as a suspect, but she deserved a win after he'd discarded her. *Spencer doesn't deserve love and happiness.*

She rubbed her eyes, smudging last night's mascara across her fingers, and she wiped them on her pajama pants. The room slowed its spinning as she willed her eyes to focus. Her pillow was lined with old makeup and her hair was a matted mess from wearing a wig all night.

She stretched her stiff muscles as she rose from her bed. As she saw news of Julissa's viral video being shared by third-party accounts, she smiled to herself. She had no idea if the killer was among the group of protesting men, but if he was, she knew the video would infuriate him. He'd come to make a statement and left trending for a different reason.

Dr. Carey understood how fame could lure a person into its grasp. All her life, she had wanted to be famous—known for something spectacular. And she'd finally arrived. Dr. Carey's fame had shot up even more now that a serial killer was after her clients. She had modest fame before as a talking head personality on talk shows, which garnered her more clients. But now every talk show wanted her, even the biggest ones on the cable news networks. They wanted to know all about the woman who stood up to a killer and refused to compromise her values.

Now that she had achieved the notoriety she craved, she felt wanted. Important. The ideals her mother ingrained—to be the best— were deep-rooted, even if her mother had failed to uphold them. The only person Dr. Carey cared about making proud was herself. Gone were the days of longing for acceptance, replaced with an insatiable hunger for fame. With Spencer gone, parts of her were no longer consumed by him. No one else had seen her softer side—the side she despised, begging to be loved. Now, she could focus on being the best. Truth be told, the serial killer was good for her business.

Dr. Carey had come too far to turn around just because some man threatened to end her and her clients. She was never one to throw in the towel or cave under pressure. She was the captain of her volleyball team, co-chair of the debate team, and now, a world-famous therapist proving that women could do anything without a man.

Dr. Carey prepared some thoughts for her upcoming all-member meeting. She pushed record on her phone to document her words. "We have modern amenities that allow us to be independent. If we want a baby, sure a man can supply the sperm, but it's a simple, emotionless procedure as far as science is concerned. The real story begins at birth, when women can choose how to raise compassionate, powerful children. Women can afford their own households, build their own savings, strip themselves of the conditioned belief that only a man could fulfill them."

The effects of last night's cocktail of pills, with molly being her current drug of choice, were starting to wear off. The euphoria, energy, and charisma of the high always left Carmella wanting more. When she first tried it, it was like comforting arms of love wrapping around her. She could envision her heart swelling with pure radiant joy, and she felt a new emotion: compassion. A bird's-eye view of the dance floor would reveal Carmella in her pink tinsel wig caressing the necks of anyone close to her. The tender laugh and genuine concern drew people in after they saw her infectious smile. Molly gave her the abundant love she lacked in reality, which always left her bitter and betrayed. The one downside of drugs was Carmella's constant confusion about her clients and whether she should give them a way out, but by morning the drug's effect wore off and she was back to her usual no-nonsense self.

Today was no exception. "Any word about who's behind the secret group?" Dr. Carey asked Julissa before closing her bedroom door.

Julissa's eyes widened, darting left and right.

"Spit it out. I need to know who's trying to undermine me so I can really make them pay," Dr. Carey said.

"No. I haven't heard anything about a secret group." Julissa avoided eye contact.

Dr. Carey narrowed her eyes. "Are you hiding something from me?" Her voice shot up an octave.

Julissa audibly gulped. "Oh, no. Absolutely not."

"Message Eden that I want a one-on-one meeting with her today," Dr. Carey said. "Don't bother me for the rest of this morning. I need to prepare for the retreat." She slammed her bedroom door.

"I'll call her and get it on your schedule," Julissa said, but Dr. Carey was already behind her door.

Dr. Carey relished a sudden jolt of energy. There was confrontation on her calendar today.

Chapter 55

Eden

Eden knew it was only a matter of time before Dr. Carey found out about the secret group. They all understood it was a risk as they grew. She'd run away before and it had worked out, but now she was finally understanding herself—her motivations and desires. The world was actually working for her this time. The universe had aligned itself perfectly, and she now had purpose: her job at Spiritual Gardens, her trusted crystals, and now her own online women's group.

But she could sense that Dr. Carey had found out about the secret group. In good versus evil, somehow the good girl always lost.

The warning email from Julissa was nails-on-a-chalkboard grating: "Heads up that Dr. Carey wants a private conversation with you," which was code for "shit has hit the fan." *How dare Dr. Carey make me feel like I've done anything wrong! I came to her for help, and now I'm being scrutinized for it. I escaped from that kind of suffocation. I'll be damned if I ever live that way as an adult.*

Eden's walls were closing in. *How did she find out?* She emailed Julissa back, letting her know she could meet with Dr. Carey online later that afternoon.

She paced her small apartment, navigating the maze of books and plants stacked on the floor. Eden sent a message to her group members letting them know that Dr. Carey was on to her. "But I promise I won't betray your trust."

After several texts back and forth, the women agreed to meet before Eden's meeting to discuss her "strategy," as Eden kept calling it. "I refuse to bow down to that woman. If I have to go into significant debt in order to stand up to her, then that's what I'll do."

Eden was all talk; she didn't know how she'd pay all the money back. Like most of the other women, she never fully read the contract and definitely skipped the fine print when she signed on the signature line. It never dawned on her that a therapist would implement such a harsh penalty for moving on.

Therapy should make us whole, not put us in debt.

Eden knew fairly early on that Dr. Carey's plan wasn't for her. The first time Dr. Carey scolded her on a virtual call in front of other members, she sucked up the tears that threatened to flow. Being critiqued, especially in front of others, was mortifying to her. She remembered having to stand in front of her parents and give a report on her school day, including the things she did wrong. She'd spend the rest of the night thinking about her mistakes and how she could be a better person. Only now, in her newfound women's group, there was acceptance, joy, and a beautiful lightness.

However, she knew she would soon have to face Dr. Carey's wrath. Eden was back in debt with no way to pay it off. She was barely making ends meet as it was. Now, the peace she'd developed within the mini-group had been erased. The emotions she had suppressed for over a year came boiling to the surface, especially the insecurity. Though it made her ashamed, she couldn't shake the persistent urge to blame herself for what was happening to her. No crystal in her pocket could quell the emotion. It had been her entire personality at one point in her life. She lost count of how many friends left her when "her ugly side" came out. For so long, she attempted to avoid others with big egos, particularly narcissists and manipulators, because they supplied the drug that fed the beast of inadequacy within her. But she quickly learned that behind Dr. Carey's beautiful exterior was an ugly, egotistical she-devil. Eden knew this monster well, as she had escaped it when she left home. *I ran away straight into the arms of an even bigger enemy.*

Eden hated Dr. Carey. She hated how Dr. Carey molded perfectly good women into shells of themselves, and she hated herself more for allowing the program to bring out that side of her. *I'm a phony. A fake wellness champion, and I'm no better than Dr. Carey.* Eden believed the words of encouragement and support she bestowed on her new group members were all regurgitated nonsense. It was nothing more than what they could read on a sentimental birthday card. Happy words from a woman with nothing left. She wanted sweet revenge, and the thoughts of Dr. Carey's demise brought up the dark desires she had pushed way down.

Eden's depression was a flame that reignited after the campers fell asleep, burning down their shelter. She was a tree with rotted roots. A call sent to voicemail.

Her fury overflowed and her stomach burned, unable to contain the turmoil. Anger sent her to the darkest places. *I wish the Cutthroat Caller would end her.* The part of her mind that tried to resist these thoughts sat back, saying, "It is your will," to all the heinous things she wanted to do to Dr. Carey. She drank her rage with a parched throat to quench its thirst.

Her former self, the one she'd run from, had a name she never wanted to hear again. A name passed down through her maternal line. One she hated because it wasn't unique or true to her personality. When Eden moved from her hometown, she had quit college overnight, telling her roommate that she had to leave for her sanity. Her lips quivered as her roommate gave her a hug and a hundred dollars, which was all she had.

When Eden first found Dr. Carey, she thought she finally belonged. She hadn't had that peace of mind in ages. Her ex would tell her she looked like a slut if she wore something too revealing.

Which, for him, included anything above the knee or anything he considered tight. He treated her as if she were incapable of original thought, analyzing her opinions and diminishing her self-worth. He thought he was a skilled artisan, and she was his raw material to carve. The final straw came when he threatened her life if she didn't act the way he dictated. She no longer felt safe and needed out.

The knock at the door interrupted her group meeting. Eden initially waved it off, but the rapping was relentless.

"Give me a second, ladies. Someone is being very persistent."

Eden straightened her T-shirt, which featured a picture of the Empress tarot card. When she opened the door, his eyes were the first thing she noticed. She knew those eyes too well—knew the hate that oozed from behind them. The jaw that would move from side to side when he got furious with her. His stiffened mouth that spewed venomous hate speech. And his long fingers that held the shiny knife up to his own lips, directing her to be quiet.

Eden lost all control of her thoughts as she walked backwards into her apartment. She nearly fell over a Buddha statue but quickly recovered, never taking her eyes off her ex. *Dylan.*

He motioned to her to turn off the virtual meeting as he stood directly to the side of her laptop. He ran the knife under his own neck, warning her to follow his orders. She knew from experience he wouldn't hesitate to hurt her. He would throw her onto the floor, smack her face, and spit on her if she didn't obey him quickly enough.

Eden raised her hand in a wave to the women who sat in silence awaiting her return. Prior to Dylan's arrival, she'd told the women, "I'll try to deny everything at first and see what kind of proof she has. Otherwise, I promise I won't be giving out any names." For the rest of the discussion, the topic of the day was ironically "How to move on from your ex."

She watched their faces as she waved. Some looked puzzled, and one woman asked, "Are we done already?" Eden hit mute and tried to make her eyes as animated as possible, but Dylan was only a couple of feet from her. She quickly removed her external camera from the top of her laptop and laid it on the side facing her living room as she minimized the Zoom screen, hoping Dylan wouldn't scrutinize too closely.

Maybe I can talk him down. Convince him not to hurt me, she reasoned. Although she knew Dylan well enough to know that if he had tracked her down with a knife in tow, it could only be for an ominous reason. She turned the laptop away from Dylan and took a deep, gulping breath.

"Well, well. Eden, is it? So nice to meet you." Dylan laughed mockingly. "I am the Cutthroat Caller, if you haven't figured that out yet." He held the knife in front of his face as the sunlight reflected off it, glinting throughout the room.

"Please, let's talk. Don't hurt me..." She stopped talking as Dylan shook his head, putting the knife back to his lips to silence her.

"You have no idea how hard I've been looking for you. When you left like you did, I actually wondered if something had happened to you. Now I know you're just a bitch who never cared about me." Dylan walked in a circle around her.

"No, please." Eden backed up right into her coffee table and fell, landing on her butt. As she scooted across the table and down onto her floor, she glanced over at the camera, praying that the women would somehow get her help or figure out Dylan's identity.

Dylan took two large steps until he loomed above her.

"Please, Dylan. Let's talk about this. I'm sorry for everything," she said as she felt around the room for some kind of weapon. Her hands found the rough natural fiber of the jute rug that she had lugged several blocks after finding it on clearance at a local furniture store. She scooted backwards until the wall was suddenly behind her, and she knew he had her trapped.

"Before I finish what I came to do, I want you to tell me why you left me."

All the evidence of Dylan's fragile masculinity flew through her mind. How he wanted to control every aspect of her life, his hot angry breath on her face, and the way she despised everything about him now.

"Let's sit down and chat. Just put your knife down first." Eden took a big gulp, staring at the shiny weapon. "Maybe you've changed and I'll come back," Eden pleaded, reaching her hands out toward his.

No way in hell, she thought, gritting her teeth.

"I'm not falling for these tricks. I was an amazing boyfriend!" Dylan gesticulated with his arms out wide. "I paid for everything! I drove you everywhere you wanted." His nostrils flared as he spoke within inches of her face.

Controlling. Possessive. Dangerous. Eden hoped Dylan's raised voice would alert a neighbor.

Barbara had left Dylan emotionally months before she physically deserted him. After meeting her college friend Lilith, she finally got the courage to find her power. In their women's study group, they formed a bond and discussed their dreams of getting out of Indiana and seeing the world. The farthest either had gone was two states to the east, so they headed west toward California. It was full of sunshine, opportunity, and no trace of Dylan. Barbara had only known Lilith for a few weeks when they made the plan, so she couldn't have known that Lilith would be so frivolous with her financial decisions. After a month of living out of a motel, Barbara ventured out on her own, which suited her fine. Thanks to her savings and a small donation from her parents, she was able to afford a deposit on a studio apartment in Hollywood, which was all she needed to shed herself of her former life, including her old name.

Eden flinched when Dylan stabbed the couch next to her head. The couch she'd saved up for months to purchase—a pale blush mid-century modern piece with tiny sparkles. Eden's heart hurt for her couch and her predicament.

"You're just like all the other women in the world. Use a guy like me to get what you need and then leave without a word. Women like that don't deserve to live." Dylan hovered over her.

Eden's eyes bulged as Dylan was only inches from her face. *Fuck, think, Eden.*

Dylan glared, approaching her with cool ease. *He's done this to the others, and now he's going to finish me.*

"You ruined my life! And now it's your turn to face the consequences," Dylan said as the first of many stab wounds marked her body. As he stabbed Eden, her voice stuck inside her chest. The rage on his face told her she was certainly dying, but she also felt the greatest weight lift. A rush of peace overwhelmed her. *Is this the nirvana I've been searching for?*

She could only think that maybe if she had carried black tourmaline on her that day that things would have turned out differently. Her final thoughts were of her secret group members witnessing her carnage, her laptop screen surely full of shocked faces. Eden's location remained unknown, so a call to the police would be fruitless; death would finally restore her identity.

She would forever be Barbara.

Chapter 56

Livvy

Eden's lifeless eyes stared back at Livvy as she watched the killer walk out of the room. Livvy's hands shook so much her brain jumbled every word that came to mind.

"What the actual fuck?" Livvy finally yelled out to the other women, whose faces were in various states of shock on the screen. "Does anyone know where she lives?" Livvy's eyes scanned the group. "Oh, my God," Livvy screamed out as the cold flush of shock singed her face. She grabbed her phone and dialed Spiritual Gardens, listening to it ring without an answer. Places like that didn't have answering machines. Those were capitalist devices.

Livvy's head swam as she tried to understand why the woman she knew as Eden was being called Barbara. The entire ordeal was a nightmare, a movie that even she didn't want to star in.

"I couldn't hear everything, but it seems like she knew this guy?" Livvy said, scanning her memory, trying to recall every aspect of the killer.

The camera angle made it impossible to see the killer's full face, but the women could see that he was thin in build, wearing jeans and a zipped-up black hoodie, and one woman had glimpsed a baseball cap. "That's good, but that doesn't narrow it down much at all." Livvy bit her lip.

"I refuse to believe I witnessed this." Denise's body trembled as she shook her head as if defiantly saying no. Her teeth chattered so aggressively that everyone on the call could hear them.

Livvy picked up her phone and dialed Dr. Carey, only to get her voicemail. "Dr. Carey, this is an emergency. The killer just killed Eden, or I guess she's really Barbara, and we don't know who to contact." Livvy's hands shook; the cell phone snagged on her stud earring. She panted on the line until a beep told her the call had ended.

Livvy bolted up from her chair, thoughts swirling as she became overwhelmed with fear that the killer was nearby. While she didn't know where Eden lived, she knew where she worked, and she assumed she didn't live too much farther.

A loud bang from the main door to her apartment building made her cower in fear. "I need to get the fuck out of here." Her knees rattled and her lips quivered as she pulled back the peephole cover to look out into the hallway. *Thank God, someone's moving in and was struggling with a mattress.*

Out on the front sidewalk, she headed off to a place she'd always wanted to go but had never taken the time to see. A well of tears stayed trapped behind her eyes for the first two blocks until she caught sight of two dogs sticking their heads out of a car window. It was so wholesome, just the right amount of innocence to break the dam, letting her emotions finally flow. By the fourth block, she was bubbling over with ugly tears. Some women could be pretty criers, but Livvy wasn't one. Her audition for a tearful part ended poorly when the casting director told her, "We like most of what we see, but your sobbing just isn't eliciting the sympathy we were looking for." Livvy's entire face showed the aching pain she'd been hanging on to, revealing the raw emotions that clung to her soul.

People stared with horror, jolting with double takes as they moved away from her. Livvy wanted to yell, "I'm not contagious!"

She wanted neither comfort nor isolation—she just wanted to forget the last several months and go back to her old life.

By the fifteenth block, the tears stopped, and her face was more resolute. The sun beamed, reflecting back the most radiant colors of soft pink and blue. *Why haven't I noticed this beauty before?* She'd lived in her apartment for nearly two years and had never once made this walk to Runyon Canyon. The Southern California air was full of wafting aromas from vendors and food trucks selling tacos and hot dogs. Laughs and chatter filled the surrounding space, drawing her forward. Once she passed the trailhead, she came upon a yoga field where a group of women were practicing warrior poses. *I really need to get back to that.* Her body propelled her higher into the hillside. Inch by inch, she was determined to get as high as possible. Even though there were hordes of people walking in the opposite direction, she felt all alone, yet there was some peace and comfort in the seclusion.

Inspiration Point was always a destination spot for her, but she'd made excuses not to explore it, typically to do whatever Alton wanted. She'd often look up at the canyon from her apartment and marvel at the majestic beauty of the mountainside. She passed women of all ages who seemed determined to reach their wellness goals. As she neared Cloud's Rest, there were plenty of hikers and tourists admiring the rare clear view of downtown. The Hollywood sign to her left was a mocking reminder of why she was here in the City of Angels. She was a stranger in California, and her recent scandal exposed her to the ugly side of fame. Her dreams were over before she'd had time to enjoy them. She sat down on a bench at the top of the canyon, soaking in the vibrant sunshine, and began to laugh. The anxiety over Eden's murder and her life predicament gave her tingling goosebumps that the sun lovingly baked under its warm rays.

She got out her phone and navigated to the secret *Year of Self* group chat where she saw that, one by one, members had left the chat until only her name and Eden's remained. The hollow lines stared back at her; the faint font showed the former group members' distancing themselves from her. She was back where she had begun before she had stepped foot inside Spiritual Gardens. The point where all of her fake LA friends had bounced on her after news broke about Alton, as soon as they realized she was no longer their ticket to a Hollywood premiere or a part in a movie.

Livvy breathed in the warm, gentle breeze that swirled at the top of the canyon. It was a pleasant contrast to the chaos she'd run from miles below. She reached into her pocket for her tiger's eye, which glowed magnificently in the sunset sun. She gripped the stone and threw it into the canyon with all her force. Livvy no longer wanted to feel connected to it, as it had come to symbolize a chapter she wanted to escape from. At that moment, grief hit her square in the chest. She hadn't known Eden long enough to mourn her, but seeing her murdered unleashed the deep sorrow she'd been holding back—the ache of losing her career, wasting time with the man she'd fallen deeply in love with, and now mourning a community of women under siege by a killer.

Livvy wrapped her arms around her shoulders and gave herself a hug. She hated this isolation. The quiet days and nights, with no hope left for a comeback. Livvy decided to make a change, aware that it would prove to be just as controversial as joining a program like Dr. Carey's.

Chapter 57

Dylan

Tinseltown was full of people chasing dreams, and Dylan was its latest inhabitant. He watched as two moving guys passed him, maneuvering furniture off a box truck. Dylan took a deep breath as he approached Livvy's apartment. Dressed in his usual outfit—a delivery cap, zip-up jacket, jeans, and tennis shoes—he carried a box he'd pre-labeled. He politely nodded to a neighbor as he passed. Distant police sirens mingled with a faraway wind chime, the perfect combination to signal impending horror. The cracked sidewalk greeted him, moss jutting out between the crevices. The hardened concrete pressed deep into the soft innards below, forcing its natural flora to the surface. As he carried the beaten-up box marked with a fake delivery sticker to the front door, he casually glanced backward to the common courtyard, where a wrought-iron bench sat in the center of the overgrown grass, which was a sign that few gathered outside. Maybe Dylan would have some privacy.

At Livvy's curved Spanish-style door, Dylan slammed the cathedral door knocker three times. Soft winds carried in a mix of scents— vanilla, hay, and blazing star plants, plus freshly cut grass that filtered in against the distant sound of a running lawn mower. These were natural comforts for Dylan, scents from home that took him away from the city lights of LA and back to the green oasis of Indiana.

He knocked with a casual authority that wouldn't alert anyone to his threatening presence. With no response, he knocked again, growing frustrated. After killing Barbara, he no longer knew where to direct his fury. It was too much to fit in his hotel room. *My time is running out,* he'd thought as he neared the end of his mission. This time he pounded his fist hard enough that the top of the door frame shuddered. There was no way she couldn't hear him.

He balled his fist and pounded on the upper right corner of the door, using the side of his hand. On the last smack, a twinge of pain shot through his pinkie and spread through the bones of his hand, and he pulled it back, wincing. He kicked the bottom of the door until it slowly gave way. It was a weak barrier against his powerful force. He gritted his teeth as he took another glance around the courtyard. No prying eyes watched as he put his back to the door and gave it a mule kick. He felt the frame give way further. Each precious nail began to loosen. What sloppy construction.

More furious kicks, then he turned to charge with full-shouldered body slams. With each one, the door pried open little by little, giving a tiny glimpse of what lay inside. He relished visions of her shielded, frightened to near death, saving her actual demise all for him.

I hope she's cowering in fear after what she's done to us.

Dylan sucked in another breath, building courage and preparing for another round. With one more series of kicks, he just knew he'd be inside to silence her. He kicked with greater fury as the door splintered and groaned under his pressure. Chunks of wood fell to the ground as Dylan's tennis shoes left scuff marks along the front side of the door. The hinges had nearly lost the battle of their lives when a voice called out.

"Yo, dude! Need me to call somebody?"

Dylan swung his sweaty head toward the pest. His face dripped, wet with fury from his fight with the door. He stared into the face of the person whose gender he held no wrath for. Dylan breathed hard through his mouth as his blood pressure plummeted back to its normal range. He concentrated on breathing through his nose as he bent down and picked up the decoy delivery box.

"Fucking bitch," he mumbled under his breath. Distant police sirens getting closer forced him to run back to his car and hide. *It can't be over yet. I haven't finished my plan.*

He had one more stop to make in Los Angeles. This would complete his agenda for men all over the world and, at last, silence Dr. Carey for good.

Murder was only part of his plan. He needed to unleash his own message into the world. He needed the counterpoint to Dr. Carey's venomous language to be remembered longer than anything she'd ever said. *Returning to the hotel is too risky.* The suffocating walls closed in on him. Hiding was his only option.

It would be much easier to hide in his native Indiana. He knew the parks like Prophetstown and Celery Bog, where he'd spent a lot of time sitting and thinking as locals and tourists passed him by. Although perhaps he was better off here, as California provided so much anonymity. The overcrowded streets made it easy to disappear. Dylan drove around the city, away from Livvy's apartment, eventually pulling up to a golf course parking lot, where he found a secluded spot in the far corner and pulled out his phone. With thoughts of his next victim, he pushed record. *If I get caught before tomorrow, at least my last words will be documented.*

"This is my final recorded video before my last mission. When you see this, I hope I've accomplished my plan to stop the world from following Dr. Carey and her bullshit."

A man drove by on a golf cart. With his window open, Dylan waited to continue as the man picked up speed.

"You all know I'm the Cutthroat Caller, and I rather enjoy that name. It gives me an official title and rank in the line of serial killers to walk this earth." Dylan sneered as he said his killer moniker. "Women have no idea how easy they have it. All my life, every woman has had an easier life than me." Dylan's nostrils flared as he thought back to all the times women had shunned him throughout his life.

"When I met Barbara, I thought everything had changed for me. Then she went and left me for no reason. How is it fair? I deserved a reason!" Dylan slammed his fist on his steering wheel, making the horn blare.

He released a big sigh, which reverberated on the recording. "Once I heard Dr. Carey for the first time, I knew I had to do something. But she refused to listen. I warned her and the fools who follow her program that they'd regret it. This blood is on her hands. She forced me to do this." Dylan glared at the cell phone camera.

With a slight chuckle, he said, "I have taken great pleasure in killing the women in Dr. Carey's program. Men from all over the world have praised me, the killer, for shutting up the pathetic cries for pity that these women have made. Society is better off without them and all the other bitches who are members." He shook his head in disgust.

A helicopter passed overhead, and he looked up with a nagging fear that they were out searching for him. "Now I am a God. I am the one men will praise for the rest of eternity. Women will know not to fuck with men and their rights ever again. I won't be the last, but I'm proud to be one of the first to actually do something. Killing those women was the sacrifice I made to improve life for men everywhere." He flashed a toothy smile.

"I delight in destroying the women associated with Dr. Carey. By the time you see this, my ultimate mission should be complete. The world will know my power and my message, and I'll go down in infamy as the man who stood up to the terrorizing feminists. I am honored to represent the men of this world and stop the incessant bitching of the weaker sex. It's time men everywhere take back their claims to our land, our God-given rights, and finally shut these women up."

Dylan hit play and listened to his words with a huge grin. *Tomorrow will be the day I become famous.*

Too afraid to go to his hotel room, Dylan got a room up the street from where his belongings still sat. He had only one mission tomorrow at 10 a.m., and then he didn't care what happened to him or his things.

His only wish was that he could inform the Mandate—the men who actually cared about him. His genuine family, as they often called each other. The men who were always in his corner. The men who weren't afraid to speak up for themselves. He teared up thinking about how much he owed them. Without them, he wouldn't have had the courage to do what he'd done. *I've come so far, and I just want them to be proud.*

Dylan tossed and turned all night. The air conditioner kept kicking on and off, eventually blowing out tepid air. It was a rotten sleep, but once the sun began to make its way through his blinds, he sprang out of bed, showered, and put on the only clothes he had. He still had the knife he'd used to kill Barbara. It had been the best knife he'd used yet. The slicing was easy and seamless. *I wish I had this knife from the beginning,* he'd thought.

In a quick stop back at the Buzzed Bee, he downed a large black coffee and a croissant. He chuckled, thinking how it would fuel him for today's main event. His prevailing thought was that maybe he was overreacting about getting caught. Maybe after today he could easily escape and return to Indiana with a whole new lease on life.

Maybe I don't have to die today.

The idea that he could escape without being caught quickly left his mind. What he'd planned for today would garner him notoriety there was no coming back from.

It would go down as the best snuff film of all time.

Chapter 58

Carmella

Today was a turning point in the *Year of Self*. Dr. Carey had felt a shift within her program after discovering the secret group, and learning Eden was murdered actually shook her to her core. She hated to admit it, but the serial killer was scaring her. *This is getting way too close for comfort.* Still, she was reluctant to do anything about it, including releasing the women from their contracts.

The scheduled interview with Renee Baldwin included Dominique Hay, the FBI agent who'd criticized Dr. Carey and her "rhetoric," as she often called it, sometimes using air quotes. Her combed, slicked-back hair, stern face, and drab navy wardrobe would contradict Dr. Carey's full face of makeup, coiffed hair, and soft clothing. Dr. Carey felt she was losing her grasp on the program with more members turning up dead. Her own sanity was slipping as she lost sleep, lost control over clients, and partook in too many extracurricular activities after dark. The escape called to her nightly these days. It was no longer just fun, but a full-blown addiction.

Dr. Carey heard her front door shut followed by the jingling of keys. *Thank God, coffee!* Julissa brought her favorite source of legal drugs to jumpstart her adrenaline and help her make it through the interview. After a big gulp, she said, "That's just what I needed."

Fidgeting with her robe belt, Dr. Carey opened her kitchen cabinets before slamming them shut. She stood in the middle of her kitchen with bare feet on the cold, stony tile. She walked to the living room and dug her toes into the carpet, wrapping her arms around herself.

"Everything okay?" Julissa asked.

"Just grounding myself. I have to deal with a very negative person on live TV today. She's trying to destroy me!" Dr. Carey swayed.

Julissa twisted the rings on her fingers. "I did, um—well, I came to tell you that, uh, it's my last day here. It's time for me to move on..."

Dr. Carey scowled. "How dare you do this to me?" She shook her head and spun away, flinging her bedroom door shut.

Inside her room, Dr. Carey slammed the rest of her coffee on her desk, and it flew into the air. "Fucking bitch," she screamed, not caring if Julissa heard. Dr. Carey hated to admit it, but the dissension from others was taking its toll. It was yet another wound to her ego every time someone didn't see how valuable she and her program were.

With the interview set to start in an hour, she focused on deep breathing as she put together her outfit. She wore a cream sweater with a small heart design on the pocket; however, black leather would have been more fitting for her mood. *You have no idea what it's like being me!* Dr. Carey raged inside her head thinking about Dominique's recent comments about her.

Dr. Carey went over her talking points out loud. "We are more united than ever." She paced her room as she got dressed, pulling on her black pants. "Death has a way of making a community stronger, and honestly, I'm overwhelmed with how much these women have come together." *That's a good line.* Dr. Carey wrote it down on a notepad next to her laptop. She applied her makeup and spritzed on a finishing mist, which gave her a freshness so she'd appear less tired.

She was thankful for modern conveniences like ring lights to give her a flawless glow.

Her stomach rumbled. Dr. Carey hadn't eaten breakfast, and the tiny bit of caffeine wasn't agreeing with her. Not accustomed to nerves, she knew today's interview was make or break. With the FBI, local cops, and her clients all feeling disgruntled, she needed to project confidence as a leader. The stakes were higher than normal today, and she could lose everything she'd worked for. She wasn't about to let some serial killer ruin it all for her.

"Julissa!" Dr. Carey yelled from behind her door. "If you're still here, I'm going to need an emergency cup of caffeine. Make it quick."

There were a few seconds of silence before Julissa said, "Okay. Be right back."

Dr. Carey took some deep breaths to center herself and practiced the mantras she often encouraged her own clients to use. "You've got this, Carmella. No one can take away your strength. You are a pillar, admired by women all over the world." At the last word, she heard the front door close and released a deep exhale.

Another cup of coffee will fix everything.

Chapter 59

Dylan

The walk to Dr. Carey's condo was comfortable and familiar. It was like a vacation spot he'd visited in the past that had kept its allure and feel. It was slowly becoming his home away from home. Thanks to modern technology and Dr. Carey's active online presence, he had been watching her every move online from Indiana, keeping an eye on many of her local haunts. He could study street views and tap into her condo board's livestreamed meetings, and Dr. Carey loved to go live on her own social media, which was a daily gift. The Buzzed Bee provided his morning fuel, but his adrenaline was keeping him fully charged for what was to come. It was nice to kick back and watch people milling about, waiting for their orders and dashing off to work. He looked for any sign of Julissa, but he must have missed her.

The weather was perfect for LA. Warm, smoggy, but not so hot he would perspire. Nothing like Indiana. It got so hot back home that even the corn would sweat. He set off toward Dr. Carey's condo, his pace casual for the first few blocks as he took in the bustling scenes around him. But when he got two blocks away from her condo, his stomach flipped. He gulped back the coffee that tried to resurface.

"What the fuck?" he said aloud. He moved closer to the side of a building, afraid he might throw up. After taking a few deep breaths, he decided maybe the coffee was just too strong, because he knew he wasn't fucking scared. *I've done this before, and I'll do it again.*

The only challenge he was worried about was getting inside the condo. He assumed there would be heightened security since Dr. Carey's program had a serial killer on the loose. It had only been a week since the protest, which he assumed would have raised security concerns. His jaw tensed as he approached the door. He squinted to see who was standing outside as a rush of people, likely on their way to work, filed out of the condo. At about an arms-length away, he nodded and easily caught the door mid-swing, walking inside. All of his nervousness was for nothing. The tenants had completely disregarded the condo board's talk of increased security, and the doorman was nowhere to be seen. Dylan loved that Dr. Carey's own ego wouldn't allow for a police presence as a security measure.

Dylan took a deep breath, hiding for a moment behind the stairwell. As he slowly inhaled and exhaled, he felt more at ease in executing his plan. He marveled at just how well it had all gone from the start. There had been no hysteria over protecting Dr. Carey; even she didn't have extra security outside, her own narcissism convincing her she wouldn't be at risk. As he ascended the four flights of stairs, his stomach fluttered. This would be the last time he'd experience life outside the condo doors. He had already planned that this would be the end of his mission, and so far, everything had been right on schedule. Finally, the world would know exactly who the Cutthroat Caller was.

Outside Dr. Carey's door, Dylan cleared his throat and raised his hand to knock. The door opened before he could make contact. Julissa appeared on the other side; her eyes grew large and her mouth even wider. Dylan tapped his finger to his lips, urging her to remain silent as she shook her head. Her hands immediately raised in a defensive stance and she moved to the side, bumping into the doorframe, to let him pass by. As he slid by, she bolted from the apartment, and he closed the door, locking it behind him. Dylan had briefly considered keeping Julissa inside with them, but she wasn't part of the plan, and having her there would make things difficult. Today was about Dr. Carey and, in some ways, Julissa had helped his plan come to fruition—she'd allowed him to access Dr. Carey's files by clicking on his phishing link, so he didn't mind rewarding her.

Inside Dr. Carey's apartment, he was surprised at how sparsely decorated it was. He'd pictured it overdone with fancy, high-priced furniture. The modern kitchen looked unused, the stainless-steel appliances still gleaming like they were freshly installed. Generic furniture from a big box store filled her combined kitchen, living room, and dining room. It was relatively small compared to how Dylan had imagined the pretentious doctor would live. Her tiny condo was far from the spacious basement he enjoyed, which spanned the length of the house. Granted, the laundry was downstairs, and he had his parents upstairs always snooping in his business, but he could spread out more than Dr. Carey could.

The light behind the closed bedroom door alerted him to movement. His heart leapt, but the added adrenaline was a dopamine hit. He felt more focused than ever before. He'd rehearsed what he'd say, but for now he needed to hide.

His plan needed to begin after the start of the interview because the best way to gain control was to catch her off guard.

Chapter 60

Julissa

She knew his face. She had seen him once before, but she wasn't sure where. Maybe it was at the coffee shop, sitting at the far table, staring. No one sat at the shop; most people were too busy at that hour. Or maybe it was the protest? She couldn't be certain since she had only seen one angle, but something about him convinced her that's where she had seen him. Yes, that was it—they'd interviewed him outside Dr. Carey's condo just a week ago, so why was he here? *He has to be the killer.* OMG. OMG. Julissa pushed the button for the elevator several times, but the doors didn't open. She sprinted down the length of the hall, holding her breath as she ran past Dr. Carey's apartment, sticking as close to the opposite side of the corridor as possible, grazing the wall. She turned her head to glance at it, but Dr. Carey's door remained shut.

She wondered what was happening on the other side. She felt the weight of her phone in her hand, but only briefly debated calling the police. *Just stay out of it. Dr. Carey got herself into this mess, and she can figure it out.* Julissa's only concern was getting the fuck out of the building and back home, never to return to Dr. Carey's sphere. She regretted ever doubting her gut and giving Dr. Carey an ounce of compassion. People like Dr. Carey preyed on others—on people with trauma who wanted abusers to like them. They sought out those soft moments where the monster was nice, treating them with tenderness. Julissa craved those fleeting moments of joy with Dr. Carey. Sometimes, Dr. Carey gave Julissa her full attention, shining her brilliant rays upon her—until she got bored. Then she snapped back to her usual hateful self. Yet Julissa became addicted to it. Her soul wanted validation; unfortunately, she'd picked someone who would never truly provide it.

Inside her car, Julissa gripped the steering wheel so firmly that her biceps shook. She sobbed so much that a man walking by craned his neck, peering through her windshield and motioning as if to say, "You good?"

Julissa waved him away and sucked up her fear. Sick to her stomach, she just wanted to be home with Bear, her oversized Maltese dog. She wanted to forget she had ever taken this job and put herself in this position. On the drive home, the guilt overwhelmed her. *Is it my fault these women are dead? Will I go to prison?* Flowing tears made it difficult to see during the thirty-minute trip to East Hollywood. As she hit every red light, her conscience screamed, "Call the police and save her!" while another part of her said, "Let him kill her and end this nightmare."

When she finally parked her car, Julissa ran inside and buried her face in Bear's neck. His beating heart instantly calmed her as she took slow breaths. When she looked at her phone, there were several missed texts from family and friends, all saying some version of, "Is that your crazy ass boss on TV? Please tell me you're safe!"

Her heart rate shot back up as she turned on her TV and immediately saw the breaking news banner. *Breaking live: Famed self-help therapist being held at knifepoint in her condo.* Julissa sank into her bed and pulled the covers up to her chin, watching the horror play out with millions of others.

Chapter 61

Carmella

Finally, *a moment of silence with adrenaline fuel on its way.* After hearing her front door shut, Dr. Carey checked her appearance in the perfectly illuminated bathroom mirror. The process of teasing and combing her hair took some time. She'd prefer the ease of one of her wigs, but no one would take her seriously if she showed up in her tinsel blue today. Some days her hair fell flawlessly into place, near salon perfection, and today was that day. With a bit of dry shampoo and a teasing comb followed by her straightener, she was ready for showtime. She applied foundation, bronzer, blush, and liner for her eyes and lips, sealing it with a mist. Although the lighting nearly made her nose blend into her cheeks, her confidence soared.

"You are the brightest light in the universe. Your inner beauty is on full display through your outer shell, and you radiate intelligence, resilience, and transcendence from negativity. You are a queen, and no one has ever come close to your brilliance. A once-in-a-lifetime diamond, a broken mold, and the envy of everyone. You have every-thing it takes to be the leader that you've worked so hard to become," Dr. Carey said aloud as she sat on the edge of her meditation chair.

She stood and stretched, pacing her room, reciting key points she wanted to make during the interview today. *Where the fuck is Julissa?* She wasn't about to break down and make her own coffee. She wanted her triple espresso and special blend of vanilla with a touch of cinnamon, all kissed with a swirl of oat milk. Her need for coffee made her cranky as she texted Julissa to return immediately. She could see Julissa wasn't the same employee she used to be, as evidenced by her consistent lateness and her poor attitude. Dr. Carey didn't have the time or desire to conduct her own interview process, but she believed she'd have hundreds lined up eager to take Julissa's position.

Ten minutes until her live interview. The annoyance of not getting her pre-show coffee had grown to full-blown anger. *A last fuck you on her hurrah out the door.* She stretched, completing an upward salute that triggered the slightest tug on the left side of her neck. She immediately released to massage the area and opened her pill drawer, downing two whites with the water left on her desk from this morning. There was no time for a complete nervous system reset on her breathwork course, so she focused on her breath of fire: deep inhales followed by forced exhales as her abdominal muscles contracted. "I am present. I am full of energetic life force," she repeated between breaths. She felt lightheaded, still craving coffee, but had no time to do anything but get her game face on.

Dr. Carey logged into the link provided by the morning show's producer, where she watched the current segment and heard the teaser, "Stay tuned for our interview with the groundbreaking and dynamic therapist, Dr. Carmella Carey. We'll get her response to the breaking news of the latest murder of another woman in her program."

There was a brief silence as Ava's image flashed through her mind. Dr. Carey frowned. *Pitiful girl.* She knew the type. Full of hopes and dreams. She had a few of that type of woman in the *Year of Self* ready for their big break. *Unfortunately, she found her way into Spencer's net before getting tangled in my web.* Dr. Carey's frown slowly turned into a mocking grin and she let out a sinister chuckle at the thought of Spencer being questioned over Ava's murder. *Serves that fucker right.*

Music came through her speakers, a bubblegum pop melody welcoming viewers to a seat at Renee's table. Dr. Carey fumed as she watched Renee feign niceties with her colleague, Bob Suney. She knew the look of a woman who hated the man sitting next to her. This was Renee's show, but for some reason the network had brought in the veteran Bob to oversee their "big interview." Dr. Carey was angry for her and decided she'd give her best answers to Renee and leave Bob hanging. Hopefully Renee would understand and pick up where he left off. *Life is a big fat misogyny game, and I'm not playing!* Dr. Carey glared at Bob's smug face on her screen.

"One more commercial break until we begin. You don't want to miss this, folks," Renee said, winking into the camera.

Dr. Carey stared at the laptop, waiting for her moment. Her hair, makeup, and lighting were absolute perfection. Her mood was utter chaos.

Chapter 62

Dylan

D ylan checked his phone for the time—thirty minutes to go before the live interview and the beginning of the end of his mission. He could hear movement behind the closed door, so he took shelter behind the kitchen island. Her condo was cast in enough shadow to prevent Dr. Carey from seeing him immediately. He could hear mumbling, and his body froze. *That bitch better not have called the police.* He had banked on Julissa to be more fearful than vigilant; to retreat rather than run for help for the boss she likely hated. Eventually, Dylan heard some coherent words that sounded like affirmations. He chuckled inside, knowing the fate headed Dr. Carey's way. No amount of metaphysical assistance could help her now.

Minutes ticked by slowly as Dylan waited. He cracked his knuckles in anticipation of bursting through her closed door while she was spewing her rhetoric, finally taking control of the interview. At last, the world would know he was the Cutthroat Caller. Before he could enter her room, he needed to wait until she started her interview so he could reinforce her front door. No way he'd come this far just to let a cop take him out before he finished his plan.

With five minutes to go, he could hear a producer talking to Dr. Carey. There were rules about being on live TV. First, they did a mic and video test. "I can hear and see you clearly." The loud producer's voice echoed into the living room. "Remember, no cursing, no shouting over others, and stay in frame." Dr. Carey responded, affirming that she understood the rules. "Stand by."

Dylan logged into the Mandate and pasted in his prepared message:

Well, guys. Today you will finally learn who the Cutthroat Caller is: yours truly. I'm sorry I couldn't clue you in sooner, but this kind of thing requires anonymity. My hope is that I'll make you proud today. I'm doing this for all of you and the future of "man" kind. I want you to know that you all have meant the world to me, and without your support, I don't know where I'd be.

My hope is that the world will be a better place after today. I hope it opens its eyes to what it's done to us. We must restore men to their rightful place, and historians will remember today as our turning point: the day men's rights reigned supreme.

I'm including my last words in a video series I've prepared for you. They're my thoughts on life, how women have destroyed us, and what needs to be done to regain control.

In solidarity,

Dylan

Dylan felt a pang of loss as he hit send and attached the video log he had prepared. *I'm really going to miss those guys.* He thought back to various posts and the happiness and purpose he'd found through the Mandate. Voices snapped his attention back to the present as he heard someone welcome Dr. Carey to the show.

It would be only a minute before his grand plan made the world gasp. Everyone would know his name.

Chapter 63

Livvy

Livvy hopped out of her hired car, which dropped her off outside of an apartment building lined with crime-scene tape. Her once beautiful Spanish-style door, which she'd believed was a powerful barrier to the world, had crumbled within minutes in the face of a would-be intruder, likely the killer. She was grateful for Eden's bravery, which had given her time to flee and rescue herself. Livvy walked toward the yellow tape that whipped against the railing beside the remnants of her door. After someone nailed a makeshift board to the splintered pieces, a uniformed officer waved her inside.

Livvy had spoken with Detective Madison at the hotel the night before and was here to gather her belongings. She had fewer than twelve hours to determine her next destination. With no one answering her calls or texts, she was running out of options. Emilio had all but dropped her. Her last-ditch effort late last night had garnered a weak response. "Sorry, Livvy. I've tried." She no longer had any connection to the secret group. Once they had all left the chat, she had no way to contact them. Their relationship was as fleeting and phony as the hollow brand of spirituality Dr. Carey was hawking.

While Livvy waited for the movers to arrive, she drafted an email to Dr. Carey and told her she was leaving and didn't care what repercussions she'd incur. But she also left a warning: "Remember, I have a voice that people will want to hear from." She hoped the subtle threat would be enough to make Dr. Carey void her contract with no questions asked, but she'd gladly do interviews if it meant exposing the fraud who took so much from innocent women.

Her mind betrayed her as it drifted to thoughts of Alton. She smiled, thinking of the good times—his soft caress, passionate kisses after a night on the town, and future plans for vacations and babies. She didn't harbor the hate she'd hoped to burn him with in court. *I'd take him back in a heartbeat.* She instantly hated herself for yearning for his love and power again. He was not only someone she'd fallen in love with, but also her ticket to stardom. He'd given her a chance when she grew weary of auditions and callbacks that never came. She wouldn't have considered herself an actor if it wasn't for him. Fame and acting were just a pipe dream, and the best she could do was walk the Hollywood Walk of Fame, taking selfies with the shiny concrete stars.

Livvy's expectations for a future in show business were low, unless it was to discuss her recent controversies. She knew that part of her life was likely over and that her reputation wouldn't protect her from being canceled. Her best bet was to land on one of the softer magazine covers with a sentimental piece—the ones at the front of the grocery store checkout with heartwarming stories. She envisioned the layout and practiced her serious smile, sometimes with crossed arms and others with soft, pillowy hands on her lap, to say, "I welcome healing and my mind is calm." She believed readers would welcome a comeback story and might even allow her back on their screens.

The sound of one of the uniformed officers' two-way radio interrupted Livvy's daydream. "It's a fluid situation. The show is still live on air. Dr. Carey is in danger." Livvy heard only certain words, but the ones that came through sounded horrible. She turned on her TV, fumbling with the remote when the batteries kept flashing low. The resulting image on her screen was terrifying.

"Viewers, we're warning you that this is a live and unpredictable scene. Please stand by as we try to determine how to proceed. We urge you to remain calm and pray," Renee Baldwin said into the camera with the most frightened expression Livvy had ever seen.

Chapter 64

Carmella

"And welcome back. We have a real treat for you this morning with our exclusive interview with Dr. Carmella Carey." Renee clasped her hands. "Let's also welcome back Dominique Hays, with the FBI Behavioral Analysis Unit. We're here today to discuss efforts to locate the Cutthroat Caller, who has been killing members of Dr. Carey's program," Renee said with an overly zealous smile.

"Yes, thank you, Renee. I'm saddened to learn that we aren't any closer to identifying a suspect in this case, and even sadder to learn of another death," Dominique said.

"Thank you so much for having me on again, Renee." Dr. Carey batted her perfectly pressed fake lashes. "Thank you, Dominique. I also share your worries. I want this killer to be caught so we can move forward with what's important here, and that's women's empowerment."

"Dr. Carey, what have you done to protect your clients? Early on, you refused to halt your program or alert your clients about the threats. You then issued a statement indicating that you would relax the rules and allow women to leave. However, you quickly rescinded. Where do you stand now?" Bob Suney raised his eyebrows.

The screen showed the two hosts in the top half, with Dr. Carey at the bottom of the frame. Dr. Carey's original smile faded to a stunned open mouth as her eyes focused on something to her left.

"Dr. Carey? Oh, dear, has she frozen?" Renee asked, looking around for the producer.

Sounds came through on Dr. Carey's feed. First there was a slight gulp, then a sticky licking of her lips and a deep breath. Her eyes widened as large as they could when a man in a hoodie came into the frame.

"Good morning. Such a lovely day for a murder in LA, don't you think?" Dylan chuckled.

Renee and Bob stared at the screen with shocked faces, eventually turning to each other and then motioning, "What's going on?" to someone invisible behind the camera. Eventually, Renee asked, "Dr. Carey? Are you alright? Let's maybe head to break..."

Dylan cut her off. "There will be no breaks during this feed. If I find out that we've gone off air, I will murder her. You need to listen carefully. I am the Cutthroat Caller, and I'm here to take back what belongs to men-kind."

With a loud gasp, Renee said, "I, uh... I'm not sure what to do. Bob? Maybe we should bring in our FBI analyst, and she can help us navigate this." Her voice shook.

"Yes, I'm here. I have contacted the authorities, and they're on the way," Dominique said.

"Let me be clear. If anyone tries to breach the front door, she's dead!" Dylan warned.

"Why are you doing this? What do you want?" Bob asked.

"Why? Because Dr. Carey and the bitches that follow her don't deserve respect or even to walk amongst us. They're what's wrong with our society. Before women's lib took over like a third-world disease, men had it easy. The world was a better place when men made all the decisions."

Renee gulped back a cry of shock and wiped a line of sweat from her forehead, motioning to someone behind the camera.

"Soon the world will know the pain you're all responsible for causing to men." Dylan produced a sharp, shiny knife and pointed it toward Dr. Carey's head. "You promote women like Dr. Carey, giving her a platform." He slammed his fist on the desk.

Dr. Carey jumped and attempted to stand, but it was futile. The edge of the knife was clear to anyone watching. He wasn't fooling around. Thoughts of escape flashed at warp speed through her mind as the knife crept closer to her neck. She felt the sting of the sharp-ened blade against her skin with each rise and fall of her breath.

Renee's body went limp and she scooted back on the couch when she saw the knife. "Oh, no. Please. Let her go, and we can just inter-view you. How does that sound?" Her voice shook like she was pleading with a cat who refused to come down from a tree.

"She's not going anywhere. In fact, I have some questions to ask her myself, since none of you has ever challenged her. All I've ever heard were softball questions." Dylan clenched his jaw. "So, are you ready to answer some real questions?" Dylan said with his hand on the back of Dr. Carey's neck.

For the first time, she spoke. She knew she had two choices. She could abide by his orders and hope that she survived, or she could be defiant until the end. "I won't answer any of your fucking questions!" Dr. Carey grimaced as his hand tightened around her neck. *I refuse to let him win.*

"I assumed you'd say that. Just like a woman to not accept defeat and whine all about it. Now, some people watching will see me as the villain, but you have to understand: I, along with my fleet of support-ers, am fed up. We're tired of the abuse, and today it ends." Dylan swung the knife around as he spoke.

Dr. Carey stared straight ahead at the screen, transfixed by her own image in the tiny box at the bottom. She watched his movements in hopes of catching him off-guard, her body screaming to jump up and tackle him. But a force she wasn't accustomed to kept her tied down to her chair. Fear wasn't an emotion she knew well. She'd rallied and spit in its face her whole life, but now it had her in its clutches.

"What do you intend to accomplish today?" Bob piped up, reading a note handed to him.

"I came here to reclaim what was originally ours, Bob. People aren't taking men's rights seriously, and I've been warning you for months. I even organized a march outside of this condo. Yet no one followed up with me or any of the men who marched alongside me. I thought someone from your show would come out, but nothing. No one bothered except one useless reporter, whose footage I've yet to see. You know how that made me feel?" Dylan leaned in closer to the laptop. "Like shit, Renee. Why are you so fucking obsessed with Dr. Carey and her lame-ass program? Tell me. Why do you hate men so much?"

"Let me interject," the agent said. "The FBI wants to talk to you one-on-one so we can move this off of the live feed. No one will get hurt and..."

"There you go. You're telling me how to run *my* mission? That's not how this is going to go down. Everything will be done on air for the world to see. I will not allow you to change my words or position to fit your narrative. The world can see how this plays out in real time and decide for themselves. Let me also point out that my video manifesto is in the secure hands of trusted men who will preserve my legacy."

Dr. Carey blinked away tears she'd tried to suppress. *Don't fucking cry.* She had never felt terror like this, but the trickle of sweat forming in both of her armpits began to soak her sides. She was used to instilling fear in others to get them to their root core, but this was different. Words were her weapon of choice, along with the tried-and-true knowledge of psychology. *Fucking coward.* She wanted to yell, but he shifted his grip on her neck, switching the knife to the opposite hand, which made her mind race with thoughts of escape. She watched him lazily fling around the knife in his hands while standing to her side, often with his opposite hand wrapped around the back of her neck, preoccupied with the discussion on the screen. Her body convinced itself to strike out at him, to disarm him, but each time she got the courage, a spike of adrenaline wreaked havoc on her muscles, seizing and paralyzing them. She remained seated. Her neck ached from his grip, and her stomach growled for food she wished she'd eaten.

"You see, I am a great man and worthy of love. These women are so brainwashed they couldn't see that I'm an amazing catch." Dylan lowered his voice, leaning into Dr. Carey's ear.

Goosebumps formed as his hot breath rippled through the tiny hairs on her skin. The vibration of his voice so close to her ear triggered the fight response in her. "If the authorities are listening, please rescue me. I refuse to answer any of his questions."

Dylan paced behind the chair, slamming books off the nearest table, sending her lamp crashing to the floor. The knife quickly reappeared on the screen, resting back on Dr. Carey's neck. "I'm in charge here, and you'll answer to me." He dug the knife a little deeper into her flesh.

She didn't feel the pain at first, but she saw the trickle of blood escape from behind the knife. She watched herself bleed onto her cream sweater. The room's perfect lighting illuminated the crimson streaks. The grisly liquid flowed onto the delicate fabric until the dainty heart shape on her sweater was covered in her own blood.

She felt the faint coolness of the air as the killer thrust his knife over and over into her body. Her neck suffered most of the wounds, with her shoulders and ribs taking several jabs. She heard the crunch, felt her inner beauty crumbling beneath her as the knife's edge scraped against her bones. With the ferocity of a caged lion, the killer bore into her body with a vengeance bottled up for too long. He was like a gas leak waiting for a spark, and today he'd finally ignited.

Dr. Carey watched her image on the screen in horror. Her once vibrant, beautiful face slowly dimmed until her mouth hung open and her eyes stared blankly at her reflection. Her striking green eyes darkened, disappearing deeper into the abyss. Dr. Carey's morning affirmation was fitting for today: *My soul is at peace no matter where I go. Peace and love will find me.*

As her earthly figure slumped over her desk, her final thought drifted to the image before her.

Vanity of vanity is all vanity.

Chapter 65

Dylan

Dylan watched as Dr. Carey collapsed in her chair and eventually slid to the floor. The finality of her death gave him a sense of calm he'd never experienced with any of the other murders. Her death meant his deed was done, and now only one last piece of his mission remained. He weighed the options heavily: end his life, or stay alive and be captured. Either way, he believed he'd be a martyr for the men's rights community, so living no longer had a purpose. He looked at Renee and Bob's shocked faces staring back at him, unsure if he was still live on air with *Wake Up LA*, but he checked his phone and could see the Mandate was lit up with comments. Renee kept covering her mouth and shaking her head back and forth. Bob sat motionless, staring at the screen, waiting for whatever would happen next.

Dylan pushed Dr. Carey's chair to the side to address the audience.

"Ladies and gentlemen, because Dr. Carey didn't listen, she forced me to do this. I wasn't born a killer, but society, specifically the women of the world, created this sad reality. My mother failed me since birth. My first girlfriend and only love was a complete failure when she betrayed my trust and honor by ditching me without an explanation. Barbara didn't deserve me. I was way too good for her and would have given her the world. She was too dumb to see through her own beliefs. She deserved exactly what happened to her." Dylan gnashed his teeth. "The worst part was she was swindled by Dr. Carey, a fake leader that women willingly signed their finances and relationships away to. I cannot comprehend how anyone could fall for Dr. Carey and her bullshit." Dylan took a deep breath, staring up at the ceiling. His phone screen lit up with messages of support from the group chat.

"Dr. Carey was the final straw for me. Society fawned over her and her program for too long, and someone had to end it. I have no regrets about what I've done. My only wish was that I had started sooner."

Dylan left the Mandate video on as he stood up and walked away from the camera. Minutes passed until finally the flash of an officer's uniform came into view and the live feed was shut off.

Local and national news had received Dylan's manifesto just minutes after the shocking online murder. An anonymous source forwarded it to a few reporters, and from there it eventually leaked online.

Dylan Foster Manifesto

I tried to be a nice guy, and that got me nowhere. Society is cruel, and the only way to get out of this is to take charge and do something myself. No one will come to change things—not our government or the weak women they allow to hold such office. No, I can't let another guy grow up and live under the oppressive regime that is feminism.

I'm writing this so you can understand how I got here, and maybe it will help change the world. Since you're reading this, I've been able to see my plan through to fruition. You should know all about it since

I planned it to be breaking news. Bigger than the OJ trial, and for years to come, it will be known as the single greatest snuff film that there ever was.

Let's start with where I'm from: Indiana, the land of jocks and girls who don't give guys like me a chance. They're a cruel group to grow up around. They sneered at me and never allowed me to fit in. I don't have height. I've always been thin, scrawny. Gym class was a nightmare because I couldn't do the mundane things that other guys my age could do. Pull-ups and weightlifting defied me, and I feigned illness as often as I could. The mocking laughs still ring through my head today. If I could add those assholes to my list, I would, but they aren't part of this plan. Someone else will need to exact revenge on them, and someday the world will mock their pleas for mercy.

I am a hero. Granted, my parents never saw this skill in me. My dad, Mr. Five-Star-General, never liked me. I was his weak son that should be dead instead of his dead namesake. I'm the kid who had to watch his parents dote on his little brother while ignoring my existence. I do not miss having a brother. Life is better as an only child, especially one whose sibling died so young. My parents were choking on the haze of grief, and I got by, but they couldn't see how much I struggled. My brother's death was supposed to be good for me, make them praise me. His murder should have been advantageous. But my parents' sorrow lingered much longer than I could have expected, and it only made them miss him more.

Of course, I thought of following in my father's footsteps in the ranks of the military. However, I often woke in cold sweats, imagining that the jocks of my youth would be my drill sergeant nightmare of the future. The last thing I wanted was to hear the same ridicule and torment that plagued me as a kid. The military life would only be to gain my father's love and approval, but that never happened.

My mother was sick. Mentally and physically. We always had to keep it private, as she never left the house except for the occasional doctor's visit. She'd spend long stays in bed and down more pills throughout my childhood and as I became an adult. My dad adored my mom more than his own healthy son. My strong military father would have sent me off to be adopted if he could, but giving me away would have highlighted his only weakness.

Why become a serial killer? You can blame it on my parents, who didn't love me, and my ex, who left me for no reason. She left me alone and isolated after I'd opened up to her. This is how they treat you. I dared to open myself up and share my feelings, and this is what I get? Barbara deserved to die for the pain she caused. She treated me like a leper, and since then, all women have conspired against me. No matter how hard I tried, I kept getting turned down. I blame Barbara for leaving me.

Let my life and story be a beacon of hope for young men going through the same thing I went through. Do not mourn my death, but praise my mission.

Chapter 66

Edgar

Nursing homes had a certain universally recognizable smell to them, no matter how clean they appeared. Virginia had been Reece's roommate for the past year, although they didn't converse. The pair were mostly mute, and no one knew what either was thinking. When Edgar first visited his wife, he felt sorrow for Virginia, who wasn't mobile. The only people who came to see her were the overworked staff, sometimes saving the confined woman for last. Edgar's heart ached knowing his beloved was their final stop.

Reece had been in a nursing home for the last year after the incessant knocks at their door wore on her mentally. Edgar hated himself for taking her to a home, but he needed the soliciting to die down, and he wasn't sure he was able to care for a wife now diagnosed with dementia. He believed this was the best course of action for the wife he loved more than anything in this world. Although he still couldn't calm the unrelenting ache in his heart; it made him reach across his empty bed only to find rough and tattered sheets. Her pillow provided only a fraction of comfort as he'd wrap his arms around it and breathe in her scent. He was still unable to wash her pillowcase after all this time.

On his way out the door, he noticed her squirming in her bed. She often dozed off during their visits. Edgar took one more glance at his wife and considered walking back inside, but she always got so excited when she saw him, forgetting he had already visited. He didn't want to confuse her or change her routine. But he couldn't resist the extra time and never knew when to cut it short, so he'd sit for a bit longer until she slept again.

After she fell asleep, he gave her a kiss on the cheek, took his hat in hand, and walked toward the front of the building, where he stood to the side as other visitors arrived. He gave subtle nods of greeting to those who entered, but saw a sizable crowd gathering around the TV in the visitor room. He stood in the open doorway behind the group to see what the commotion was about.

"Shhh, shh. She's coming up next," Edgar heard one of the staff announce. He had no idea who was coming up, but based on the size of the crowd, he assumed it was someone important.

The TV volume blared. "Welcome to *Max Logan Live!* Viewers, we have an exceptional show today as Alton Shaw is making his first appearance since his exoneration of all sexual assault charges. It's going to be a real doozy of a show." Max fist-pumped into the camera.

A few of the women standing near Edgar groaned.

"Alton, please fill us in on how you're doing since the verdict was read." Max leaned in.

"Thank you so much for having me. I have a new lease on life. It was a real witch hunt, but the truth prevailed. I've always maintained my innocence, and I'm just glad a judge saw through these lies." Alton looked around, nodding at various friendly audience members who cheered him on.

"And my what lies they were. You had five women come forward against you. How did you stay positive?" Max rubbed his chin.

"It was really tough. I can't say that I was positive at all. I hit rock bottom. I drank too much, and I just floated through the days. I was angry with everyone for allowing this to happen to me."

"Don't we know it. #MeToo has destroyed many men, and I'm

glad you made it out safe." Max looked straight into the camera and let out a whistle.

"It was all like a religious experience leaving the courtroom. My lawyers and my mom accompanied me. I had to make plans for my estate should they find me guilty. Naturally, my assets would go to my children, but I certainly didn't want their mother to be in charge of it." Both men chuckled.

"Shut up, loser," a woman in blue scrubs yelled at the TV. Edgar stared at the backs of heads in disbelief.

"I can completely understand that. Our ancestors would be rolling over in their graves to know what feminism has done to us. It's time for a shift, and with your acquittal, we're going to get back on track." Max slapped his knee.

"Thankfully, I had successful lawyers, and life is looking up. It's a hard road to pave here in Hollywood to get my name back. Even though I've been proven innocent, people have written me off. Actors I've made household names—and gotten handsome checks for so their children could attend elite schools—have all turned their backs on me. The few who support me would ruin their careers if they came forward." Alton scowled.

"What a shame." Max shook his head.

"It is a shame. But I'm determined to get back out there. Maybe I'll look into indie films. They eat that shit up globally, and they're more tolerant. Not like the #MeToo police we have here." They both snickered.

Max raised his eyebrows. "A little birdie told me you have a secret surprise that you brought with you today?"

"That's right. We've had a rocky road, and I admit I wasn't my best self, but things are changing for the better."

"I told you!" one nurse whispered loudly to another.

Max stood up. "Ladies and gentlemen, I don't think you'll be prepared for who you're about to see."

The sound of heels on a concrete floor boomed through the speakers of the TV. She walked out on stage to a smattering of applause—the kind of polite clapping of people had no clue what she might say or do.

"Livvy! Welcome to the show. And I can see that you're glowing. How far along are you?"

She took a deep breath. "Five months." Livvy's eyes shifted side to side, taking in the audience.

"Now, last we all knew, you were going to speak for the prosecution against Alton. What changed your mind?" Max leaned close to her.

When she sat silently for several seconds, Max cut through the dead air. "Cat got your tongue?"

Livvy kept searching the crowd. Her eyes moved as if watching a game of tennis.

"She's being coy. She and I have a mutual understanding, and honestly, our breakup was based on some false misrepresentations. But we're all good now. Livvy moved into my Malibu home, and she's been in nesting mode ever since." Alton grabbed Livvy's limp left hand.

* * *

Livvy sat frozen in her chair. No words escaped her lips after she declared how far along she was. It had been several months since she'd been in front of the bright camera lights.

Have they always been that bright?

When she first left Runyan Canyon, she was too afraid to return to her apartment, at least alone. She had no place to run and all of her acting gigs were done. She was officially washed up. Her career wasn't going to beat both Alton and Dr. Carey, not in Hollywood. She was faced with a decision: cooperate and enjoy a lavish lifestyle or return to her hometown, the one she never wanted to see again. Of course, there were other options—trying to make it on her own, getting a regular job, but the truth was, she still loved Alton, and that made her decision much easier.

She felt Alton's tight grip on her hand, although he didn't need to do that. She didn't need any reminders to behave. She would always have his back, and he would always provide a luxury car and top of the line bed for her back. Livvy and her baby would live comfortably for life.

* * *

Edgar heard grumbling throughout the room. The growing tension was one of disgust and betrayal, the kind he'd known toward Dylan. His chin dropped to his chest. He could no longer muster the strength to show courage in the face of disappointment. He'd had enough. He turned, not understanding the allure of programs like this. A small part of him hoped he might learn something about his own son, but he knew better. He walked toward the electric sliding doors.

"Ma'am," he said to one stranger with a nod as he placed his hat back on his head. He could see he startled her as her right hand moved to her heart. He knew people didn't converse as much as they used to, plus maybe people knew who he really was—the father of a serial killer. Dylan's unmasking as the Cutthroat Caller meant Edgar's life was now intertwined with his son's image, forcing him to isolate himself from the community and its usual activities. He was now a black sheep because of his son's crimes.

Edgar hopped in his truck and took off down the winding road. He had to brake hard for a family of deer with the buck standing guard, staring back at his Chevy. He passed by all the familiar city haunts that were both a comfort and a curse to him. Maybe if he had moved his family away, gotten his wife in to see a different doctor... Life was so much easier when viewed in reverse, intending to grade your past. As he pulled into the cracked concrete driveway, there was some comfort in knowing that he was home. The house was the haunted echo of all that he had lost. He felt he deserved it. He could handle the blame because the house, with its tormenting reminders, was his prison. The lost joy of laughter, baby cries, even his wife pleading for help. He deserved whatever the house gave him.

Edgar was used to adapting to a new way of living. The military taught him to never get too comfortable. But his new normal was life as the father of a serial killer, and he had to accept it. His profound guilt and shame lessened as the days went on and he learned to separate himself from the son he despised. When he was in the military, he'd spent endless nights out on a mission, which kept his focus back on Indiana. Life as a soldier couldn't take him away from the drama that lived inside his home. His remorse for leaving Reece there with Dylan weighed heavily now that he understood the monster he'd left his precious wife to deal with.

God only knows what Dylan said and did to poor Reece. He'd never forgive himself for leaving her alone with a psychopath. He blamed himself even today and likely would until his final thoughts. There was no longer any hope for grandchildren since Dylan carried the family DNA to his grave. The Foster clan would now end. While Edgar had found peace with this, it still didn't take away the ache of it. His home was now empty, and he hadn't gotten used to the feeling of living alone. The entire time he was away, all he ever wanted was to be home, and now that it was empty, he wished he were back on assignment. Sure, there were temptations over there. Sure, he'd watched several comrades risk it all for one night of fun. But Edgar wasn't that man. He was fully, wholly, a man devoted to his sweet wife. If only he could have rid the world of Dylan. One thing Dylan was right about was that Edgar Jr. would have been a much better man.

Following Dylan's livestream, Edgar's front door was constantly bombarded by people wanting the scoop. Edgar wasn't watching when it happened, but he eventually learned what his son had done when the police arrived at his door.

"Mr. Foster? We'd like a word with you about your son. Have you been watching the drama unfold on TV?" the mustached cop asked, holding his hat in his hand.

"What drama?" Edgar's mood soured. "I honestly haven't kept up with him. Why is he on TV?" Edgar scratched his head, turning to the dusty television.

All of his life he had wondered who his distant son really was, and now he knew for sure: a killer.

"I'm at a total loss for words, but feel free to look around. He lived in the basement. I just ask that you leave his mother alone," Edgar said. Soon cops and reporters littered his dead-end street, and pieces of yellow tape lingered for months in his yard. If his family was alienated prior to the murders, they now became like direct descendants of the Salem witches, complete with the Devil's Mark. The neighbors didn't even feign looking away; they openly gawked, trying to get a glimpse of the murderous family unit. Were they grieving? Were they guilty by association? How could they raise such a child? Edgar didn't blame them. He'd probably thought worse of others in similar situations. He wished he could yell, "I hate who my son became, too."

Back at home, Edgar fixed a cold sandwich and sat in front of the still-dusty TV, wishing for good news, but those days were over. All news was bad news, and he had seen enough misery for a lifetime.

Chapter 67

Bailey

The sweltering heat from the steam bath filled the tent as Bailey sat in a prayer circle amongst strangers she'd met only minutes before. There was nothing subtle about the scents, and the palo santo overwhelmed her nose. Sweat poured down her face as she blinked away the moisture in her eyes.

Someone gave her a wooden cup filled with ceremonial ayahuasca tea, and she drank it all, wiping her mouth with the back of her hand. She'd come to Costa Rica to escape her immense grief after witnessing what happened to Dr. Carey. She'd immediately given notice at the law firm and existed each day since then with such a deep longing, her sense of purpose snuffed out. This retreat was her last-ditch effort for connection.

She shed tears as someone guided her back onto the woven pillow. Her body convulsed with deep belly cries.

"I miss you," she kept repeating.

Someone dabbed a cool rag over the top of her forehead as her entire world spun in a hypnotic dream. The dizziness overwhelmed her as her stomach churned. She noticed a pail next to her as the person behind her attempted to comfort her, reassuring her, "You'll be fine."

She couldn't be sure what was real or part of the trip. She'd read up on what to expect, but her logical mind was of no use. This realm wasn't about order; it was all upheaval.

When Bailey first saw her, she tried to reason that it was all an illusion. Dr. Carey was absolutely dead, but yet, she stood in front of her.

You're so real and alive.

Bailey's body weight lifted, and all of her worry and sorrow floated above her and drifted from the tent. She was weightless and free.

Dr. Carey mouthed something that Bailey couldn't hear. Bailey leaned closer until she was within an inch of her mouth, but then she felt something slimy enter her ear. Bailey jerked away, attempting to cover her ear with her right hand. Instead, she felt skin and hair, a head—Dr. Carey's. The beautiful head of Dr. Carey was now attached to her own long neck, and they slithered in unison as their tongues jutted out, their eyes darkening and their skin turning a slick green. They communicated by staring into each other's eyes; they were each other's twin flames, a two-headed snake, lovers trapped in opposite dimensions. Dr. Carey's head snapped and gnawed into Bailey's with a meaty bite as a thick venom seeped inside. Bailey's thin paisley muumuu soaked with sweat as she fell back onto the pillow, only feeling a shock of cool at her forehead.

When she awoke hours later, she immediately knew her next move.

Through death, Dr. Carey and I will be closer than ever.

Chapter 68

Dylan

Dylan's new reality was bleak: a hospital room with cold shackles to keep his already immobile body on the bed. Spittle crept along his jawline, landing on the front of his starched gown. After a cruel year of no longer being able to ambulate or urinate on his own, his bed was his constant companion. While his body reaped the damage of his failed suicide attempt, his mind was still stuck inside Dr. Carey's apartment. Dylan often revisited his body as it lay on Dr. Carey's floor. He watched as the pulsating flow of blood sprayed with each heartbeat until he eventually convulsed, stroking out before paramedics rescued him. The only sound was a faint sizzle of his own blood gushing out of the knife wound he'd sliced through his neck.

As he lay dying, he could only stare at the rug on Dr. Carey's floor. He saw the remnants of items left under her couch: a silvery wig, white pills, and a lacy thong. The thought of Dr. Carey returning home from a night of partying danced in his head. He imagined himself following her into the apartment, where they'd make out on the edge of her couch with her silver wig and thong finding their way to the floor.

The cruelty of the iron shackles holding his already immobile body in place was another dagger to his ego. Diagnosed with locked-in syndrome after suffering catastrophic lack of blood circulation to the brain. While he hadn't moved in a year, there was a very slim chance he could still regain mobility.

Dylan's lawyers successfully got continuances for his trials because of his hospitalization. Nobody from the Mandate came to visit, and he had no idea if his message had gone viral like he'd hoped. They provided assisted communication, but Dylan found it frustrating to learn and difficult to spell out, "Has my manifesto transformed the gender constructs of our time, usurping power from the feminists and restoring it to the capable hands of men?"

Like every morning, Dylan woke to find himself stuck inside a hospital room attached to various tubes, a worse prison than his previous self could ever have imagined. He could hear the beeps and suction sounds of the machines regulating his life. His eyes stared despondently at the ceiling, blinking every few seconds. The hospital smelled of freshly opened bandages, with a strong odor of disinfectant which nurses used to clean the scars on his neck. Restrained to the bed by metal locks, Dylan was completely helpless—an unseen weight pinned him in place with paralyzing intensity. The near-fatal injury from his slice to his neck, stabbing and tearing the carotid and vertebral arteries resulting in an ischemic stroke, reduced Dylan to just his eyes.

Dylan first felt the slight shift in temperature: a negligible breeze hit his skin, then a shadow came across his face. He glimpsed a woman checking the machines at his side. *A nurse.* They came so often he couldn't keep up with who each one was. He could see only her profile as her brunette hair hung down to her chin. Dylan noticed a heart tattoo on her left wrist, just above the edge of her hospital glove. He could only read the end of her name tag, "OW."

Dylan heard her pressing on the touch screen next to the bed before she eventually turned to the various machines. He heard a switch snap, and then there was a powering-down sound. Dylan immediately sensed a warmth. His breathing deepened, way down into his diaphragm where they always tell you to breathe, but his lungs wouldn't expand, so his breathing grew shallow. The tube in his mouth no longer felt plastic. It now felt like hard metal. He gagged, but even if he could move, he wouldn't be able to pull it out with his hands cuffed to the bed.

The nurse leaned close to Dylan's ear and said in a nearly inaudible whisper, "You will see darkness, but don't worry, you'll see the most beautiful stars. They'll be breathtaking, the most overwhelming and haunting diamonds in the sky to guide you along the journey. You'll find solace, peace, and love. But this stop won't be for you. You'll pass by your victims, who will point you on your final way. You'll keep going, well past the twinkling lights, into the inferno of devastation. You will suffer for eternity after what you've done to women, including my soul sister."

Willow leaned back and watched as Dylan spat against the tube. His eyes darted left and right, rolled back and forth, searching and seeking, finding only more misery. The nurse's face started to shift. Dylan wished he could rub his eyes. He saw the face of his once cherished Barbara. *Please save me.* But there was no saving him. The face became Stacy and her welcoming smile, then turned to Margaret's serious gaze, to Eliza's hopeful joy, to Nora's wistful nature, to Ava's innocent pleas, to Dr. Carey's eager dreams. Death. *I'm dying. Save me. Help me. Why is this taking so long?*

His thoughts raced as his body lay helpless. Willow checked her watch. Her hair swished as she turned to check the door. The gurgle of phlegm stuck in Dylan's throat. His eyelids twitched as his heart stuttered, trying to pump life into his body. The overhead speaker announced, *Code 1, Dr. Hobart. Emergency Room.* He heard footsteps outside the door. Distant chatter, even louder laughter.

Dylan drifted back to his childhood house, to the room he shared with his short-term brother. On the morning of his brother's death, Dylan waited until his mother's midday nap, which usually lasted two to three hours. Baby Eddie kept the household up several hours each night, which he didn't appreciate very much. *Baby Eddie is a nuisance that needs to go away.* Dylan never formed a bond with his younger brother. He'd never experienced a hatred so deep and never would again until decades later, when he laid eyes upon Dr. Carey. Eddie was his first true enemy, and by default, he despised his parents for bringing the child into this world. Every time he heard them use his father's name, the hatred dug deeper into his soul. Even at five years old, he knew the burden of loathing. The deep desire to silence the crying baby, the fuming rage of jealousy, and the knowledge that there was only space for one son in this family.

Dylan knew the drill. Fake sleep while Reece peeked inside his room. She'd lay Eddie in his crib, where he'd fuss around a bit until he finally relaxed with his pacifier in his mouth. Reece left the room, leaving the door cracked open about a foot. Dylan waited for a time he didn't know how to tell, but he watched the dust particles drift through the sun's rays, his sleepy body willing itself to rise to carry out the deed he'd been fantasizing about. Baby Eddie never smiled at Dylan. In fact, he always squirmed anytime he got near him. Sure enough, he inched away as Dylan approached. The pacifier came loose from his gaping mouth, his face turning red. Dylan panicked as he didn't want his mom to hear the impending screech coming from Eddie's lungs. Faster than he realized, he leapt onto the crib, scaled the top, and landed with a thud on top of Eddie, who let out a single yelp before Dylan placed a pillow over his mouth to muffle the cry. *Hope Mom didn't hear that.*

At forty pounds, five-year-old Dylan was twice the weight of his sibling and could use his size to pin a pillow onto him. It surprised him that Eddie wasn't squirming and, other than the initial yelp, he didn't hear any sounds. But when he pulled the pillow away after just a minute, Eddie moved again, so he promptly put the pillow back over his head. Dylan immediately knew it would take much longer. He got the idea to kill Eddie with a pillow after seeing it on a TV show, but in that case it was a comedy. The character being killed came up gasping for air because they didn't do it long enough. Even his parents laughed, which made him think it would be a perfect plan.

The longer Dylan held the pillow, the more he worried about how long it was taking. He thought he heard his mom's footsteps. Every creak was her opening the door. He wondered what would happen to him if she caught him in the act. *Will they send me to jail?* Dylan knew about prison because his dad often told him he would end up there if he didn't straighten up his act. He had no idea what that meant, but he assumed his dad didn't like his attitude. Dylan's arms grew tired, aching from the pressure. His hands left an indent in the crib mattress from how hard he pressed down. As he slowly lifted his body away, he watched for any signs of life, but found no movement. He could see Eddie's mouth was open, and when he pushed on his face, there was no response. He attempted to put the pacifier back in his gaping mouth, but it kept falling out. Dylan pulled the blanket up over Eddie's head, jumped over the crib, and scrambled back into his own bed, covering himself to his chin.

It felt like another hour, maybe two, before his mom came into the room. He feigned sleep, watching with his eyes slanted shut. She shuffled into the room and put her hand on Eddie's chest. As she uncovered his head, she cocked her own to the side, her mouth agape until it became wider than baby Eddie's. Dylan only wished he could have stifled her yelps.

* * *

As Dylan lay in his hospital bed, he wished that the ghost of baby Eddie would come to give him the favor of a quick, sweet death. A pillow to the face, not too short but long enough to escape the hell of this existence forever. But Dylan knew the death he gave to Eddie was similar to the fate he had just experienced.

A final heartbeat.

Dylan finally succeeded in dying. There would be no trials or long prison sentences, nor an even longer wait for a death date.

Dylan's final thought drifted to whether he would be remembered as a hero, a true luminary when no one else had the courage. Dylan and Carmella had that in common. Both wanted to be notorious: rule breakers made famous by their views. Their actions unknowingly linked their names forever, like those of an old, feuding couple. The one-page article about their lives would include both of their names, cemented together for eternity.

As Dylan took his final breath, he still hadn't heard from his dad, but his dad hadn't been there for him when he was born. He wouldn't be present when he left this earth.

Chapter 69

Julissa

She held the jagged key in her right hand and slowly turned the handle. The condo door opened to a room filled with soft blankets, the fuzzy kind on furniture displays, and an inviting dark gray modular sofa. An oversized mirror hung above the fireplace mantel, which made the room appear much larger. The tenth-floor unit gave way to a city skyline that differed from the one she'd viewed in Beverly Grove, peppered with other tall buildings surrounding downtown. At night, the city lights looked like twinkling stars or falling snowflakes. Julissa no longer felt the trepidation she once did when she worked for Dr. Carey, the constant pins and needles feeling that she'd feared had permanently altered her nervous system. Now she could stretch freely like the well-worn elastic in her socks. Her new employer had the same vision for women's empowerment. While using some of the same buzzwords as Dr. Carey, she seemed to want a fresh approach. Her demeanor alone was softer, more engaging, and trusting.

"I'd love for you to join my team. I admire what you did for Dr. Carey, and I want that same dedication here." Julissa replayed the job offer in her head. "I saw firsthand the errors of the *Year of Self,* and with you by my side, I believe we can create a magical program."

Julissa flipped on the fireplace and rubbed her hands in front of it to catch some warmth. She crawled into the oversized chair in the corner, which was perfect for reading or working on a writing project, or even a brief nap. The room smelled of leftover Christmas cookies, sugar with cinnamon, and glowed from the white light garland that lined the ceiling trim. Even in the heart of Los Angeles, it felt a bit like a Hallmark movie set in Vermont, with all the snuggly, homey vibes.

She took a deep breath as a smile overcame her, one that shot straight from her belly to her head. She was finally in harmony, and she hoped her new job would be her sanctuary away from the chaos of her previous position. A cozy retreat from the old life that still haunted her. The nightmares of those clients of the past had slowly faded, replaced by the beautiful normality of her tranquil new life.

She browsed through the emails without finding any death threats, which was already a plus. These emails were full of joy and elation, all from people seeking a higher purpose and meaning. The women could freely express themselves and find acceptance when pursuing life changes. Julissa had kept in contact with members of the former *Year of Self* program and taken it upon herself to keep tabs on them, many of whom Julissa had convinced to join the newly formed group. She couldn't shake the guilt that she was the one who must have let the Cutthroat Caller into the system. *I allowed the killer into our group.* She still couldn't banish the pervasive thought.

Julissa greeted her new boss as she entered through the front door. No longer filled with dread, she was eager to welcome her new employer in. Grocery bags full of fresh fruit and vegetables stocked the fridge and countertops. "A healthy body creates a healthy mind" was a tenet of the new program. Gone were the caffeine fixes and bottles of pills.

"Are you ready for today's big event?" Julissa asked from the comfort of her chair.

"Absolutely. It's going to transform this community in such divine ways." Bailey smiled warmly.

Since Dr. Carey's death, the group of women that remained in the *Year of Self* had kept up via a new online chat group. They were survivors of both Dr. Carey and Dylan Foster. Their deaths bonded them like nothing had while the two still lived. With their deaths, a community of accepting women connected through their mutual hatred of the pair.

Julissa watched Bailey get comfortable on the couch next to her. They lit incense on top of the fireplace mantel and said a brief prayer before logging in.

"May this fragrant offering bring us peace and stillness. In your presence, we bow," the two said together before nodding toward each other.

Julissa grabbed the white ultra-plush blanket that was draped on the arm of the couch and pulled it around her legs as she balanced her laptop on her lap. She brushed her hands along its lush material, prompting goosebumps to form up and down her arms. As she logged in to the team meeting, there weren't multiple slides of women joining the online call like there were with Dr. Carey, but there were enough. A smaller community meant more personalized attention, which Julissa preferred. She could see how valuable Dr. Carey's program had seemed at the start, but as it grew, so did her ego.

"Ladies, I've been thinking hard about the direction of our program. I know most of us come from the old *Year of Self*, and that's been traumatizing, to put it mildly." Bailey chuckled.

Julissa smiled, knowing how far they'd all come. Some women on the screen nodded in agreement while others shook theirs in disgust at memories of the past.

"One thing I think Dr. Carey did right is to create rules."

Some women raised their eyebrows in question. Julissa squirmed in her chair. A sudden pulse of heat shot through her body and she uncovered herself from the blanket.

"I mean, life is full of rules, and we can't just be these free spirits all the time. Now, life would be great if we could just be ourselves, but rules help us. Rules are necessary." Bailey looked around at the faces on the screen, doing her best to make eye contact with each member.

Julissa suddenly felt like she was sinking into the overly padded chair. Her skin flushed, and she kept trying to reason with herself that maybe she was misunderstanding.

"Julissa has informed me we've reached the fifty-member mark. That's phenomenal. Although fifty personalities can be...a lot." She laughed, then quickly narrowed her gaze. "So, I want to impose rules to keep us fair and balanced."

Fair and balanced. This sounds familiar. Julissa stared blankly at the screen, afraid to gulp.

"Oh, and in order to be fair and balanced and for everyone to feel a deep connection, I'm going to need to charge for this service," Bailey said. "I appreciate the donations, but they're just not reliable."

Julissa sank deeper into the chair. Its false edges buried her whole. She couldn't crawl out of it even if she wanted to. It had become a sinkhole that was too dangerous to attempt a rescue. She sat motionless, a perfect soldier on the outside. On the inside, she was a frenzied mess. Her new boss made so many promises, including that the program would have no rules and would always to be free. Julissa had only come back to the group under those stipulations and was happy to take a small fee in order to be part of the team. She'd even joked to her friends she was like a paid volunteer, giving more to the program than the menial income it gave back. "But I'm not there for money; I'm there to be part of something great," she'd told her best friend, P.

A bead of sweat trickled down Julissa's cheek. The fireplace was no longer cozy but baking her alive.

"Let me see what else. From now on, you can call me Frost. Hmm, Dr. Frost," Bailey told the wide-eyed group.

The other women on the call sat motionless. A few of them

blinked, signaling to Julissa that they remained connected. The shock was evident from miles away.

Julissa tried to get up from the sunken chair, but it became a vortex. Unable to move, she sat staring at the screen. Wishing for an earthquake to swallow them all whole and end this nightmare she couldn't wake up from.

"Now, ladies, let's start with our first rule..."

Julissa's belly shook as she sniffled.

A cult born of a cult is still a cult, and it had Julissa trapped in more ways than one.

A letter from nicole

Dear readers,

I want to say a huge thank you for choosing to read *The Signature Line*. If you enjoyed it and want to keep up to date with all of my latest releases, you can sign up for my newsletter at nicoleannbury.com. I will never share your email address, and you can unsubscribe at anytime.

I hope you loved *The Signature Line*, and if you did, I would be very grateful if you could write a review. I'd love to hear what you think, and it makes such a difference helping new readers discover my book for the first time.

Thank you so much for reading!

Nicole

Acknowledgments

There are several people I need to thank for helping me along this writing journey. First, I thank my editor, Meg McIntyre, with Phantom Pen Editorial for her phenomenal eye in helping make this book into my vision. There were many beta readers along the way; however, I could not have made so much improvement without the keen eye of my good friend Amanda Watson. She is the friend we all need, giving us the honest feedback that makes us better.

I'm so grateful to the ladies in my writing group, Quill & Cup. When I joined four years ago, I dreamt of having my book in my hands, and now I have my second published book. I just know that without Ania Ray and Quill & Cup's guidance and comforting faces along the way, I wouldn't be this far into my writing journey. I am so grateful to have met my thriller feedback partner, Mica Merrill Rice. She is an amazing source of inspiration, and I can't wait to see where our partnership takes us. I'm also very thankful for early feedback from Courtney Burger. Her enthusiasm for my story helped fuel so much creativity, which was a tremendous support.

I am so grateful to my family for their encouragement, especially my parents, for instilling my creative spirit at an early age. I watched them follow their dreams, and it's something I know I want to emulate. I am so thankful to my husband for our home and the life we have and the space for me to fulfill my writing dreams.

About the Author

Nicole Annbury currently resides in Indiana with her husband and three cats. Although she's originally from Missouri, she spent part of her youth in California.

The Signature Line is Nicole's second novel after her debut, *The Final Sentence,* came out in 2025. She's currently drafting her third novel titled, *You Can Leave.*

When she's not writing, she enjoys nature walks, true crime documentaries, reality TV viewing and going on drives with her husband.